DEANNA GREY

ISBN 979-8-9878955-1-1

First Edition: February 2023

Editor: Heather Rosman

Beta Readers: Muddled Ink Editorial, Alexia, and Lisa

Cover Design: Books & Moods

Contents

Content Notes

This book includes:

Brief mentions of childhood bullying and body image issues
(discussions are never graphic and the bullying never depicted).
On page sex scenes.

For the girls who used to beat all the boys in elementary school races.

Chapter One

Sam

The air smelled stale. The linoleum floors shined with fresh wax. And she was in my spot—again.

For the last two weeks, Aderyn Jacobs beat me to the best, and my most coveted, view in Harry's Bait and Goods.

The first few times, I let it go. When I needed time to think, I came here. She probably did the same thing. The only problem was, when something was on my mind, the last thing I wanted was company. So, I had to stand opposite where she stood.

Unfortunately, the view on the north side of Harry's indoor pond was far inferior to the south. Where I stood barely got any sunlight from the overhead windows. The larger fish avoided this darker area. And most of the indoor trees were planted close to the edge where entering customers could enjoy the view.

Boxes of new merchandise had been stacked against the wall behind me, so naturally, employees began walking back and forth to manage the pile during slow hours. Their constant movement is what convinced me to confront her. I could only take so much daydream interrupting.

"You're in my spot." I wanted it to sound like a joke, but the words came out more serious than I'd intended.

Jacobs straightened, eyes going wide at the sound of my voice. The look washed away when I moved closer. Her shoulders relaxed.

"Oh. It's just you. Hi, Morgan."

I raised an amused brow over her lackluster tone. "Hi, Jacobs. Well? Do you have anything to say for yourself?"

She blinked, confused, still half-lost in whatever she'd been thinking about. I stood next to her, leaving more than enough space for someone to fit in between us.

"Excuse me?" she asked.

"For the past three semesters, I've come here and stood in this very spot," I explained, pointing at her feet. "Rain or shine, no one's stood in front of this exhibit for longer than a few minutes. Then, you start showing up."

Jacobs was the captain of the girl's hockey team. Most people liked her and went as far as calling her friendly. Our interactions usually centered around arguing about ice time, and "friendly" never came to mind when I thought of her. She was painfully blunt and never one to shy away from speaking her mind. Even when smiling, I could see the 'don't-try-me' in her eyes.

"Sounds like a you problem," Jacobs said with a nonchalant shrug.

She rested her forearms on the glass fencing, turning her gaze back to the pond. The muscles in her arms flexed as she leaned across the railing to get a closer look at the koi fish swimming in the murky water.

Jacobs was built like a tank–sometimes she seemed just as large as the guys on my team. Like usual, her hair was in cornrows that stretched down her back. Unlike usual, she wore a dress. It was tight around her wide waist and included a slit revealing one of her long legs. Her dark brown skin contrasted with the white beautifully. When she wasn't in full hockey gear, Jacobs usually wore sweats and baggy tees. I wondered what was the reason behind tonight's dressier fit.

"I'd be more than willing to come up with a schedule to share," I said. I wanted the spot back. No, I *needed* it. Harry's was my perfect place to escape campus. It was quiet enough to disappear and pretend my life outside wasn't falling apart. Pretend I didn't have to figure out what to do about a corrupt athletic director using my team in his gambling scheme.

Jacobs snorted, turning her gaze back to me. "Share? Are you joking?"

"I think it's only fair since it's obvious we both like it."

"It's first come, first serve," she argued. "You can't claim a spot is yours in a store you don't own. Besides, this place isn't as exclusive as you think. Someone else suggested it to me."

"Really?" I frowned, trying to think of who else might know about the quiet wonder of Harry's. "Who?"

She smiled wide enough to reveal a crooked canine tooth. The way her brown eyes danced communicated she was pleased to know something I didn't. "Your boy, Lincoln. He said this was the perfect spot to think."

I scoffed. "I'm the one who told him. He came all of one time and complained about the poor lighting and unhelpful employees."

"Which is the best part," Jacobs noted under her breath.

"Exactly. Thank you."

She chewed on her lip, trying to stop her smile from growing. "It's nice we agree but that doesn't mean you're getting this spot back. I need it to think. I've got a lot on my mind."

"Same here."

She raised a brow. "What do you have to worry about?"

"Hockey," I said, simply. It was a general answer, but still the truth. The dirty details were for people I trusted—the number of which I could count on one hand.

Jacobs laughed. It was a rich and deep noise that made me want to inch closer to her. She didn't seem to notice when I did. I told myself I only wanted to subtly urge her to the left and reclaim my spot.

"You're not worried about hockey," she said.

"And how do you know that?"

"I can see it in your eyes."

My smile wavered for a second. I was a professional bullshitter with countless years of experience and enough professional references to blow my competition out of the water. So, there was no way she saw through my half-lie. Right?

When Jacobs realized I wasn't going to share anything, she shrugged and said, "Fine. I'll bite. What does the great, magnificent, wondrous Samson Morgan have to worry about this hockey season?"

"Wow. Great, magnificent, *and* wondrous? Using my whole name, too." I chuckled. "You got something else you want to add?"

Her mouth turned downward. "No," she said dryly.

"You sure? Because it sounds like you have something to say. We got beef I'm not aware of?"

Jacobs shook her head hard enough to make her braids sway back and forth. "I don't have anything to say...Other than, I think it's hilarious that you think you can come over here and push me out of a spot because you want it. It's annoying. This isn't campus. This isn't the rink. I'm not going to fall to my knees for you."

I grinned at the assertion. "Never expected you to fall to your knees."

"Yeah, right." She waved her hand across the pond. "You've been staring at me from afar for the past twenty minutes. It was like you were practicing for the lead role in a romantic comedy."

"I wouldn't need practice for that. Trust me."

Jacobs laughed. "You sure? Word on the street is you only have experience with the physical parts of the role."

"You've been asking around about me?" I teased. I slept around...often. Sex had become the perfect way to decompress from everything in my life. I liked keeping things casual and made sure to find partners who preferred the same. Casual was simple. Low stakes. I saved the risk-taking for the ice. Because with a hockey stick in hand, I had control.

"I don't have to ask around about you. People talk all on their own. And you're surprisingly always great in their eyes," she said with a little bite. In a steadier voice, she added, "Don't even get me started on the banners."

"Banners?"

"Come on. You forget posing for the photos on every corner of campus?"

"Oh, those banners. They're up now?" I asked, genuinely surprised.

"They've been up for weeks." She shook her head. "You'd think a bar fight would make the school reconsider using you guys as campus role models."

I unconsciously brushed my fingers across the edge of my jaw. There was still a decent bruise from last week's post-game fight. A few of us got into it with some disgruntled guys looking for revenge. The fight was rough enough for the cops to get involved. There'd been a few arrests but none of my teammates among them, thank God.

"Is that your issue? You're jealous," I figured.

"No. Why would I be jealous of you?"

"You tell me, 'Miss Have You Seen Your Banners'?"

She took a breath. "I...fine, maybe I compare myself to you on occasion. It's hard not to when you're my counterpart."

Her shoulders sagged at the confession like she'd been holding a hundred-pound weight over her head this entire conversation.

My forehead wrinkled. "Counterpart?"

"Yeah, you know, you're the guy version of me," she explained. "First Black captain of Mendell's hockey team, competitive as hell, loves the attention of a full crowd, favors your left side on the ice—"

I frowned because no one was supposed to know I favored my left side. I'd trained myself well to cover it up, I hadn't received a note since high school.

Jacobs continued, not noticing my shock. "Thighs that could crush a man. Looks great on a ten-foot banner—I would totally rock that banner if they ever gave me the chance." She paused for a second, considering her next words. "You know, the only difference I've found between us is you can't keep a relationship and I can't stop having them—even if they're bad for me. But there's some intersection in that too, I'm sure."

"That so?" I was still reeling from her extensive observation.

"We both suck at romance," Jacobs murmured with a sigh as she rested her chin in her hand. "See? Practically twins."

I tried to digest everything, wondering if I should take her last assumption as an insult. "Can't keep a relationship? I don't try to keep a relationship."

"But if you did try, you couldn't." Jacobs' voice was flat and eyes slightly glazed over like the conversation was starting to bore her.

I frowned, taking her words as a challenge. I've never done well with people telling me I couldn't do something. "I could. No doubt. You on the other hand..." I trailed off, letting her assume the worst.

"What?" Her brow wrinkled when she saw me shaking my head. "What?"

"You wouldn't last a day in a casual relationship because you clearly care too much."

"I care an appropriate a-a-mount," she stammered.

I scoffed. "Really?"

Her nose wrinkled at my question. "Yes, really. I could do what you do easily."

"You sure about that?"

"Of course. I could do it ten times better," she said as if it were a known fact in the universe.

"Wanna bet?"

"Yes." Jacobs froze, shocked by her confirmation. "I mean...what is it we're betting exactly?"

I smiled at how her lips pressed together. Any athlete worth their weight knew how to handle uncertainty with a straight face. Jacobs stared at me like I was a wall in the way of her goal. I'm sure my look was no different. Even off the ice, we found ways to make up competitions. We were always going to crave a battle of some sort.

I suppose she was right. We were a lot alike. That fact made me more comfortable in her presence. I didn't know her well, but at least I understood a part of her that others probably wouldn't. The part of her that loved to be a winner.

"Casual sex," I said. "No more than a few months. No catching feelings."

Her expression clouded.

"Yeah, I thought so." I looked her up and down. "Bet you're just coming from a date and ready to commit yourself entirely."

My guess was a shot in the dark, so I was surprised when her mouth twisted in embarrassment.

"Not entirely," she grumbled, looking at the water again. "It was a rebound date. I haven't gone out with someone in two years. So, I might have been a little rusty and a little starved for romance. Sue me."

I whistled. "Two years? Why the long stretch?"

"I had a girlfriend...and she dumped me last semester."

My smile vanished. "Sorry."

She waved away the apology. "It was a long time coming. I'm fine."

We both went silent, and the air was heavy with how not fine she was.

I wracked my brain, trying to come up with something to distract her. Insulting Jacobs about her dating life had been a terrible move.

"You know what? I think you deserve the spot," I said, tapping my hand on the railing.

"Why?" Jacobs didn't look or sound thankful. She squinted in my direction, suspicious.

"It's a lucky spot," I said with a shrug. "I'm going to tell you something no one knows, okay? So, keep this between us."

"I'm definitely telling everyone," she joked with a smile and leaned closer to exaggerate interest. "Go on."

I chuckled. "I stand here and make wishes sometimes."

"Wishes?" Her eyebrows squished together.

"Yeah, right as the light from the sunset gets at a perfect angle." I pointed toward the windows above. Jacobs' gaze followed my hand. We were only minutes away from sunset. I moved closer so she'd have an easier time seeing where I pointed.

"See that baseball lodged in that tree branch?" I asked, my voice low since she leaned in close enough for me to feel the warmth of her body. My breathing hitched for a second when I smelled peppermint and rosemary. Part of her shoulder brushed mine. My stomach tightened at the feel of her warmth.

Jacobs stood on her tiptoes, trying to get a better look. "Yeah, I see it."

"It's m-m-magic." I winced at my stammering. The nerves turning in my stomach reminded me of when I was a kid. It'd been a long time since I tripped over my words in a conversation.

"Okay." Jacobs drew out the word, sounding skeptical.

"Make a wish when the sun hits it and it'll come true," I whispered, watching her take a breath. I thought she was going to do it and felt excited about being able to make her disappointment disappear for a moment. But, after a few seconds of silence, she shook her head.

"There's another place where we differ." She looked at me, not at all fazed at how close we stood. "I don't believe in magic, Morgan."

I cleared my throat, trying to not feel embarrassed about my confession and my serious lack of control over my drumming heart.

Jacobs let out a dry laugh. "And I'm not going to take the spot because you feel sorry for me and my breakup. Have it. Make your wishes."

"You don't know what you're missing," I said when she pushed away from the railing. "It really works."

"I'm sure it does." She walked backward as she spoke. "But I like to get my dreams the old-fashioned way. Hard work."

"Everyone needs a little help now and then," I teased.

"Good night, Morgan. Happy wishing." She gave me a small smile before leaving.

I tried not to feel some type of way about how the space felt empty now that she wasn't here. My spot was mine again. I claimed it, anticipating relief and only feeling loneliness.

The sun finally hit the baseball, and I made my wish.

Chapter Two

Aderyn

I 've always wanted to be a crier.

Crying seemed like such a perfect way to express myself after my most recent breakup. But anytime I tried, I felt numb. So began my journey to find something to trigger an emotional reaction. Cue a bait shop and Samson Morgan.

A few weeks ago, I started using this bait shop as my main place of escape. I rarely ran into students from campus. The employees were never too nosy or too helpful. The landscaping of the pond and the indoor waterfall was downright mesmerizing. And Morgan's frequent presence eventually became the cherry on top.

He came as often as I did. Always later in the day. Usually before game nights. I suppose the water and fish made him feel something, too.

At first, it'd been irritating sharing the shop with him. I couldn't get away from this guy on campus with those damn banners everywhere. And now, he'd somehow found my quiet spot. But, after a few times, I got used to seeing him and even anticipated it.

Morgan always triggered clashing emotions in me—it was the opposite of numbness, so exactly what I needed right now. I wanted to roll my eyes at his perfect smile and ask him a billion and one questions about how he was so good at being a captain. He was charming when he wasn't being a show-off. Interesting when he wasn't around a crowd of people.

When he approached me tonight, it broke the spell. I preferred admiring him from afar like he was some distant planet in a far-off galaxy. Morgan always maintained orbit on the opposite side of the shop. And I remained on mine. I preferred things that way because there was no expectation. No need to act a certain way. Once I opened my mouth, I put my foot in it.

I was snappy with people I admired—one time I met my favorite actress, pretended to not know her, and asked her to not block the walkway. I used the same clipped tone on Morgan. I left him behind in the bait shop, cringing on my way out.

"You're so ridiculous," I cursed under my breath as I exited the shop.

A teen on their way to clock in gave me a look, and I quickly shook my head.

"Not you," I promised. "Me. Definitely, me. Sorry."

The employee didn't look impressed, and I didn't blame them. With even more to cringe about, I started down the sidewalk. The sun was dipping behind the horizon and the parking lot looked emptier than when I first showed up. I didn't feel like going back to my dorm yet. I lingered outside the bait shop to figure out my next move.

The air smelled of fried fish. Across the street from the bait shop was a small restaurant set on the lake. There weren't many cars in the parking lot, but the cute fairy lights and scent of greasy food drew me forward. So, I followed my nose. Maybe I could drown my feelings in a pile of fries and tilapia.

A woman with graying hair greeted me as soon as I came through the door.

"Welcome to Shells. My name is Wendy," she said, giving me a kind smile. "How many are in your party, dear?"

"Just me." I smiled, still trying to shake off my embarrassment from running into Morgan. I needed to get over it. He didn't give a shit about me. He barely acknowledged my existence on a good day. I'm sure whatever I said to him had already been forgotten.

"Booth or bar?" The host grabbed a menu and led me toward the seating.

I scanned the restaurant to find only one couple eating in the building. A few servers were playing cards at the bar. And the bartender was building a wall of saltshakers. Busy night.

"Booth, if that's okay," I said.

"Of course." She whipped out a cloth to give the table a wipe before gesturing for me to sit. "Your server will be Janis. She'll be right with you."

I slid into my seat. "Thanks."

The menu felt a little sticky when I picked it up. I made a face and pulled a wet wipe from my bag. Janis laughed when she saw me cleaning the lamination and asked what I wanted to drink.

"Water's good," I said while examining a concerning stain blocking a few of the dinner specials.

"It's tap," she warned with a raised eyebrow. "No lemons."

"Got Coke?"

"Off-brand. Kind of flat but still pretty good."

I shrugged, not feeling energetic enough to drive across town for more options. "Eh, works for me."

Janis turned on her heel to grab my drink. I studied the menu, noting how good everything sounded. Baked lemon pepper salmon with creamy mashed potatoes and seasoned vegetables, grilled tequila lime fish tacos, or blue crab cakes with fresh basil and pickled mustard seed. I wondered if they did delivery.

"Well, if you wanted to go out, you should have just asked."

I froze. When I looked up, Morgan was slipping into the seat across from me. He'd shed his sweatshirt from before and now had on a distractingly tight, black, long-sleeved shirt. Morgan's skin was a gorgeous shade of deep brown. He was never without a perfect lineup and waves in his short, dark hair. A breath caught in my chest at the teasing smile he wore. That smile always lit up his eyes and made the curve of his jaw more defined. He was one of the most handsome guys I've met.

"What are you doing here?" I laid down the menu with a frown.

"Same as you," he said, leaning back to get comfortable. "This is the second time today you're in one of my favorite spots. I'm starting to feel this is less of a coincidence and more like your way of flirting."

I scoffed. "I got to both places first. If anyone is flirting, it's you."

"You got me," he said with an easy wink.

My cheeks burned. "Is this seriously your booth of choice? Do you go around town just pissing on everything to mark your claim?"

"No, not piss. I do things the old-fashioned way." He chuckled at his attempt at a callback.

I narrowed my gaze, unimpressed.

"I carve my initials," he explained.

No way. I scanned the table for some indication of faux ownership. He let me search for a few seconds before he laughed.

"I'm joking, Jacobs." He nudged his chin, gesturing to a booth near the windows. "That's my spot. And I didn't carve my initials in it—though I probably should now that I have to contend with you wherever I go."

"You always this territorial?"

He leaned forward, placing his elbows on the table. The closed distance made his next words surprisingly intimate. "When I'm allowed, yes. Very."

My mouth went dry. Janis showed up just in time with my drink. I grabbed it right as she set it down. They both looked impressed by my nonstop gulping. She asked what he wanted to drink, and Morgan didn't take his eyes off me for a second as he ordered.

"Good?" he questioned when Janis left.

"Incredible." I pulled away from the cup. The flatness of the soda made it perfect for downing and calming my nerves. "If you're so territorial, why are you over here bugging me?"

"Because I thought it'd be more awkward if I sat over there than if I joined you here."

He had a point.

"Unless, of course, you prefer sitting alone." Morgan moved like he was going to get up.

"No, no," I said a little too quickly. "It's fine. Stay. I...I'm sure you're not horrible company. Besides, if you've been here before you can tell me what to avoid on the menu."

"Now that I can do." Morgan looked excited at my invitation and spun the menu around so he could get a proper look. "Let's see what we got for house specials today."

I watched him drum his fingers against the table. The beat was familiar and oddly soothing. As he murmured to himself about the excessive amount of cod dishes available, I tried to work up the courage to ask him a question without revealing how much of a fangirl I was.

I started playing hockey at four years old. My mom put me in a rec league because there were no beginning classes for figure skating at the time. Once I got a hockey stick in my hands, I became obsessed. When I wasn't playing, I was watching games on TV or in person. Most of my allowance growing up went to tickets, merch, and equipment.

When I started looking for colleges to play hockey for, I went to a game where Morgan was playing. I'd never seen someone so confident with a puck. Most of the professionals I studied didn't have shit on his technique and he'd only been a freshman at the time.

Since my family used to live a few towns over, I caught most of his games. When it came time to enroll, I didn't have enough money to spend my first year at Mendell. And there weren't enough sports scholarships to go around. But, by my sophomore year, my stepdad got a job working in the athletic department. Tuition became astronomically more affordable.

I transferred in a heartbeat because I wanted to be close to greatness. And now, a large part of that greatness sat right across from me, and I couldn't figure out how to not sound stand-offish.

"Any allergies I should—" he started.

"How old were you when you started playing hockey?" I blurted and winced at talking over him. "Sorry, my bad."

Morgan chuckled. "No worries."

"And no allergies," I shared.

"Started in middle school," he said, looking back down at the menu.

"Middle school?" My eyes widened. Most players I knew started as early as they could. The earlier you started, the better off you'd be.

"Yeah. On the weekends with my friends," he said. "You opposed to salmon?"

"Salmon's fine." I nodded. "Weekends only? No rec leagues?"

"Nah. I barely learned the rules until I made my high school team." He looked up, gaze searching for our server.

"Wow, that's..." Impressive. Far more impressive than I thought his background would be. I'll be damned if I admitted it though. "You come from a family of players?"

Maybe it was in his genes? Maybe he came from a long line of athletes?

My mom had thrown the shotput in high school. Placed second in the state. I got my large build from her. And learned to love my muscles from watching how much she loved hers. Most of the women in my family were built thick. And we all competed in some kind of sport. It was in our blood to compete and win.

He laughed. "No, absolutely not. My dad's a preacher turned dentist. His dad's a preacher turned alcoholic."

"Oh."

He gave me a half-shrug. "Not a lot of money in preaching."

Janis appeared with refills for our drinks. Morgan asked if it was okay to order for me and I nodded, curious about what he'd choose.

"If you hate it, you can throw the tomatoes at me," he permitted.

"Don't worry, I will."

He laughed at my ready agreement.

"So, you're just a natural on the ice, is that it?" I asked.

Morgan reached for a packet of sugar to pour into his iced tea. "I guess one could say that."

"Unbelievable."

"Are you doing that comparison thing again?" He gestured between the both of us. "Because you know they say that's the thief of all joy."

My shoulder sagged. "It just kills me not to get to the bottom of things. You have this wealth of knowledge and skills you've got from raw talent."

He sipped on his drink, considering my words. "You looking for advice?"

"Always."

"Why? From what I hear, you're the best thing to happen to the women's team in years."

I perked up. Sure, he wasn't directly complimenting me, but it was close. "Really? From who?"

"Overheard Coach Bella bragging about you. And our head coach constantly wishes you could play on our team."

My stomach fluttered and I smiled to myself.

"Might have caught a few of your games, too," he added.

I looked up, surprised at his confession. The women's hockey game turnout was pathetic in comparison to the men's. I'm talking barely enough people to fill a row. The guys' team rarely came to the women's games—even though, as a rule, we showed up to all of theirs to cheer them on.

"From what I've seen, you're good," Morgan stated, simply. "Is there some problem I'm not seeing?"

I thought for a moment. "I want it too much."

I wanted to be the best so much it hurt. My desire wasn't just because I wanted to win. It was because I loved the security I got from being on the ice. I was addicted to the feeling. When I played well, I became untouchable. Nothing compared to feeling strong enough to take on anything in the world.

"And you think I don't want it?" Morgan asked.

"Well...no, not like me. You're a natural, you don't have to want what you already have. Even under pressure, your delivery is nearly flawless. I see it in how you interact with your team, too. You're a leader, through and through. I fuck up every chance I get because..."

"You want it too much," he repeated.

"It's painful," I assured. "It bleeds into other stuff, too. The more I want something, the further away it gets. Hockey, relationships, grades, everything."

There was a lull in the conversation, long enough for me to realize how open I was being. Morgan was easier to talk to than he looked. It was all in the eye contact. The undivided attention. He didn't look away when I was talking, and because of that, I could see every change in his expression. His unbothered brow and nods let me know his ear was a nonjudgmental one.

"Want to know something really embarrassing?" I asked since I was already knee-deep in sharing.

He smiled. "Of course."

"I asked my girlfriend to be my girlfriend on the first date. Who the hell does that?"

He chuckled and raised a brow. "When you know, you know?"

I snorted. "No, I didn't know. I just wanted to be all in immediately."

"Interesting. Can't say I relate."

"How do you do it? Not fall for the people you sleep with? Not want to be all-in?"

Morgan shook his head. "I don't think my advice is going to help your situation."

"Oh, come on."

"It's not," he promised. "Besides, I thought you said you could do what I do easily? Why would you need my advice?"

I opened my mouth and then closed it again. Okay, sure, I got a little bigheaded earlier. Might have bitten off more than I could chew. Morgan grinned, seeming to know I'd been all talk. My face flushed in embarrassment and pride.

"I did, didn't I?" I nodded. "And I can. Given the chance, I could best you any day of the week."

"Love to see you try."

Without thinking, I declared: "Game on."

He paused, disbelieving. "Yeah, right."

"Really." I sat taller like good posture would save me from barreling headfirst into a pile of shit. "We'll start with sleeping around. If I catch feelings, I'm out. If you give in and sleep with multiple people, you're out."

His expression changed to something unreadable.

"I thought you were..." He shook his head. "You said you had a girlfriend before...sorry, I shouldn't have assumed."

"Assumed? That I'm straight?" I asked, my forehead wrinkling.

He nodded.

"I'm bi," I clarified. "And what does that have to do with...oh. *Oh*. You thought...?"

"Yeah." He laughed, and for the first time, it sounded strained.

My mouth went dry. Our food came just in time for me to gather my thoughts and have a moment to myself to figure out what I needed to say to clear up our misunderstanding.

"I didn't mean you and me sleeping...together," I whispered because suddenly, the restaurant felt quiet enough for the cook to hear me in the back.

"Right, of course." He gestured to his head. "Mind in the gutter. Always."

"I'd never sleep with you," I continued while looking down at my plate. The baked salmon, mashed potatoes, and vegetables looked heavenly. It was a shame my stomach was turning with too many nerves for me to enjoy the first bite.

"Never? Well, that's a long time," he noted, tone one part teasing, two parts disappointed.

I choked on the fish. Morgan held up my Coke when I couldn't stop coughing. I guided the straw to my lips, and he kept the cup steady as I drank.

"Are you serious?" I gasped once I was finally able to speak. "You would want to..."

"We could keep one another accountable that way." He set my cup down. "You prove you can walk away easily. Or I prove I could do romance easily if I wanted."

From the sound of his voice, I think he took my criticism at Harry's far more seriously than I thought. Huh. Why did that make me feel proud? I kind of liked the idea of getting under his skin. He was always so put together on campus. Until his bar fight, I didn't think the guy swung a punch out of the rink.

"You want to become fuck buddies to prove you're a romantic?" I laughed. "Do you know how ridiculous that sounds?"

"It could be interesting. You'd be free to sleep around, of course."

My smile faded. "What?"

"I play the all-in role, you play the...player. Come on, tell me you're not at least a little interested."

I was, and that was the scary part. "It's a silly idea."

"But fun. Look, the further we get into the season, the more we'll need an escape. And, if I'm being honest, finding a decent partner can be draining. I need a break from the constant bar hopping and party going."

It was hard to keep a straight face when the hot center forward you admired offered to sleep with you.

"I thought Harry's was your escape?" I tried to buy time.

"It's getting a little crowded." He winked. "Don't you think?"

"Ridiculous," I repeated, unable to hide my smile. "Reckless, too."

"Reckless, how?"

"We're captains. Leaders."

He gave me a one-shoulder shrug. "So?"

"We're supposed to be setting an example."

"Jacobs, I'm not suggesting we fuck on the floor of locker rooms or something."

My stomach dropped at that visual. I could barely pay attention to the rest of what he was saying because...sex in the locker room with him could be kind of hot. I hated that I thought it'd be hot. Sure, I wasn't immune to Morgan's looks but it was usually easier than this to manage my thoughts about him.

"What happens between us, stays between us. Tell your teammates to mind their business. I tell mine that constantly," he finished.

I chewed on my lip.

"Hey, no pressure," he said in a serious tone. "I'm half-messing with you."

"And the other half?"

"Would enjoy blowing off steam while also proving you wrong," he said. "I could be a full-fledged romantic lead if I wanted."

"Fine."

Morgan blinked, surprised. "Fine?"

"I'll consider it."

His wide smile encouraged heat to form between my legs. "Well, let me know once you make up your mind. Either way, no hard feelings. You can still hang out at my spot. Any of them."

"Wow, you're so generous," I joked.

"Consider it a preview, Jacobs." He smiled and reached to hold up my drink for me again when I choked on another bite.

Chapter Three

Aderyn

I swiped my student ID to unlock the women's weight room doors. Mary Yoon, my roommate's girlfriend, and our team's starting goalie manned the front desk. I made a beeline for her when I noticed she was chewing on her wispy, black curl. That was never a good sign.

Mary dropped her book as soon as she saw me, failing to mark what page she was on.

"I need you to put me out of my misery. After you do, remind Jas they're the love of my life and will inherit all my fortune—which is fifty dollars in Bath and Bodyworks gift cards, but still," she said.

"Good morning to you, too," I teased, leaning on the cold, granite counter.

"Is it?" she asked. "Because after I clocked in, I had to watch some guys cart out half of our weightlifting equipment."

My smile disappeared in an instant. "What?"

"Half of our shit." She snapped her fingers. "Poof...well, not poof, poof, of course. It took them two hours to get everything out of the door."

"This better be a joke." I stood on my tiptoes to look behind her. Sure enough, there was an alarming amount of space on the workout floor.

"Did they give you a reason?" I asked.

She shrugged. "Something about the equipment being a hazard because it's too old."

"Too old?" I laughed, humorlessly. "Of course, it's too old. Most of this shit's been here since the early 2000s! We told them that at the beginning of the semester."

"Well, they finally listened."

"Did they tell you when we'd get replacements?"

Mary gave me a knowing look.

I sucked the back of my teeth in frustration. "Are you kidding me? So, we're going to start a queue line for the few bench presses we have left?"

"I can make us a real cute sign-up sheet," Mary offered. "I've gotten good at Photoshop this semester."

The women athletes at Mendell were great despite—and not because of—the school. I learned very early on in my college career, women's sports programs were hardly ever given the attention and funding we deserved. We often got by with hand-me-down equipment from the men, subpar uniforms, and inconsistent transport to and from games.

"I bet you the guys are sitting pretty on some brand-new equipment," I said under my breath, thinking about the men's weight room just next door. It felt like every time I walked by their room, there was something nice and shiny to admire.

"I heard they get gift bags stuffed with free clothes and energy snacks every weekend." Mary sighed and looked wistfully into the distance. "What I'd give for Nike to notice me. My sports bras have seen better days."

"We're going to do something about this," I promised. "Where's Coach Bella? Is she in her office yet?"

Mary looked unimpressed with my determined declaration. I've gotten riled up plenty of times this season. I'd spoken up and complained constantly to coaches and anyone else in the athletic department. Each time, they convinced me that they were "working on it." That I had to be "patient."

"They're just going to spew the same old stuff." Mary shook her head, already looking defeated. I couldn't have that. Especially come later at practice. Defeatist attitudes spread faster than the flu around here.

Every single time one of my teammates walked on campus and saw how much this school didn't invest in them fucked with their heads. This wasn't just about being good on the ice. It affected their lives outside of hockey, too, making them think they weren't important because the school treated them this way. I'd know since I went to war with my self-worth on the regular.

We shouldn't have to. Deep down, I knew I was one of the best. I knew my team was, too. We could make history. Mary (an excitable goalie who was Korean), Jas (a quiet, steady, Black woman who dominated in their ring wing position), Kaya (a Black, fiery left-wing player), and I were a record number of women of color on a starting line-up in the league this year. We could change the game...if we got the support.

Mary seemed to read my mind because she said, "Kaya thinks it's pointless to complain."

My jaw tightened. "Kaya doesn't know what she's talking about half of the time."

"I don't know. I kind of agree with her."

"Don't go to the dark side on me, Mary." I massaged the sides of my neck, trying to formulate a plan. "We need solutions, not negativity."

"I could start teaching a Pilates class in the morning. People underestimate how toned you can get with some dumbbells and a mat," she said, eyes shining a bit. The girl was passionate about her Pilates.

"Good. That's one option." I pressed my knuckles on the desk, trying to think of something else. A few rowdy guys passing by outside pulled me out of my thoughts. They were on their way to a state-of-the-art facility to complete their workout in relative peace. They didn't have to worry about equipment being removed by higher-ups or being ignored by them.

"What are you doing?" Mary asked when I pushed away from the counter with an admittedly alarming, determined look on my face.

"Going to see something." I grabbed my gym bag from the floor.

"Ryn, I wouldn't," Mary called after me.

"I'm just looking."

"What's the point?"

"To satisfy my morbid curiosity." I flashed her a smile that was supposed to be comforting. "I won't make a scene. Promise."

Mary scoffed. "That's what you said last time."

"Well, it's this time," I said and shoved the door open.

S tudent athletes got a lot of perks on campus. Free meals, seemingly limitless sports drinks, and separate workout facilities from the rest of the student population. Those perks were, of course, under lock and key so the school could make sure the "right" people were being taken care of. So, I had to wait outside of the men's weight room to sneak in when one of them used their card to buzz in.

"Good morning," I said in an exaggerated perky voice when the guy I slipped in behind glanced at me. He simply raised a brow, not caring enough to ask what I was doing. The guy working their front desk didn't even look up when I passed by. He scrolled through his phone and offered me deuces.

"Have a good workout," he mumbled in a bored voice, keeping his gaze on his screen.

"Thanks," I muttered and stepped into what looked like heaven on earth. My eyes went big and my heart skipped a beat. I was in love.

The men's weight room was two times larger than ours. Their equipment was shiny, new, and abundant, just like I expected. So, fucking abundant it brought a tear to my eye.

Guys spread out in the space—not a queue in sight. Perfectly maintained battle ropes (fraying? They didn't know her) were lined on the far wall. Power racks had pegs for band assistance exercises. Their adjustable weight benches adjusted without them having to put in copious amounts of elbow grease. What a concept, I know.

"Assholes," I laughed to myself.

Honestly, I shouldn't blame them. It wasn't their fault the athletic department invested more money in the men's teams. But still, my blood wouldn't stop boiling every time one of them let out a laugh or called out a joke to each other. The energy here was far less bleak. Even the lighting seemed brighter.

"None of that yellow light shit," I mumbled to myself as I admired the light bulbs overhead.

I made the decision then and there to claim one of the lockers for my gym bag. A few guys side-eyed me, but there was no protest about my presence. Best believe I was going to milk this for as long as I could. I tugged on my weight-lifting gloves. The material was old and peeling. I wrapped athletic tape around my wrist to secure the fabric because the straps were broken. Once my gloves were in place, I made my way to the benches. The plan was to get in a proper session without having to stuff cotton back into a torn bench seat.

When I chose my bench, I didn't realize Morgan was two seats over until I placed on my weights. As soon as our eyes locked in the mirror, his face broke out into an amused smile. I frowned back.

Morgan wore a black muscle tee that hung loosely around the arm area. His red shorts barely reached his knees, showing off the hard curve of his thighs and calves. My chest felt heavy at the sight of him. I took a deep breath to recenter myself. I was on a mission and couldn't let his presence distract me.

We hadn't spoken in a few days since our dinner at Shells. I avoided Harry's because I needed to think and steel my resolve. Being fuck buddies with a fellow captain would be all kinds of complicated. Neither of us needed complicated.

"Morgan," I greeted with a firm nod.

He couldn't hold back a chuckle and didn't even sound the least bit formal when he replied, "Jacobs."

I foolishly hoped that would be all. He'd go on with his reps, and I'd start mine—just two college athletes enjoying a quiet workout.

"Are you in the right place?" he asked teasingly.

I straddled my bench and leaned back. "No doubt about it."

A few guys to our right were glancing my way and whispering now. They wore looks of disapproval and maybe a bit of disgust at my presence. I tried not to take it too personally. I was here to make a point and of course, some people would take issue. Their feelings didn't matter. Showing people we deserved proper equipment did.

I wrapped my hands around the steel bar, took a breath, and lifted it off the hooks. After fifteen reps, I replaced the bar with ease. Morgan was still watching me through the mirror. When I met his gaze there, he raised a brow.

"You got something to say?" I asked him because I couldn't challenge the guys a few feet down without making a big scene. Morgan was close enough and far less intimidating.

"I do, but I don't think you're gonna want to hear it." He grabbed a towel hanging on the edge of his bench and used it to wipe his neck. I chewed on my bottom lip as I watched. Sweat was never sexy to me. It didn't matter who was sweating. But something about how Morgan's biceps flexed and relaxed as he cleaned himself made my pussy clench.

My jaw stiffened at the feeling, and I quickly laid back on the bench and got in another set.

"Say it. I'm dying to know," I said sarcastically when I put the bar back on the hook.

Morgan opened his mouth but stopped short when someone greeted him.

"You said you were going to wake me," Lincoln complained with a smile that indicated he wasn't pressed. Mendell Hawks' starting goalie was an outgoing guy who knew and got along with everyone. Lincoln was willowy for a hockey player. His brown skin was a few shades lighter than Sam's. And his hair was grown out just enough to curl at the ends.

When Lincoln saw me, his eyes brightened. The nerves that'd been building in my chest, thanks to the still whispering guys, subsided.

"Hey, how's it going, boss?" Lincoln offered me his fist. I smiled and bumped my fist against his. Leave it to him not question my presence for a second. Lincoln was a roll-with-the-punches, the more, the merrier, kind of guy.

"Not too bad," I said. "My morning got screwed up because of some missing equipment, though. Had to search for greener pastures."

"Damn." Lincoln's forehead wrinkled. "Sorry to hear that."

"No worries. It's not your fault." I said the last part while looking at Morgan. He hadn't removed his gaze from me for a second, even when exchanging a handshake with Lincoln. It obviously wasn't Morgan's fault either but a petty part of me wanted him to experience just a minuscule level of guilt for not making me feel as welcome as his friend had.

"Here, let me spot you." Lincoln moved into position behind my bench.

"Thanks." I smiled. "That's so nice of you to offer."

I spoke in a sweeter tone to Lincoln and Morgan noticed immediately. All humor faded from his eyes. His mouth set in a hard line. He watched me lift as his friend cheered me on. I got through my next set without breaking a sweat. Morgan huffed, obviously impressed even though he didn't say it.

"You're an absolute beast, Aderyn," Lincoln complimented once he helped set the bar back in place. "You coming for blood at your next game? You guys are up against Monroe, aren't you?"

I nodded, surprised he was familiar with our schedule. "They got the best of us last year. I don't plan on it happening again."

Lincoln laughed. "Hell yeah. That's what I'm talking about. We need your kind of energy around here. The guys have grown a bit sluggish this year. What do you think, Sam? We should finally steal her for our own, right?"

Morgan didn't answer immediately. The amused glint in his eyes said he agreed, but not in the way Lincoln was suggesting. I swallowed at how his gaze lingered on my face, taking me in like I was the only thing in the room.

"Grab Jacobs a drink, will you?" Morgan said in a firm tone. It was his captain's tone. The one I heard when I'd catch the end of their practices. Or, in the middle of their games. It was deep and so damn commanding I almost got up to do it myself.

My pussy clenched again. So much for a steeled resolve. God, I used to be so good at steel resolve. This was embarrassing.

"Got to show her just how green the pasture is," Morgan added.

"Right," Lincoln agreed. "What are you up for, Aderyn? We've got it all. The fridges are literally overflowing."

"A water's fine," I said.

"You sure?" Lincoln's shoulders sagged, disappointed. "I mean it when I say we have everything."

"She's sure, Link," Morgan said, finality in his tone.

"Alright. Wasted opportunity if you ask me, though." Lincoln turned and left toward the break area.

"You serious about your equipment?" Morgan asked as soon as his friend was out of earshot.

"Why would I lie about that?"

He nodded. "Right. Well, I'm sorry. But you know if one of the coaches finds you in here, you'll get kicked out. Potentially get a strike. I heard Bella runs you guys harder than Haynes runs us."

"Getting a strike or being kicked out is the point, though," I said with a grin.

He tilted his head to the side as he studied me. "Is it?"

"Think of my presence as a silent protest."

Morgan scoffed. "Silent?"

"Well, I didn't come in here causing a scene. And I certainly wasn't the one who started talking."

"Nothing about you is silent, Jacobs. You don't have to open your mouth to make noise. Your entire presence is hard to ignore…" his voice faded at the end of the sentence like he'd lost the willpower to continue.

"I'll take that as a compliment," I joked. This wouldn't be the first time I'd been told I'm too much. I've been too big, too bossy, and too difficult for most of my life. I won't lie, it stung hearing him say it in an off-handed sort of way. But I wasn't going to change for anyone. Didn't want to and couldn't –even if I tried.

"It was," Morgan said.

I froze. He repeated what he'd said with more firmness than the first time. My heartbeat picked up. I heard a hint of admiration in his words this time.

"On the other hand," he continued and looked around to make sure we still had relative privacy. "I must be very easy to ignore. Or, at least, avoid."

My body warmed. He was talking about Harry's.

"I'm not trying to make you feel some type of way," he said.

"And I don't," I lied.

His hands fidgeted with the hand towel he still held. "Well, good for you."

"Great for me, actually," I tried to one-up him. "I'm great."

He shook his head. I nearly lost it when he bit down on his bottom lip in a failed attempt at lessening his smile. That damn smile with its perfect curve and undeniable charm. He knew exactly what he was doing with that smile.

"I just need to know I didn't scare you away with my...suggestion," he said in a low voice.

"You didn't. I've been busy." Busy trying to figure out if I was crushing on him because I admired him, because he was hot, or both. Would either be an issue? No. Not yet. Not if I kept my feelings to myself. Because I was already beginning to lose the bet: I couldn't successfully be with multiple people like he could. It was annoying as hell to know I was failing at something, even if the bet wasn't in action.

"Really?" Morgan didn't sound convinced.

"Yes," I confirmed. "And I've given your suggestion some thought."

"We can pretend like it never happened," he said, quickly, as if he'd been waiting for an opening to say that. "It was a weird idea."

"I thought it was interesting. It'll be even more interesting when I win." I don't know what possessed me to say it. Maybe it was him trying to backtrack right when the space we kept between us was closing for the first time since I started attending Mendell. I'd had a great time the other night—even though I probably didn't seem excited to be sitting across from him.

I wanted more.

Morgan rubbed the back of his neck. "You pullin' my leg, Jacobs?"

"Not at all."

He took a deep breath, still looking skeptical.

"But if you want to back out." I shrugged. "Go ahead. Sometimes it's best to admit defeat early. Saves energy."

Morgan laughed. "I see what you're doing."

"I'm just a good sport. I'll respect your forfeit."

"Forfeiting's not in my nature." He tossed his towel over his shoulder and stood up. "Let's get breakfast when you're done."

My hands felt clammy. Not because of impending competition—I was more than capable of holding my own—but the dangerous look in his eyes. Like he had an ace up his sleeve.

"Where?" I asked.

"There's a nice spot within walking distance. It'd be my treat. Then we can talk. Set up some ground rules."

"Oh...okay. Yeah. Sounds good." I nodded, feeling like a bobblehead on a dashboard.

He smiled. "I'll meet you out front."

Chapter Four

Sam

D ust + Dawn was a small, on-campus breakfast spot for students. The line was nearly out the door when Jacobs and I got to the restaurant. Inside, the walls were a pastel green and white shelf displays overflowed with fresh-baked pastries.

"My personal favorite's the Cat in the Hat," I said while we waited. The menu was a slideshow displayed on a TV above the counter. When I first got here, the number of options was overwhelming and the cursive font on the screen was a headache to read. So, much like at Shells, I thought it might be helpful to offer her my recommendations. "Or the Wild Things."

She frowned, squinting at the menu. "Wild Things?"

"They're jelly-filled doughnut bites," I explained.

Jacobs fake gagged. "Please, don't tell me you like jelly-filled."

"Please, tell me you do." I chuckled at how she bunched up her lips as if someone was currently trying to force-feed her the doughnuts.

"They're disgusting. They smell awful and are a disgrace to all doughnut kind."

"Damn, *all* doughnut kind? Did you meet up with them and ask?"

"Yes. It was a privilege and honor to be in their presence."

I snorted her deadpan tone. We hadn't been together for more than a few minutes and my cheeks already hurt from how much I was smiling.

Jacobs continued studying the menu, tilting her head to the side when she noticed the theme. "Is everything named after a children's book here?"

"Nah, they switch it up every semester. Last year, everything was Marvel-themed...until they got a cease and desist letter."

"Damn," Jacobs said. "Wait, so the options change every semester? That's annoying. Your favs are just gone?"

"It's the same food," I quickly assured. "Different names."

"Same selections but you gotta learn the new names every few months?"

When I nodded to confirm, she laughed and said, "God, I hate gimmick restaurants."

I exaggerated a huff, pretending to be offended. "What are you talking about? They're the best. Why not make eating out an experience?"

"It's all theatrics for no reason," she argued and waved her hand toward the menu. "Just be straightforward and tell me what you sell."

"You would choose to ask for a ham and cheese sandwich over getting to say something like, give me the Terminator?"

"Yes," she confirmed without hesitation.

I tsked but still wore a good-natured smile. "Boring."

"I didn't realize you were so into fluff," Jacobs noted. "Always took you for more of a straight-to-the-point guy."

"I'm into a lot of things. Some of which you might know if you stop thinking you can learn everything about me from what you observe at the rink."

Jacobs chewed on her lip for a moment, gaze avoiding mine as she tried to hide her embarrassment. I bumped my shoulder against hers to remind her I was only playing. It took a whole lot more than harmless assumptions to offend me.

"Touche, Morgan," she said after a few seconds of silence. "Tell me what you like and don't like again?"

I listed off the things worth trying and avoiding. Jacobs nodded, seemingly interested in getting one of my suggestions. But once it was time to place our order, she got the one thing I said I didn't enjoy on the menu: The Giving Tree. Also known as apple pancakes.

I smiled when she picked up her plate, knowing she was being contrary on purpose. She gave me that same proud grin she had in the weight room. The one that caused her chin to tip up a little. I bit down on my inner cheek, imagining pressing my lips against hers to melt away every ounce of smugness in exchange for something more primal. It was a vivid thought that I pushed away as soon as it appeared.

Once we got our food, she led the way to the outdoor seating. The sun was out, making it warmer than usual. Jacobs wanted to enjoy the heat while we could, and the sun seemed to enjoy her in return. Her dark brown skin looked beautiful in the light. I tried not to stare as she flipped her braids over her shoulders and gathered her hair in a band. She had to tilt her head back, exposing her neck as she secured her hair. I swallowed the lump in my throat.

"How long do you plan on protesting in silence?" I asked as I unwrapped my Cat in the Hat (a ham, egg, and cheese croissant).

Jacobs shrugged, kicking her feet up on the empty chair at our table. She often took up any available space around her. I'd be lying if I said I didn't think it was fucking hot.

"Until everyone's as pissed off as I am about the situation," she said.

"Have you talked to your coaches?" I asked. The look she gave me was piercing.

"I must come off as a complete clown to you." She opened her plastic fork and stabbed at a few pieces of pancake.

"No, clown's not the word I'd use," I teased.

"What would you use then?"

I hesitated for a second. I wasn't sure if my first answer would offend her or not. Jacobs was a challenge. And not in some weird, notches on headboard way. Ever since we finally talked about something outside of hockey, her presence pressed against me like a bump in a mattress. When she walked into the weight room this morning, I couldn't help but feel excited I'd finally have another shot at learning more about her.

I had no business focusing on Jacobs. There was too much on my plate with upcoming games and figuring out how I was going to deal with the new information about our athletic director, Stoll. My to-do list was longer than I-95. Yet, I willed the clock to tick a little slower, so we got more time.

This wasn't just about our sex bet—though that was undeniably appealing. It was about the look she had in her eyes the other night. It was the same one I had whenever someone challenged me. There was a fire in her gaze.

The other night, when Jacobs told me how badly she wanted everything, I remembered when I used to be that way. That was before coming to Mendell tainted everything. Before Stoll cast a shadow on hockey and made the future uncertain. I wanted to find my way back to that feeling. I wanted to be more like her.

"Determined," I settled on. "You're used to fighting for what you want."

"Nice save." She licked whipped cream off her fork. There was no seduction in the motion but my dick hardened, nonetheless.

I hadn't hooked up with anyone since a party a few weeks ago. My stress levels were through the roof, rising each day. Our bet would be a very welcomed interruption to my life. Maybe I'd finally be able to relax.

"So, when I win," Jacobs started with a smile. "What do I get?"

"When you win?" I played dumb.

She nodded. "When I prove I can sleep around casually without catching feelings and you fail at sticking with one partner—"

"So sure of yourself?" I leaned back in my seat. I was also sure of myself. Jacobs sounded like a textbook romantic. Falling for someone on the first date? Absolutely wild.

"Very sure," Jacobs agreed. "Now, what do I get?"

I rested my arms on the table, leaning in closer. "What do you want?"

She tapped her fork on her lips. The action resulted in more whipped cream transferred onto her skin. I watched her tongue as she licked it off. A frustrated groan threatened to rise in my throat. I took a sip of water to silence it.

"Your O'Ree jersey," she decided with a devious look in her eyes. She thought I was going to deny the request.

I raised a brow. "That it?"

"It's rare, expensive, and signed." She laughed at my nonchalant response. "I thought you'd put up a fight."

"It's yours," I promised.

Her eyes widened. "Wait, for real? I was half-joking. Morgan that jersey's a collector's dream. A piece of Black history. He was the first Black hockey player in the NHL."

"I'm aware." My uncle got it when he was a kid and passed it on to me. I had the jersey displayed back at the house I was renting this semester with my friends. She'd probably seen it there at one of Lincoln's parties. The excitement in her gaze almost made me consider letting her win. But I wouldn't go down easy.

Jacobs' shoulders sagged when she realized why I was so chill with 'letting the jersey go.'

"You're that convinced you can beat me."

"I am," I confirmed.

She rolled her eyes. "Fine. I get the jersey. What about you?"

"The satisfaction of proving you wrong."

"Boring. Come on, you can do better than that," she teased.

"Fine." I thought for a second. "You buy the rest of my meals at Shells until I graduate. And give up the Harry's spot. Northside is your side."

Jacobs snorted. "Alright, bet."

"Perfect." I grinned. "So, guidelines and rules?"

"We start with STI testing."

"Naturally," I agreed. "And with each new partner you have, we'll get tested again."

She readjusted in her seat at the mention of new partners. "Right. How do I know if you're only having sex with me?"

"You'll have to trust me. Like I'll just have to trust you're sleeping with other people."

"Fair," she agreed.

"I'll make it easy on you," I said. "I'll give you some tricks of the trade later. Help you beef up your flirting game."

She eyed me, suspiciously. "Why?"

"I'm nice."

Jacobs snorted and I laughed.

"Also, I don't mind leveling the playing field. I have years of experience doing this. Besides, you did ask me for advice. Begged might be a better word."

She frowned, obviously embarrassed. "I wasn't completely myself that night."

"You seemed fine to me."

"What's our time frame?" she changed the subject quickly.

"I'm thinking three months."

"Why?"

"Playoffs will almost be over by then. We'll be able to readjust our focus for finals."

She nodded. "Okay, three months. You're monogamous and I'm casual."

"Hello, Casual," I teased, earning me a roll of the eyes.

"The first person to crack loses."

I stretched out my hand. "Deal?"

"Deal." She gave my hand a firm shake.

"Good luck." Our hands stayed connected, even when the shake was long over. "Not falling for me and all that."

Jacobs scoffed but I could tell by the slight twitch of her eye she was nervous. "Keep your luck. I won't need it. You're not as irresistible as you think."

I grinned. "We'll see about that."

Chapter Five

Aderyn

Me: **Meet me at my place tonight?**

It'd been a few days since our breakfast, and Morgan insisted on letting me make the first move. He'd left my text unanswered and unread for the past three hours. I kept listening for my phone to vibrate and cursing myself when I was disappointed at notifications that had nothing to do with him.

It was already happening. I was becoming invested, and I hadn't even slept with him. I asked for tonight because I wanted to rip off the band-aid ASAP. Waiting for him felt like a slow, painful removal.

"This okay?" Kaya asked after setting down the last cone. "Ryn?"

I blinked and looked up. "Sorry. What?"

She gave me a look. Kaya confused a lot of people with her sweet, heart-shaped face, lavender-colored coils, and butterfly earrings. She looked harmless. In reality, the girl could check a body like a beast and curse like she'd spent most of her life in prison. We met last year and got close instantly. Like me, she was a large Black girl who was told she wouldn't get a boyfriend because she lifted too many weights. We bonded over our "undesirability" and obsession with being the best.

"You alright? You've been out of it all fucking morning," she said.

"I'm fine just..." I shook my head and scanned the cones she'd laid down on the ice. I needed to shove this whole "bet" thing into the furthest corner of my mind now. Practice was in less than ten minutes. I needed to be focused to run drills.

"You worried about the department meeting?" Kaya skated closer to hear me better. She'd lost hearing in one ear, and partial hearing in the other after getting sick as a kid.

"Yeah." I nodded, grateful for the excuse to label my mood. "I don't think they're going to be fair."

Coach Bella promised to address our budget concerns at the upcoming athletic department meeting. We all hoped it'd lead to restoring our equipment, but the longer the meeting went on, the less likely that was going to happen.

Kaya leaned on her hockey stick. "When are those bastards ever fair?"

I sighed. "You're right. Still, I can't help thinking there's something more we can do. Coach Bella and Lucy said the reason we don't get more money is because they think we can't pull the crowds."

"But we dominate the league, Ryn." Kaya looked pissed at the idea of having to put in more effort. "Who cares about pulling a crowd?"

"They do. It's a business." I couldn't blame her for being annoyed. Like all student athletes, we slept, ate, and breathed our sport. Morning runs, afternoon workouts, late-night study sessions, and weekend drills. Every minute of every day our bodies and brains were on high alert. None of us had time to breathe or have a social life outside of our teams and other athletes.

"If our games don't start selling tickets, we'll have to get used to the short end of the stick. No audience means no advertising dollars. No advertising, then no sponsors. Without sponsors, we can say goodbye to new equipment and uniforms. If that happens, we stop attracting top talent, and we start losing. It'll become a vicious cycle. The Mendell women's hockey team legacy will be no more."

Kaya threw her head back and groaned. "God, I didn't think coming here would make me feel like a second-class citizen."

"Welcome to women's sports. Now, stop moping and help me think of an idea to attract more people. If it's butts in seats they want, that's what we'll give them."

My friend pinched the bridge of her nose, already over brainstorming. "I don't know. Maybe it's time to talk to your dad?"

I frowned so hard I nearly pulled a muscle. "Absolutely not. You know that's off-limits."

"I don't see anything else that'd help us get a leg up. The guys have the privilege of using what's between their legs to attract crowds."

I snorted. "I don't think they see it like that."

Kaya gave me a look. "Come on. You're telling me most of this college crowd is cheering because they love the sport? No. They're there for the eye candy. What we need is a different approach: Nepotism."

"I'm not talking to Warren. End of discussion."

Warren was my stepdad and Athletic Director at Mendell. He'd been the main person to encourage me to try out for Mendell's team when I was panicked about making the cut. That was as far as I'd let him interfere with my life on campus.

Only a few girls on the team knew we were family. I didn't want anyone to think I got where I am because I knew the AD. I'd played hockey long before my mom remarried. Warren had only been in my life for five years. I loved the man to death, but while I was on campus, we acted like strangers. That's how it'd stay.

"Well, guess we could always play games topless," Kaya joked in a dry tone. "We'd be eye candy then."

I tapped my finger against my chin. "You might be onto something."

Her eyes widened. "You're shitting me."

"Yes and no."

"I love this sport. But there are some lines I'll never cross. If I'm topless, it's going to be for cold, hard cash."

"Fair enough." I nodded in agreement. "But I'm not saying we need to put on a show for the crowds."

"Good. Cause I'm a shit dancer unless I'm drunk."

"When you're drunk it's even worse."

She smiled. "But in an endearing way, right?"

"No." I laughed. "Not even close."

Kaya clicked her tongue against the roof of her mouth in disagreement. "You have no idea what you're talking about."

"I do, actually." I perked up a little at the thought of my plan. "We'll show people who we are underneath our helmets by using our socials. People care more when they feel personally connected. It's called something... I learned it in my Marketing course last year."

I snapped my fingers, trying to figure out the term.

Kaya raised a brow. "What are you going on about?"

"Parasocial," I practically screamed. "Parasocial relationships."

She frowned at my sudden giddiness. "You're giving me nothing to work with, Ryn."

"Come on. I'll explain on the way."

I grabbed her hand and pulled her behind me. Most of our teammates were still in the locker room getting ready. I needed to gather my inner circle for a vote. Before we did anything, I wanted unanimous agreement.

"I'm not showing any kind of skin for a thirty-dollar ticket," Kaya protested. "They'll have to raise the prices."

"Babe, my idea is going to do more than sell seats. By the time I'm done, that'll be the least of our worries."

Chapter Six

Sam

"You still with us, Captain?" Lincoln asked.

"Yeah." I looked up from my phone. "Just give me a s-second."

I winced at my stuttering and quickly replied to Jacobs. A simple "yes" seemed enough. It didn't take her long to send a thumbs-up.

"Are you okay?" Finn, my best friend, leaned against my bedroom doorway while Lincoln made himself more at home on my beanbag. Henrik, our team's alternate captain and voice of reason, was staring at my corkboard in silence. The wrinkle in his brow made me want to go on another long-winded explanation as to why I'd waited to tell him and Lincoln about our gambling athletic director, Stoll.

"The guy's room is drowning in red yarn and stolen spreadsheets," Lincoln answered for me. "The answer's obviously no, Sam's not okay."

I frowned at Lincoln. Yes, I'd become a bit obsessed with the photos Finn had recovered from his phone. Those photos revealed a ledger tracking bets on hockey games made by people in Mendell's athletic department – and likely expanded outside the college. Stoll was meticulous in keeping records. He was also smart about what he wrote down. No full names or bank statements. His notes in the margins made no sense but probably meant something to him.

"I'm f-fine." I pushed out of my desk chair to join Henrik in staring at the corkboard.

Finn nodded, taking my word for it. Henrik knew better.

"You've been stammering a lot," he said in a calm voice. He didn't take his eyes off my board as he spoke. "Maybe you should step away from this for a few hours. Consider taking this stuff down, too. Sleeping with it up can't be easy. Or healthy."

My skin burned at his mention of stammering. Here's the thing about growing out of something you did as a kid—you never really do. Parts of what happened are forever etched into your bones. All it takes is one trigger to remind you of who you used to be.

When I was younger, when I spoke, my mind went into hyperdrive. I'd stumbled over the easiest sentences, making it near impossible for me to get through a simple conversation in a decent amount of time.

It wasn't until I was a senior in high school that I could have a full conversation without tripping over my words. The fear and embarrassment of taking forever to get my point across haunted me. Which was why I worked my ass off to become the captain of Mendell's hockey team. What better way to face your fear than to stare it down directly every day?

It was my job to keep the guys in line. That involved plenty of public speaking. Pre-game pep talks, post-game speeches, media interviews, and lots of one-on-ones. Talking became effortless.

However, for the last few weeks, that'd been changing. The idea of reverting to the bullied kid from high school scared me shitless. That boy had been so afraid. And alone. So, I pushed the thought away.

"I'm meeting someone later. That'll distract me," I promised, quickly. "I'll take the board down in a few days. For now, I wanted to make sure we're on the same page."

"The page you've been hiding from us for the past few months?" Lincoln asked. "Sure."

"It's not his fault." Finn rubbed the back of his neck. "I didn't have the photos. I couldn't remember how to get them."

Finn had a brain injury last year and didn't remember a lot about his life from before it happened. Whenever he referenced the incident, there was a tightness in his voice. I couldn't imagine what he was going through. He was doing much better, but his loss of memories still got to him occasionally. It got to me, too.

We'd been so close to losing him and my stomach always turned whenever I was reminded of it. Grateful didn't even begin to describe how I felt when he finally woke up. Amnesia or not, he was still our Finn. Our family.

"Still could have clued us in," Lincoln said, his tone a bit gentler this time. He also got uncomfortable thinking about Finn's injury.

"Knowing now or later changes nothing. Relax," I said.

"I've been talking to Stoll like he's done nothing wrong," Lincoln argued.

"Exactly," I insisted in a clipped tone. "And that's how it's got to stay until we can go to the Dean."

"When will that be?" Henrik asked, his voice unaffected by the emotions coursing through the room. His most enviable skill was remaining calm under pressure. Hen killed in his right-wing position because nothing ever got too overwhelming for him.

"As soon as I get more concrete evidence. Something with full names or maybe even bank deposit receipts. Because, if we're wrong—"

"Are we wrong?" Finn raised a brow. He trusted me when I spoke about the past. I didn't take that trust lightly.

"I highly doubt it," I promised him. "But on the off chance we are wrong, or he makes himself look innocent, we need a smoking gun. This move could get us on the bad side of the AD and all the other higher-ups in the school. They'll ask us how we got photos of his personal things."

"How did we do that exactly?" Lincoln asked.

I smiled a bit. "Pretty sure Finn was a spy in his past life."

"Seriously?" Finn shifted his weight from one foot to the other, eyes wide with concern. I kept forgetting he didn't understand a lot of jokes, or he took them literally on instinct. That was getting a little better since he started dating our roommate, Naomi. She teased him constantly. But he still had a way to go.

"No, I don't think you were an actual spy." My assurance made Lincoln snort. "But you were a pro at sneaking around. We used to do it all the time back home. I was the lookout and stalled people if they got close. It was hard to get past a kid repeating the same thing over and over."

"Where was Henrik during all this?" Lincoln wondered. "Sounds like a missed opportunity. Why bench an MVP?"

Henrik's shoulders stiffened at the suggestion of his potential involvement in our illegal antics. His past as someone with "sticky fingers" was something he did his best to avoid talking about.

"We didn't need, Hen," I said, simply and shot Lincoln a 'shut-up' glare.

"Wait. You're saying you played lookout while I broke into Stoll's office?" Finn asked.

"Nah, you got these photos rogue. Snuck into his office before a game and texted me after," I explained. "You were totally reckless. I was so proud. It was a very 'my baby's all grown up moment.'"

Finn rolled his eyes when I laid a dramatic hand on my heart.

"We keep this to ourselves before blowing the whistle," I told them. "Because if Stoll or anyone aware of his extracurriculars finds out, they could get rid of the evidence."

"Makes sense," Henrik agreed with a curt nod. "While we wait, what should we do? Because breaking and entering isn't a risk any of us should take...again."

Finn's ears went red. Lincoln shrugged and said, "I'd take one for the team if it meant ending the jackass."

Henrik laughed, humorlessly. "You're the opposite of light on your feet. A whole security team would be on you in a heartbeat."

"Really? Guess I learned from the best," Lincoln joked. "Remind me how you got caught again?"

"Okay. Okay." I held up my hand when Henrik started for Lincoln. Finn stepped in too, nudging Lincoln back.

"J-Jesus." I shook my head. "Chill out. Both of y-you."

Finn met my gaze. "You sure you're alright?"

I rubbed my forehead, feeling the tension of a headache coming on. "I'm fine."

"You're taking a break," Henrik decided for me, his expression as concerned as Finn's. "There's plenty of time to figure this out."

Except I wanted to figure this out now. The longer this went on, the more I felt like I was failing them somehow. Failing my team at being their leader. They voted for me because they trusted me. The main part of my job was to look out for them. I needed to do this right.

"Just listen." I blew out a breath and gestured to my wall. "The data on these sheets include income and outcome numbers. Transactions. Next to them are initials. The most frequent match-up with players on the team. I doubt that's a coincidence."

"Look at Miss Marple go," Lincoln said.

I rolled my eyes. "On the sheets we have, one initial appears only once. J.W."

"Who is it?" Lincoln asked.

"There's only one guy on the team with those initials," I explained.

Finn's expression cleared with realization. "And that guy acts buddy-buddy with Stoll."

"Okay." Lincoln shook his head, still confused. "You guys know I love a good mystery, but this is real life. You need to share with the class."

"Jack Whitfield," I said.

"Damn." Lincoln's eyes widened and he shook his head. "Are you serious? That a-hole talks a lot of shit, but helping someone commit fraud?"

Henrik nodded in agreement. "That's quite an accusation, Sam."

"He's said a few weird things to me," Finn confessed, crossing his arms over his chest. "If he's not involved, I think he still knows something."

I nodded. "His initials aren't listed as frequently as the others. This could mean he only recently learned about it. If he's new, then he's not too far gone. He might not be all in yet. It's a place for us to start. I'm going to talk with him. We have a rapport. But we all need to be friendly and open with this guy. If he's got his guard up, he's not going to spill anything."

Finn gave me a look.

"Right, right. Look, Henrik and I will worry about the friendly bit. You and Lincoln keep your ears open," I said, pointing directly at Finn. "I don't have the time to become besties with everyone on the team. Try to get someone to talk."

"We can do that," Lincoln assured.

"Perfect." I nodded."We need to make sure we're treating Stoll the same while still watching him like a hawk."

There was silence for a moment before Finn laughed. "I see what you did there this time. Like a hawk. Funny. It was—a funny joke."

"Very cute." Henrik's agreement and small smile helped Finn feel less awkward about pointing it out.

"Was it?" Lincoln asked with a teasing grin.

I broke out into a smile. Even through the stress, these guys knew how to lighten a mood. "It was. Now, get to work, team."

The campus was a twenty-minute drive from our house. I was grateful I finally had my car this semester. Though it'd been fun with Finn chauffeuring us around at the start of the school year, I found comfort in the familiar.

My hand-me-down Mazda3 felt like all the good parts of home. My older sister had driven it down one weekend when she'd interviewed for a grad program on campus. When I thought about the good parts of home, she was in most of them.

As if sensing my nostalgia from across the country, Eden texted,

Eden: Hey, jerk. You haven't called Mom in two weeks and now I'm the one getting yelled at. How is this my fault?

I laughed to myself and waited until I was parked in the lot outside of Jacobs' dorm before responding,

Sam: Everything's always your fault. Them's the rules.

I shot a quick 'here' text to Jacobs before getting out of the car. She lived in one of the older dorms on campus. The building was at least ten stories with a black iron gate out front that buzzed loudly anytime one of the students used their card to get in.

Eden: You joke, but I need you to understand this is my reality as the oldest. The baby of the family always gets it easy. That's why I'm gonna make things hard for you if I get accepted into the program. Get ready for 24/7 embarrassment.

Sam: When.

Eden: What?

Sam: When you get accepted. Not if.

There was a pause in the conversation. I looked up, thinking I saw Jacobs finally coming down to let me in. Instead, it was a group going out for the night.

Eden: Damn it. I try to threaten you and you're nice, asshole?

Sam: Guess I'm just the bigger person.

Eden: Whatever. Call Mom. And thanks for believing in me. That program's my dream.

Sam: Next fall, it's reality.

I smiled when she sent a middle finger emoji along with a heart.

In our family, I got the athletic gene. Eden got the smarts *and* athletics. She had skipped at grade, been a straight-A student in high school, an award-winning mathlete, a state champion skier, and accepted into an Ivy League university. She hit a few bumps in her undergrad but still graduated cum laude last year. Now, she had her sights on becoming a physical therapist. There was no doubt in my mind she'd succeed.

The sound of giggling girls walking by made me look up from my screen. Out of habit, I flashed them an easy smile. One of them, with long legs and gorgeous dark eyes, seemed intrigued and slowed her friends down. They feigned interest in reading a plaque in front of the old dorm building. I almost pushed off the car to join them before remembering the bet. Was flirting a part of the rules? Flirting was always fun and usually harmless.

I chewed on my lip, trying to decide. Before temptation grew too large to ignore, Jacobs opened the gate. She took one look at me, the girls—who were still throwing flirty glances in my direction—and figured out what was going on.

She wore a superior look as I approached her.

"You ready?" she asked in a mocking tone.

"Definitely." I nodded and tried to keep my expression unassuming.

"You sure? You're not forgetting something? A number, perhaps." She wiggled her brow.

"I already have the one number that matters. Yours."

She snorted. "Good one."

Jacobs stepped aside to let me in. She wore dark sweats and a white shirt that barely covered her stomach. Her hair was hidden underneath a red scarf that matched the color of her lips.

As I followed her into the building, I watched the sway of her hips. Jacobs walked like the hockey player she was. Full power and force behind every step. The scent she left behind made me want to take deeper breaths. She smelled sweet, like something from a bakery. My mouth practically salivated.

Jacobs caught me checking out her ass when she pressed the elevator button. I didn't even try to hide my approval, which earned me a playful head shake.

We waited in silence as the elevator came down. Once the door slid open, I let her walk inside first. She pushed the button for the tenth floor.

"You look nice," I said in a low voice as the doors closed.

Jacobs pressed her back to the wall, eyes on the climbing numbers. Our ascent felt achingly slow when I noticed her nipples poking through her shirt. Was she not wearing a bra?

"Thanks." She finally looked at me. "You, too."

I placed one hand on the wall behind her and the other underneath her chin. "Never seen you in lipstick. You wear it for me?"

She laughed. It sounded nervous and shaky, so I released her. My hand remained right above her shoulder, though.

"No. I'm coming from somewhere," she said.

"That somewhere someone else's bed?" I was genuinely curious. Had she been able to start her side of the bet before we'd even begun? If so, I hadn't been expecting that.

"Maybe." She smiled and shook her head when she realized she couldn't play along. "No."

I chuckled. "Good."

"Doesn't mean you're winning, Morgan. I saw you out there."

"Looking for a violation? Cause nothing happened."

"It was hard for you, wasn't it?" She raised a brow. "Not flirting with them."

"No," I said, voice low and eyes flickering down to her lips. "But something's hard for you."

A cute sound came from the back of her throat. Jacobs' eyes flickered down to my crotch for a quick second.

"You're corny," she managed.

"And your pulse is racing," I whispered, glancing at her neck. "Could I...?"

I leaned in slowly, waiting for her to stop me. Jacobs breathed deeply and nodded. When my lips brushed against her jaw, she reached out, placing her palms against my chest. Judging from her sharp inhale, I think she wanted something stable to hold on to.

I slowly worked my way across her jaw and to her neck. Her skin was warm and silky smooth. I kissed the racing heartbeat with a promise to speed it up ten times faster.

She sighed as I continued to press gentle kisses across her skin. My hands found their way to her waist, squeezing her tightly, pressing her hard against the wall.

"How many floors?" I asked in a hoarse whisper, too entranced with her smell to pull away and check for myself. I wanted every second.

"Three," she breathed. I'd parted my lips and lightly bit her neck. I thought her nipples were hard before, but now they practically cut through her cotton top. The darkness of her areolas was more noticeable through the fabric this close-up.

I sucked on the bite before pulling away. Seeing the mark left behind gave me an unexplainable amount of satisfaction.

Jacobs sighed, clearly frustrated, and readjusted her shirt before the doors opened. A couple of girls on the other end smiled and greeted her before letting us walk out. They looked a little curious when they saw me get off behind Jacobs.

"Are you cool with people seeing us together like this?" I asked once we left the elevator behind. A hickey was far from inconspicuous.

"I don't really talk to anyone on my floor," she said simply. Her voice was still heavy from our close contact. I smiled, pleased she wasn't able to bounce back easily. "And my friends are gone for the weekend. So, no one's going to see us. We're safe. I wouldn't have invited you if we weren't."

I nodded. For some reason, I felt a little disappointed about being kept secret from her friends. But I've always kept most of my flings away from the guys, so I couldn't blame her.

Jacobs stopped in front of a door that was covered in superhero fandom stickers. Her name was written on an oversize post-it note with her major (Sports Medicine), year (sophomore), and pronouns (she/her). In addition to her name was that of her roommate, Jasmine Valentine (Physical Therapy, sophomore, she/they).

When I stepped into the room, I instantly guessed which side was hers. "You like purple?"

Everything from the bedsheets, tapestry and house slippers were various shades of purple.

Jacobs shrugged with a smile. "Maybe a little."

Outside of the purple decor, her wall was covered in posters of women athletes. Not just hockey players but swimmers, dancers, runners, and golfers.

"Those who came before me," she explained as she hurried to shove some clothes into the closet.

"They all attend Mendell?" I moved to get a closer look at the photos. The Mendell Hawk logo was displayed prominently on a lot of the uniforms.

"Yup. Some of the best of the best." She joined my side. "That's Karmen Walters. She still holds the 400-meter dash record for the school and the county. She qualified and got fourth in the Beijing 200-meter dash. That was after giving birth to twins."

I whistled, impressed.

"Right?" Jacobs beamed. "The dancer's Ellie Cho. She danced at Morston Hall in New York. She's the first Black-Korean dancer to earn a principal role there."

I smiled as Jacobs rambled, interested in her shine more than any of the athletes. She glowed talking about the people she looked up to.

"This is amazing," I said when she paused to take a breath. "How come I haven't seen these photos down at the athletic center?"

She shrugged, light fading from her eyes. "It takes a lot to get on those walls. Tons of competition, of course, and well, cis men tend to be the preference."

"Right." I frowned, feeling bad for even wondering why.

"You don't have to look so guilty." She climbed onto her bed. It'd been raised from the ground to accommodate large trunks stored underneath.

"Sorry." I joined her.

"Don't apologize." She waved her hands back and forth. "If you really feel guilty just do something about it."

This conversation was going in the opposite direction of where I'd originally thought after our moment in the elevator. But surprisingly, I didn't mind. I wanted to hear her talk. I wanted to learn more about her outside of what happened in the arena.

"I would love to," I said. "Just have to figure out how."

There was a devious look in her eyes. I raised a brow, intrigued.

"What?" I asked when she didn't say anything.

"Nothing," her voice was innocent, yet I was highly suspicious. "Well, I have a tiny favor to ask you."

"Go for it."

"Well, two tiny favors."

My stomach flipped, nervous at her tone. What was I getting into? Right then I realized Jacobs might be more dangerous for me than I'd originally thought. I was ready to accept both favors without asking questions because I hoped I'd get to see the shine in her eyes again.

I wasn't like this with people. I didn't connect like that. I cared about my partner's well-being, of course. This felt different. I wanted to give her something without anything in return.

"Go on," I said, playing up the hesitation in my tone.

"Let's focus on the here and now first," Jacobs decided, perking up a bit. "Could I tie you up?"

I chuckled. "What?"

She dug underneath her blankets and fished out a long, silk scarf. "Tie you up. It's something I've always wanted to try."

Chapter Seven

Aderyn

I n the beginning, I was nervous about the whole thing. Our moment in the elevator gave me the push I needed. He'd looked so into me. Like the sight of me in sweats and a T-shirt was mesmerizing. Of course, I knew he looked at a lot of women that way. Still, there was something undeniably addicting to being desired. Especially by this man. His mouth on my neck told me this was going to be far from some lukewarm experience.

Morgan didn't look at me with disapproval when I told him what I wanted to try. If anything, he seemed intrigued. Excited, even. Based on the clearly visible imprint of his hard dick on his pants, I assumed he was excited.

"This is something you've done before?" Morgan asked as he got comfortable on my bed. Like in every room, he took up most of the space. I don't think I'd be able to get the scent of his cologne out of my sheets even if I bleached them. I prayed I wouldn't be able to.

"No, but I've done the research," I said as I twisted a scarf between my fingers.

He laughed a little and looked impressed. "Research?"

"On how to make it comfortable," I explained. "Um, you don't have to say yes. I was only throwing it out as an option. There are plenty of other things we could try."

"No," he said a tad quickly and then, cleared his throat to add calmer, "I won't lie, it's a surprise that you'd want to try it for our first time together."

I shrugged. "First time's as good as any, right?"

His smile made my clit swell in anticipation. "I suppose so."

"Have *you* done something like this before?" I asked.

"Once or twice." He glanced at the scarf in my hands. "I was on the other end, though."

I nodded. That made sense. For some reason, being tied up didn't feel as appealing to me as seeing my partner restrained. Especially a guy as large as Morgan. The guy was basically a mountain and looked strong enough to break out of almost anything. "Got a safe word?"

"A few." He nodded and then, met my gaze. "I like to change them with my partners. Do you have an idea for one?"

I chewed on my inner cheek as I thought. I should've come up with some before but the thrill of learning new tying techniques stole my attention. "Puck?"

He snorted. "Excuse me?"

I frowned at him. "I don't know, I thought it was something we'd both relate to."

"Sure," Samson agreed. "But it sounds a lot like 'fuck' and safe words are supposed to be something we wouldn't normally say. Something out of the ordinary."

"Right, right. Of course."

"How about…" Morgan looked around the room. He stopped scanning when he found something on Jas's desk chair. "Halo?"

Jas's old Halloween costume was an angel. Earlier this year, we went to a costume party as the devil and angel on Mary's shoulders.

"Halo works," I agreed.

Morgan smiled, pleased. He offered me his hands, palms face up. "How do you want to do this? Should I stand, sit, or kneel?"

I pressed my lips together, doing my best to keep my head on straight and not laugh. Finding the humor in a situation was usually how I managed to get through awkwardness—I've laughed through plenty of arguments.

But sex shouldn't be laughed at. It was supposed to be serious and hot. Especially when tying your partner. Super especially if said partner was the gorgeous captain of the hockey team.

Morgan noticed my inner battle and asked, "Is everything alright?"

"Yeah, of course." I let out a heavy breath.

He rested his hands back down in his lap. "You sure?"

"I'm more than sure," I insisted and gestured for him to raise his wrists again.

"Jacobs, we don't have to do this tonight. We'll figure something else out," he said, voice gentle. I raised a brow at his tone. He sounded sweet. Like he'd throw away a night of sex in exchange for...what? Movies? Dinner? We weren't anywhere close to dating. I was banned from it, and he had no interest in the concept.

"You don't want to have sex tonight?" I asked.

"No, I do. Of course, I do," he said.

"Perfect. Me too. Now, give me your hands."

"I was just saying, if this is too much, too fast, we can slow down. I know you romantics like cuddles and candlelight." The smirk on his face made me glare. Morgan thought he already had me beat.

I playfully shoved his shoulder. "Shut up before I find another scarf and shove it in your mouth."

He chuckled. "Damn, I forgot how much I love a bossy woman."

My stomach flipped at his confession. I had to avert my eyes so he couldn't see how his words affected me.

"Tell me what else you're gonna do to me," his perfectly deep tone warmed my core. "I'm very open-minded—just so you know."

"I thought—" I tightened the scarf dramatically "—I told you. To shut. Up."

He nodded, biting down on his bottom lip. I used one hand to keep his wrists together while the other secured the scarf. When I realized this was the longest I'd touched a man in years, my breathing shallowed, and I felt a tightness in my core.

I didn't usually find men beautiful and saved that adjective for the women I liked. But Morgan was beautiful. His jawline was strong, covered in a nicely maintained beard. His lips were wide, perfect to kiss and be kissed. If he wasn't so good at hockey, I think he'd be great on the big screen.

He looked unattainable. My heart started pounding with uncertainty. Maybe I should stop before I got in over my head?

"I don't think it's tight enough," Morgan's voice forced me to put my downward spiral on pause.

"It's fine," I said and finished tying the knot. "I didn't want our first time to be too intense."

He licked his lips and nodded. "Okay. Whatever you want."

I stared at his mouth for a second. I was a serial monogamous and kissing was my kryptonite. Kissing came first, followed by a family dinner invitation, and then thoughts about expensive vacations we couldn't afford as college students. But I'd still make the vacation Pinterest board, dreaming of going in the future, because that's what I did. I fantasized until I got hurt by disappointments and break-ups.

Morgan's mouth turned downward with worry. "I'm starting to feel like this isn't the right move, Jacobs. I don't want to do this unless I know what you're thinking. Talk to me. Tell me what you're thinking."

"Nothing in particular. Just...." I shook out my hands to relax.

Get it together, Ryn.

"You probably should have stripped before I tied this," I said with a nervous laugh.

He gave me a one-shoulder shrug. "Still could with your help."

Right. I could do that. I was perfectly capable of undressing Samson Morgan without losing my shit.

I flexed my fingers before reaching for his waistband. He looked unimpressed at my graceless attempt to unbuckle his belt.

"You alright there?" he teased. "Need some help?"

"I've removed a belt before," I said in a flat tone. "Thanks."

"Could have fooled me."

I sighed and pulled back. "Your commentary isn't helping."

"Well, neither are your butter fingers.".

My expression darkened. He flashed a smile that was supposed to wash away my annoyance. And hell, it almost did.

"I'm joking, Jacobs," he promised in a genuine tone. "You seem nervous. I want to help you relax."

"It's not working."

"Clearly," he agreed and then, scooted closer so my thigh overlapped with his. I swear this man's thighs could put someone in a coma by either sheer force or exposure. They were a clear indication of religious adherence to leg days. I've always been a sucker for thick thighs and his were amazing.

"Come here," he instructed, wiggling his leg to beckon me.

"On your lap?" I asked in an uncharacteristically squeaky voice.

"Yes, on my lap." He chuckled. "Or is that too scandalous for you?"

I swallowed and followed his order. When I moved onto his lap, I hung one leg over his and wrapped my other leg around his back. I could feel his hardened dick pressed against the bottom of my ass cheek. My pussy grew wet knowing he was still turned on through my failed belt removal. Morgan lifted his arms, so his tied hands were behind my back, pulling me closer to him.

"Why did you want to tie me up?" He was close enough that his lips grazed the same spot from before in the elevator. I had a birthmark shaped like a mountain near my pulse. Morgan seemed bent on memorizing its placement with his lips. I swallowed as he pressed a kiss on my skin.

"I thought it might be hot," I murmured back.

"Well...is it?" He nuzzled his nose against my neck, breathing in slower. I think he was smelling me. From the sigh slipping from his lips, he seemed like he enjoyed my scent. Knowing that something about me was turning him on made me feel sexy and more confident.

"I don't know. I feel like I'm not using it to its fullest advantage," I said.

He made a low noise of agreement. "Try the belt again. Close your eyes, go fast, and don't think about it."

I followed his instructions exactly, not allowing myself to think about what I was doing and who I was doing it with. His belt was off in a heartbeat.

"That's a good girl."

His praise sent a spark down my spine. His being restrained was supposed to be a power play on my part. But he was still in control. From how he whispered instructions into my ear to how he remained calm.

Shit, *I* was supposed to be in control. I wanted to be more upset about losing it so early on but couldn't. The challenge of winning it back excited me. Morgan excited me.

"What are you going to do with it?" He pulled back to look into my eyes. When he realized I was confused he added, "The belt."

My stomach flipped. The ball was in my court. Morgan looked needy and desperate for something. His dick swelled, and I knew that anticipation was just as thrilling as whatever I decided to do.

"Fortify my scarf," I said.

He chuckled and lifted his hands, placing them in front of me. I wrapped the belt around his wrist, hoping the scarf provided enough cushion between his skin and the rough, leather surface restraint. I made it a little tighter since it was easier to maintain friction.

Feeling more comfortable, I reached for the zipper on Morgan's pants. Once they were removed, his boxers were next.

Morgan had no shyness about sitting in front of me, half-naked. On the other hand, my heart jumped into my throat when I got a good look at his dick. My pussy grew wet, preparing to accommodate his large girth.

Fuck.

Morgan leaned back on my bed, resting his head on my pillow casually. He looked like he owned the place. "What now, Jacobs? I'm at your mercy."

Despite my nerves, I smiled. "Is that right?"

He held up his wrists. "As much as I'll ever be."

I took a deep breath and crawled on top of him. I straddled his torso, still in my sweats and crop top. Having a half-naked hockey player underneath me was empowering. I pushed his T-shirt up to expose his stomach. His chest rose and fell quickly. My breath caught in my throat when I felt how fast his heart was racing.

I pressed my lips to his chest, kissing right over his heart. His skin was warm to the touch and smelled less like cologne and more like something more natural.

Morgan whispered something I couldn't make out but from the furrow of his brow I knew it wasn't sweet or romantic. The look in his eyes was pure erotic filth.

His body tensed as I moved further down. I could hear the belt buckle click now and then as he strained against it.

"All good?" I teased, peering up at him from halfway down his body.

"Damn," he breathed when he saw how close I was to his dick. "I mean, y-yes. It's...I'm good... This is f-fine."

"Just fine?" I tried to bait him because he looked on the verge of falling apart. The clean, put together, bring me home to your mother guy had vanished. He was replaced with a man who could barely string together a sentence.

"Yeah... just f-fine..." his sentence transformed into a moan when I licked the tip of his dick. The bead of pre-cum tasted salty on my tongue and made my pussy squeeze, desperate it be put inside me. The groan Morgan let out confirmed his agreement.

I hadn't heard a man groan in ages. His was partly stifled because he didn't want to fully let go. That holding back was sexy. He was providing more of a challenge. Could I get him to be louder?

"Give me one sec," I said before hopping off the bed and hurrying over to my dresser.

Morgan let out a sarcastic laugh. "Sure, of course. Take all the time you need. I'll be here."

I dug through my layers of clothes to find my purple vibrator. Morgan raised a brow when he saw what I'd retrieved.

"You're trying to make this as torturous as possible, aren't you? Trying to get me to beg for a taste?" he joked as I slowly stripped out of my clothes.

"Of course." I smiled at him and resumed my position at eye level with his crotch.

Whatever complaint he'd been ready to share disappeared as soon as I took him fully in my mouth. Morgan strained against the belt again, trying to reach for something he could hold onto. I used one hand to help my mouth work up and down his dick. With the other, I positioned the vibrator on my clit.

The stimulation I got from his dick and the vibrator made my ears buzz. I'm ashamed to say the high I got from scoring a goal didn't hold a candle to the flame that was tasting Morgan while grinding against my vibrator.

As I tried to get him deeper into my mouth, I also pressed the vibrator inside of me. My pussy tightened around the toy and my tongue added pressure around Morgan's shaft.

"Jacobs," he begged.

I kept letting up and loosening my grip when it seemed like he was getting close. I could feel the frustration in his body. His thighs flexed and his stomach tightened. I pulled back and smiled when he growled in protest.

"You're a sadist," he accused, his breath coming in hard puffs as I drew light circles with my tongue around his tip.

"I try my best," I agreed. "It's fun seeing a guy like you want it so bad he's forced to beg."

Morgan laughed, sounding frustrated. He raised an eyebrow when I completely pulled away from his dick to catch my breath.

"Let me see how you touch yourself," he said, voice dark and demanding.

"What about you finishing?"

He shook his head. "I want to see what you're doing to yourself. What's making that pussy sound like fucking music. I want to watch you."

Heat traveled through my body at his insistence. Morgan moved to sit upright, proving his seriousness.

"Sit on my lap again." There he went using the demanding, captain voice, acting like he wasn't tied up with his own belt. When I rolled my eyes, he said, "Quit being a brat. Come here. Now."

My throat tightened at his shortness of tone. He was fed up. Genuinely pissed at my attitude. That should, in turn, piss me off. Except it didn't.

No one in my life spoke to me like he did. Not even my coaches could demand things from me. I did things in my own time. I was hardheaded as they came. Until now, I guess. Because I did exactly as Morgan ordered. I moved onto his lap, my legs encircling his waist.

He lifted his arms, securing me in his restrained grip. There was just enough room between our crotches for my vibrator to fit.

"Go on." He nodded, looking down at my pussy. "Play with yourself."

I chewed on my lip as I placed the vibrator on my opening. He moaned, watching the toy circle my swollen clit. This close, I could see the dark desire in his eyes. Morgan didn't look away. He didn't ask me to touch him either. For now, we both got off on my pleasure alone.

My heart pounded at being watched. Morgan paid close attention to every bit of my movements. I put on a show and moved the vibrator in wider circles, wanting to impress him. Just like I wanted him to see me on the ice, I wanted him to see me here, too.

"There you go," he whispered when I moaned from the pleasure. "You see what listening to me gets you?"

I laughed. "Shut up. This would be so much better if you were quiet."

"You don't mean that." Morgan met my gaze. "Look at me and tell me you don't mean it and maybe I'll give you a reward."

"Reward?" I asked, breathless from his dangerous smile.

"A reward," he confirmed with a nod. "Say it."

I briefly and foolishly considered brushing him off. But I couldn't. Not when my pussy was this wet and he was this hard underneath me. Whatever he wanted to give me, I'd take. No matter what I had to do to get it.

"I didn't mean it," I said.

"Really?" he faked like he was hurt over the matter. Morgan pressed his forehead against mine. "You sure, Jacobs?"

"Stop messing around. I promise I didn't mean it," I said and was cut off when his lips pressed against mine. Goddamn kryptonite.

Morgan pulled me against him and parted my mouth, tongue grazing against mine. I grabbed his shoulder with my free hand, holding on as the building tension in my core neared its peak. His kiss was firm and rough. Morgan bit my bottom lip, uncaring about the mark it might leave behind.

I pulled away from his mouth when my orgasm captured me. I could take a lot of things but coming while also making out with him felt impossible. I could only take one soul-consuming sensation at a time.

My head tilted back and my mouth parted as I came. Morgan moaned right along with me and did something that surprised us both.

His dick twitched, cum spilling onto our thighs. He let out a deep moan and leaned forward to capture my nipple as he continued to come on both of us.

"Fucking hell, Jacobs" he whispered against my skin.

There'd been no need for physical stimulation. Morgan climaxed from simply watching me. The sight of it triggered another orgasm ripping through my body. Morgan pulled away from my breast when he heard my whimper. He kissed my neck, helping the ecstasy linger as I rode the vibrator. We were both out of breath by the end of it and collapsed on the bedsheets.

"*Shit.*" Morgan chuckled once we got a handle on our post-orgasm tremors. He glanced down at the mess he made. "I can't believe that happened."

I took in a deep breath and got up to grab a towel from our bathroom. He murmured a 'thanks' as he wiped his thigh. I did my best not to stare but even the smallest glance made my nipples harden again.

"You ever done that?" I claimed a spot beside him on the bed. "Come without someone stimulating you?"

"Never."

I smiled, feeling proud. He let out a disapproving grunt.

"It's because you spent the majority of the time teasing me," he said.

"Excuses, excuses."

Morgan scoffed but didn't argue. Instead, he held up his wrists. "Untie me."

I did as he asked, swallowing my question about him leaving. He moved to tug on his underwear, pants, and shirt. But he didn't start for the door.

"What?" I frowned when he lingered on the bed.

"Should I stick around and cuddle?" he asked, grinning.

I sucked the back of my teeth. "Shut up and get out."

"You sure?" He wiggled his brow. "I don't mind."

"We're done." I nudged his side with my elbow.

Instead of moving off the bed, Morgan leaned in close and kissed me. It was quick and unsatisfying. As soon as I started leaning in, he pulled away with a knowing smile. He teased me once more like he was going in for another kiss, only to simply hover close enough for me to feel his breath against my skin.

"I can see it in your eyes, you know," he said.

"Get out," I whispered against his mouth, no force behind the words.

"You're right," he continued. "You got it bad. Such a pesky habit, falling so easily."

"I'm not falling," I denied and hopped up—still naked—to open the door for him.

Morgan followed me and lingered in the doorway.

"Maybe if you're fast enough you can catch up to those girls," I taunted.

He shook his head and placed his hands on the top of the door frame. I gulped at the sight of his muscles stretching out and his shirt rising to reveal a bit of his stomach.

"I'm all in on this, Jacobs," he reminded me.

"And I'm not."

"Perfect. Call me when you're ready for more."

I folded my arms over my chest. "I will."

He winked, gave me a final once-over, and then, started down the hall.

One truth and a lie: He didn't look back, not even when he had to wait for the elevator. And I didn't feel disappointed.

Chapter Eight

Sam

A s I tugged on my glove, the memory of Jacobs' hands on my wrists gave me pause. I let myself get lost in it for a second, going back to a few days ago in her dorm.

I imagined her exhales, her smiles, and her shudders. The way her legs felt pressed against mine, squeezing. The way that sweet moan escaped her throat when she climaxed. That mark on her lips left behind by yours truly. I hadn't seen her since and wondered if it was still there.

"Hey, see you out there?"

I looked up at Henrik's question. My cheeks burned as I panicked about him guessing what I was thinking by just looking at me. My dick had hardened a bit because of my imagination. I pulled my other glove from my locker, trying to look busier than I was.

"Yeah, yeah," I said, quickly. "Go ahead. I need a minute."

He gave me a weird look but started out of the locker room. I followed him at a slower pace. Most of the guys were already on the ice, getting ready for warm-ups. The air in the arena was cold and crisp. My teammates called to one another, joking around before practice officially began. The sound of scraping skates along the ice and hockey sticks making contact with pucks grounded me. This was home. This is what I needed to give my undivided attention to.

I pushed away thoughts of Jacobs and started toward the sidelines.

Well, you were right. She's a good distraction.

A nagging voice in the back of my mind dared to ask, *are you sure it's only a distraction?*

I scoffed. I was being ridiculous. Of course, she was only a distraction. I never wanted anything more from the women I slept with. I didn't need anything more.

Couldn't handle more, even if you got the chance. Especially with a girl like her.

"Alright, that's enough," I grumbled to myself.

There were a million other things I needed to focus on.

Like, how careless Lincoln had been in the goal these last few practices. I needed to remind him to take every moment in the rink seriously.

I needed to ask Jack why he was being so timid while defending. Lately, he'd been pushing against everyone like they were glass. He'd never been one to turn down a good body check.

Then, there was the new guy, Ben. He'd confided in me about his drinking problem. I had to keep an eye on him for any slip-ups with the hope things didn't escalate.

This was why I enjoyed being the captain. I got to learn more about the guys, to see parts of them they didn't show people. Sure, most of the time my teammates leaned into their egos and tried to mask their problems. But being their leader afforded me a sort of automatic trust. I took that trust seriously.

Helping them gave me purpose and unique insight into myself. It helped me to realize I had an incessant need to feel important. I liked having a role and a place. I liked being relied on. It made up for my uncomfortable experiences around guys my age when I was younger. I frowned at the bad memories. I shook my head, trying to get my mind back on present problems. My brain seemed bent on bringing up shit in the past that didn't matter.

"Sam." Jack paused in front of me and removed his helmet.

"What's up?" I rested my elbows on the boards. I planned to continue watching on the sidelines until Coach Haynes and our assistant coaches showed up. Sometimes, it was easier to feel the overall mood of my team after getting a bird's eye view from off the ice.

"Finn said you wanted to talk." Jack looked annoyed. He always did. I think someone could give this guy everything he'd ever want in this world, and he'd still find something to mope about. His lack of satisfaction worked to the team's advantage during game time, turning him into a force on the ice. Afterward, it was a headache trying to have a decent conversation with him.

"Did he?" I looked for Finn. He was in the middle of a conversation with our second-line forward. Our plan had clearly been to play this as casually as possible. What possessed him to send Jack my way?

"What?" Jack looked over his shoulder at Finn, too. "Was it a misunderstanding?"

"No," I said, quickly. "I just—"

My attention was stolen when the doors on the other end of the arena burst open. A few of the women's hockey players came out on ice. My stomach flipped when I saw Jacobs among them.

I remember the first time I saw Jacobs fully suited up for a game. She looked like she'd been born to play. Born ready for battle of any kind. And now, as soon as her skates connected with the ice, she demanded attention. Jacobs wasn't graceful by any means. Every one of her strides was made with fierce determination. That determination was oddly more beautiful than grace. I bit my inner cheek at the thought of such a powerful person allowing me to watch her orgasm.

I cleared my throat and turned back to Jack to renew my investment. Jacobs was done taking up so much of my head space.

"I wanted to ask if you were coming out this weekend," I said. "A bunch of us are getting together at Dade's. Karaoke."

"Nah, that doesn't sound like my kind of night."

"Come on," I encouraged, giving him a light punch to the shoulder. Jack shot me daggers, which I promptly ignored. "It'll do you some good to get out. You need to bond with the team."

"Sounds unnecessary."

"It's vital," I argued. My eyes strayed to Jacobs again. She was doing what she did best, riling up the guys so they'd accept a face-off challenge. It was hard not to smile as she tried to intimidate my teammates.

"Campus life can be isolating," I continued, carefully. "It's nice to have people you can count on. To get those people, you gotta foster connections. You gotta let them get to know you."

Jack didn't buy my impromptu advice session. "Did someone say something about me? I know I'm not exactly winning MVP or Most Charming Teammate of the Year anytime soon. But I do what I came here to do. And I do it well."

"Right," I agreed. "And no, no one's said anything."

He raised a brow. Here we go. I was going to take a risk and throw a line.

"I just know you're close to Stoll," I said.

Jack shifted his weight from one leg to the other. "And?"

"He did me a favor once. Afterward, I felt kind of isolated."

"That so?" Jack refused to give me any kind of reaction.

Damn, respect.

I'd have to offer a little more than a vague confession.

"He bailed me out when I'd had a little too much to drink," I shared in a low voice.

He scoffed, disapproving. "Used your one call on him?"

"His card was in my pocket," I explained with a shrug. "I didn't know anyone else in town. It was my first time away from home. I couldn't exactly call my folks, you know?"

"And let me guess, you never made the same mistake twice?"

"Maybe."

Jack chuckled. "Look, Sam, I know what you're doing."

"And what's that?"

"You're trying to create a connection of sorts between us. Trigger an emotional response in me. But I'm not missing a connection in my life. I don't have much of a heart. But I do have a brain."

I nodded, impressed by his straightforwardness. "Okay. You got me."

Jack looked over his shoulder to make sure we had privacy. "So, let's be frank. You want to know about Stoll's little side hustle, right?"

I blinked, surprised at how forthright he was being. I thought I'd have to dance a little to get him to even admit being close to the guy.

"What side hustle?" I tested.

"The one where he makes up excuses for certain players to sit out when we're winning a game."

And there it was. "You've talked with him about this?"

Jack gave me a shrewd look. "Come on, I'm not offering you information without something in return."

My expression clouded. "What do you want?"

"You got anything better than the approval and connections of a respected athletic director?"

My jaw tightened. "How about knowing you're helping your fellow teammates get a fair shot? Isn't that enough of a return investment for you? Do you realize how many lives this affects? Or are you too selfish? This isn't about winning or losing. It's about someone profiting off our hard work. You want to be a part of that?"

Jack's posture went rigid. "It's not that simple."

"Really? Then, please, explain to me the intricacies," I demanded, enunciating each of my words hard.

Before he could say another word, Coach Haynes's whistle sounded in the air. I straightened, looking over at our coaches making their way toward us.

"Dade's," I said. It was a command this time. "Or I'll track you down on campus. And you know I don't like wasting time like that."

"Fine," Jack said through gritted teeth.

Coach Haynes was getting close so I smiled like nothing was wrong.

"Ready to get to work, boys?" he asked.

"Ready," Jack said.

"As we'll ever be," I agreed.

Chapter Nine

Aderyn

"**Y**ou won the vote," Kaya reminded me. "So, why are you stalling?"

I shook my head and ignored the puck whizzing by. Jas hurried after it, two guys on their tail. We were in the middle of a semi-serious face-off that I'd instigated. Kaya noticed me getting distracted by Morgan and pulled me aside.

"I'm waiting for a good opening," I said.

"Girl, fuck good openings. We need a yes or no."

"Why are you rushing me? You hate the idea."

"Yeah, which is exactly why I need this over and done."

My gaze turned to Morgan again. He didn't have any gear on, so he wasn't joining us just yet. Which meant I had to go to him. The thought of it made my stomach knot.

We'd only exchanged a few mindless texts since that day in my dorm. Most of which I sent, and he barely responded. His nonchalance about the situation made me take notes on how to adopt his reactions. I needed to be more like him if I was going to survive three months.

"If I'm going to make a fool of myself online, I'd rather do it sooner than later," Kaya continued.

"We're not going to make fools of ourselves," I promised and added in a lower voice, "Hopefully."

"I heard that." Kaya frowned.

"Do you want cool perks and a decked-out gym or not?"

She sighed, pausing like she could think of a response other than her eventual, "Yes."

"Exactly. So let me work my magic."

"Your magic needs to work a little faster. We have a game coming up. The sooner we start the hype train, the better."

I blew out a breath. "Alright, alright. I hear you."

She nudged my shoulder for a final push in the right direction. As I skated toward Morgan, my shoulders pinched. He'd moved from his original spot near the boards, closer to the benches like he was leaving.

"Hey," I called, my voice sounding airy.

He paused and raised a brow when he saw me. Coach Haynes greeted me with a polite nod but focused most of his attention on calling out orders to his team.

"Got a minute?" I asked in a low voice.

"Maybe even two." His smile made me feel less anxious about this situation. He was so good at that.

"How do you do it?" I asked out loud before I could stop myself.

Morgan tilted his head to the side, confused. "Excuse me?"

I laughed off the embarrassment. "Sorry. You're good at not being weird about you know what. I wanted to know how. But that's probably cheating, right?"

He gave me a one-shoulder shrug. "I told you I'd give you some tips. Still don't mind doing it. Knowing something is one thing, executing is another. You of all people should understand that."

I nodded. "I do."

"Great. I'm a bit busy now but come to Dade's later. I'll give you a quick lesson."

My heart did a silly, little flutter. Needed to ask him how to nip that in the bud, too. "Thanks."

"No problem. That it?"

"One more thing." I winced a little at having to ask him for so much. "I can do shit for you, too, by the way."

"What?"

"Favors, I mean. I'm not as naturally talented as you are on the ice, but I have a few tricks up my sleeve."

He smiled. "That you do."

My cheeks warmed at the knowing look in his eyes. I took a deep breath before ripping off the band-aid. "I come to you again, completely humble, requesting your assistance."

"Humble? You?" Morgan shook his head. "Has hell frozen over?"

"Of course. That's why you and I are here, right?"

He chuckled. "What do you want?"

"I saw your team's social media account has a large number of followers. You've all done well branding your individual accounts, too."

"Yeah, getting a leg up in the self-promotion department helps those of us wanting to go pro. The NHL only pays so much for so long. Brand deals could stretch for years after retirement."

"Exactly. Very smart, looking forward and all that."

He studied me, catching onto where I was going. "Women's team going to start a joint account?"

"We already have one," I said, voice quieter than before. Here came the part I'd been dreading.

"Really?" Morgan pulled out his phone and asked for our handle.

I mumbled, having to repeat it so he could hear. Morgan pulled it up and swiped through the few videos posted.

"Who are these girls?" He looked at the people on the ice, seeing if he could find someone he recognized.

"They graduated four years ago."

Morgan whistled. "You guys haven't updated your joint account in four years."

"There's been a lot of changes in command on the women's team. Players transfer in and out a lot. It's hard to keep things consistent," I explained while keeping eye contact. Determination began to take over, replacing my embarrassment. I shouldn't feel ashamed about my team. We'd come far. Despite the many roadblocks, we were the top competition for the other teams in the league.

"We've been focused on building a strong team. It's like Maslow's pyramid. Got to focus on the basics first. Now, we're ready to move up."

Morgan nodded. "Makes sense."

"Here's where you come in. I need your..." I hesitated when a slow smile formed on his face.

"Yes? What do you need?" he encouraged in a purposefully sensual tone.

I frowned, trying my best to ignore the heat between my legs. "Stop that."

"Just trying to be helpful," he said, feigning innocence.

"Whatever." I glared. "I need your help with getting people excited for us."

"Excited?"

"Yes. Encourage people to buy tickets for our games or to come out and support us during fundraisers. Get them excited to support us. You know it does wonders for morale if there's a large crowd cheering you on."

Morgan nodded. "Yeah, of course."

"My team needs a morale boost. And the department could use an excuse to start supporting us and stop treating us like an afterthought. So, I want our teams to work together. It'll just be for a few months. A few videos to get the ball rolling on our account. We'll tag you guys in everything, of course, and expect vice versa."

"Social media requires more effort than you might think," he warned. "It's a part-time job."

"My girls and I will take care of everything," I promised. "We'll even edit some videos of just your team for y'all as a thank-you."

Morgan glanced down at his phone again, looking at our dead page. "Alright, I don't see the harm in it. We could use some new faces on our page anyway. You've got yourself a deal."

I was so excited I wanted to hug him. So, I did.

The action shocked us both. It was a quick motion. I reached over the boards, and he caught me. Morgan encircled his arms around my waist slowly, like he wasn't sure what was happening. As soon as his familiar scent hit my nose, I knew I made a mistake. He was warm and solid against me. We'd climaxed together, so it felt silly being anxious about a fully-clothed hug. But, there I was, heart racing because his grip tightened slightly when my skates started to slide. He was trying to keep me steady.

As quickly as I grabbed Morgan, I let him go. Pulled away before I did anything else weird and random. The smile on his face made me want to melt into my skates.

"We can talk strategy at Dade's," I suggested in a shaky voice. "I have a list of ideas. I'll invite you to the Google doc."

"Organized. I like it." He sounded a little out of breath, too. Morgan flexed his fingers for a second. Did I come in too hot and accidentally hurt him? I winced at the thought but couldn't get my mouth to force out an apology.

"First drink's on me, okay?" Morgan asked.

I nodded, giving him a smile. He winked before starting his trek back to the locker rooms. I did my best not to let my gaze trail any lower than his shoulders. My fingers shook a bit from my slip-up.

"What's the verdict?" Kaya stopped near my elbow. Her voice was calm enough for me to hope she hadn't witnessed the hug. If I was giving myself a hard time, I knew she'd take advantage of the opportunity to tease me.

"It's a go." I let out a nervous laugh. "They're going to help us."

"No shit— I mean, great." She forced a smile. "You know how much I love any excuse to shake my ass."

I snorted. "Girl, no one's shaking ass. Yet. We lead up to that."

"Dear Lord, please put me out of my misery," she begged to the ceiling.

I looked up at the ceiling, too. "Not yet, Lord. I still need her until the end of this semester."

Chapter Ten

Sam

My sleeping schedule has always been bad, but it'd been particularly horrible this year. I dragged myself across campus most days feeling like a cocktail of frustration, anxiety, and depression. My friends knew me well enough to figure out I didn't have the energy for karaoke. And I knew them well enough to convince them I needed this.

"I can't flake out on Jack," I said when Henrik and I pulled up to Dade's. "I'd lose the little credibility I have with him. Then, who'll get him to talk? Finn with his silence or Lincoln with his motor mouth?"

"Jack's actually coming?" Henrik looked doubtful.

"He i-is." I checked my phone as we got out of the car just to be sure I didn't have some last-minute cancellation text. Thankfully, neither of my invites was bailing. So far.

"I've been known to persuade a person or two," Henrik offered.

I patted his shoulder, thankful for his solidarity. "It's fine. I want to do this."

"You do know you have other people you can count on, right?" Henrik opened the door for me. "Don't think I haven't noticed your speech patterns. I have half a mind to call Eden myself and get her to talk some sense into you. You need sleep, and maybe a relaxing hobby like puzzles or something. Finn could teach you to knit?"

"Call? You and Eden finally graduated to calling?" I teased because it was too good of an opportunity to pass up. "Done with the emails?"

Henrik's face didn't betray the embarrassment I knew he was hiding underneath his unbothered brow. "That was one time and it was a misunderstanding."

I laughed. "It was more than one time, man. We were all in that pen pal program and I remember you sending more than one email."

"Two tops," Henrik promised, mouth barely opening as he spoke. God, he was good at pretending. I wondered if he was doing it for his sake or mine.

"Now, stop changing the subject," Henrik ordered and ran a hand through his dark hair. Yeah, he was definitely doing this for his sake.

"I'm fine," I said, only willing to get back on track because Hen looked desperate to avoid the topic of my sister. "Or I will be soon."

He nodded, not looking convinced but willing to leave things alone for now.

Dade's was a small, Roswell-themed bar complete with UFO piñatas and green alien decor. The place was already alive with people crowding in the seats closest to the tiny stage. Some woman was singing an impressive rendition of *My Heart Will Go On*. The crowd cheered her on, swaying their arms back and forth like they were at an actual concert.

I scanned the place for our group—hoping to find one specific person. Once I found her, I did my best to keep my expression neutral and not betray the increase in my heart rate.

Outside of that one night in Harry's, I hadn't seen Jacobs in anything other than sweats or baggy uniforms. Seeing her wearing non-workout clothes got me going. The brown dress she wore fell off her shoulders. Her hair was out, soft coils framing her round cheeks. She was at a table with her friends. Someone said something that made her throw her head back in laughter. Jacobs pulled off sexy effortlessly.

"Target spotted?" Henrik teased.

I frowned, afraid he'd noticed my staring. "What?"

"Jack. With the others." Henrik nudged his chin toward a table in the back. Jack, Lincoln, Finn, and Naomi had all squeezed into a booth.

I started in their direction. We had to pass Jacobs' table to get to theirs. Our eyes locked. I nodded, acknowledging her presence. She gave me a smile and gestured at her empty glass.

I held up a finger. "I got you, beautiful. Give me a second."

One of the girls at Jacobs' table said something that made her frown and she immediately broke our eye contact. I willed myself forward, trying to ignore my growing frustration for having to leave her be for now.

"So, theoretically," Lincoln was saying in an uncharacteristically low tone for him. "How would someone flirt with someone who's shy in a way that doesn't intimidate them? Theoretically."

His question had been directed to Naomi. Our roommate gave him a knowing smile and asked, "You said theoretically, right?"

Finn snorted at her teasing and wrapped his arm around her waist, pulling her closer to him

"Never thought I'd see you ask for relationship advice," I noted and settled in a spot next to Jack, who didn't look up at our arrival. His fingers ran up and down a sweating glass of water. This guy was the poster child for 'I want to be anywhere but here.'

"It's a thought experiment, not relationship advice," Lincoln said in a dry tone. "And I only want Naomi's opinions, so you all keep your comments to yourself."

"Just Naomi's opinion?" I nodded thinking about Naomi's best friend. Celeste could barely make eye contact when she greeted people. Since the beginning of the semester, Lincoln had been curious about her, always lingering when she was around.

"In my experience—" Jack's voice surprised us all "—don't make her feel weird for not talking, you'll make a long-lasting impression."

Lincoln recovered from his shock faster than the rest of us. "Decent advice but, no offense, I assumed that was a given."

Naomi laughed and patted his hand. "I don't think you need pointers."

I chuckled at Lincoln's confused look. Most of the time, he was too nice to realize that the world wasn't as accommodating as he thought it was.

"Let's get drinks for the table," I said to Jack.

He opened his mouth like he was going to protest, then realized this was a ploy for us to talk on our own. I took drink orders before heading to the bar.

"Got experience with shy girls?" I settled on a stool, waiting for the bartender to get a free moment.

"Why?" Jack looked suspicious like he was sitting across from an FBI agent.

"Your advice to Link."

"Oh. Right." His shoulders relaxed a little. "No, not really. I have– had a best friend on the quieter side. She taught me a lot."

The bartender came over for a second, interrupting our conversation so I could put in our drink order.

"What do you have on Stoll?" Jack surprised me once again by talking so freely.

I gave him a one-shoulder shrug. "Some pages from his ledger."

"Names? Addresses? Any type of damning identifiers?" Jack shot out the questions like bullets from a gun.

"Initials." I swallowed a sigh. "Just initials and numbers."

Jack let out a dry chuckle. "Not a lot. He could deny everything, and you'd get suspended for stealing private property."

"Why do you think I'm keeping this to myself? I know I need something more substantial before accusing him publicly."

"Like an invite to a dinner he hosts for the guys he 'likes best' on the team?" Jack raised a brow.

"No shit?" I whispered. "This is for the guys he has in his pocket?"

He nodded. "Every now and then, he asks us to invite players we think can keep the secret."

My forehead wrinkled. "How many know?"

Jack hesitated.

"Look, I'm not going to rat the players out or anything," I promised. This was about Stoll. None of my teammates had his kind of power.

"Don't treat them any differently either. They have their reasons, alright? They're just trying to get by with the cards they've been dealt."

"Of course."

Jack's protective tone shocked me. He looked torn as he continued to talk about this. Maybe my first impressions of him were wrong. Maybe he wasn't as selfish as I thought.

"Stoll doesn't want the number to be too big. But he'll listen to me if I tell him you can be trusted with an invite."

"You're getting me in the dinner?"

"On the condition you can act your ass off, yes," he confirmed.

"I can."

"You sure? Lately, you've been a little..." he trailed off, gesturing to his face.

I rubbed my cheek. "What?"

"Not yourself. Red in the eyes. You look exhausted, man."

"I'm fine," I grumbled, pissed that it was so noticeable to people outside my circle.

"Snappier, too." Jack smiled, indicating he was half-joking. "Maybe get more sleep?"

"Thanks. I hadn't considered that, but you have a point," I said, dryly.

Jack nodded. "I'll text you the details about the dinner. It's in a few weeks. Stoll holds it at his house. He's friendly and welcoming. Honestly, if he wasn't committing fraud, I'd say he was a decent guy."

I snorted.

"All the doors in his house stay open. He has a no closed-door policy," he added in a lower voice.

"Including his office?"

"Including his office." He nodded meaningfully.

"You're more helpful than I thought you'd be."

"I'm a lot of things people don't think I'll be," he teased.

"More selfless, too."

He frowned. "Okay, let's not go getting in over our heads and spreading that around."

I laughed. "Wouldn't dream of it."

"Sleep," Jack reminded me again. "So you can act normal when the time comes."

"Don't worry about me. I got this."

"Right. Well, as interesting as our socializing has been," he said as he studied the growing crowd around us. "I think I've had enough for the rest of the year."

"Thanks for coming."

He shrugged. "Thanks for reminding me there might be another way."

"Y ou ready?" I placed my hand on the back of Jacobs's chair.

"For what?" One of her friends with light purple hair and an ever-present scowl gave me a once-over.

Jacobs popped out of her seat with more energy than I expected. Had she been anticipating this moment with excitement? That possibility made me smile from ear to ear.

"I'll see you guys later," she said, not meeting their gaze.

"No rush." Mary smiled at us like she was in on our secret. "You can keep her all night if you have to, Sam."

I chuckled. "Might have to take you up on that offer, Mary."

Jacobs led the way through the crowd. I followed without a word because she seemed to know exactly where she wanted to go. We ended up at a round pedestal table in a quiet corner of the building.

"This okay?" she asked, sounding more breathy than usual. "Didn't want us to have to yell over the singing."

"It's perfect." I followed her gaze back to her friends—who were still watching us. "What's going on with them?"

"They think we're a thing," she said.

"Aren't we?"

Jacobs snorted. "You know what I mean."

The shyness in her eyes made me want to take her chin between my fingers. I wanted to watch every moment her expression changed to memorize each small detail. That desire was unfamiliar. I chalked it up to only being with her for the past few weeks. My body was confused at the change of pace.

"What did you tell them?" I asked.

"That we're working together on the social media for the team."

"And?"

She frowned. "There's no and. At least, not to their knowledge."

"Thought you wouldn't be able to keep it to yourself."

The crease in her forehead deepened. "And why's that?"

I reached over to place a hand over her fist. Quite early on, I noticed how much she squeezed her thumb in between her index and middle finger when she was anxious. Jacobs' finger went sheet white when she didn't know what to expect.

"Your body language gives away a lot," I explained. My hand still rested on her. She stared down, watching as my fingers gently tugged open her own. Her palm was warm, like mine. I absentmindedly traced the lines on her hand before pulling away. My heart sank at the separation. Going home alone tonight was going to be difficult. I wanted skin-to-skin contact. Kissing and touching. Breathless moans with desperate pleas.

"I figured they'd guess something was up and you wouldn't be able to lie about it," I said.

"I can keep a secret," she argued with no real surety behind her voice.

I shook my head, smiling a bit. "Not when it comes to body language, you can't. Lesson one, learn how to communicate what you want when you want."

She nodded with a determined look in her eyes. Her lips parted as she paid attention. Every inch of my being wanted to move closer and place my mouth on hers. But not tonight. I was supposed to be helping her focus on someone else tonight.

"Morgan?" she asked, taking note of my weird pause.

"S-sorry...um..." I shook my head, clearing out all the space in my brain occupied by her. "Your shoulders, you give away everything with them."

Jacobs frowned and touched her bare shoulder. Her fingers traced across her collarbone as she tried to figure out what I meant. The act was so unconsciously sexual.

"On and off the ice, you turn them to what you want," I said, careful not to let my eyes linger on her skin. "And away from something that scares you."

"I'm confused. What does my technique on the ice have to do with flirting?"

"Everything," I promised and then moved to her side of the table. "Do you mind if I—?"

She swallowed and nodded. I gently placed my hand on her shoulders, urging her to relax them away from her ears, and turned toward me. The touch was innocent enough. I ignored the spark traveling up my forearm. This was a natural reaction to touching a beautiful girl.

"When you're playing, you're stiff in your upper body." My voice was lower because of how close we were standing now. Karaoke was still going on in the background and people were walking in the aisle next to our table. But everything felt muffled now, like there was a wall blocking us from everyone else.

"Really?" Jacobs looked confused.

I nodded. "You grip your stick too tight, and allow the puck to get too far away from you when you pull back for a pass or attempt a goal."

I could see the wheels turning in her head as I spoke.

"Probably the same thing happens with flirting and dating," I continued. "You think too much, and it affects the outcome."

She let out a dry laugh. "Story of my life. I'd kill to not think too much. I'm a rusher, too. Like going from one thing to the next without really thinking things through."

"It's possible to slow down. It takes practice." I removed my hands from her shoulders and lightly touched her elbow instead. "Look around and pick someone you like in here."

"Like someone I want to flirt with?"

I smiled at her widened eyes. "Yeah, but no pressure. We're practicing. You can fuck this up as much as you want."

"Okay." She licked her lips and scanned the crowd. While she searched for someone, I studied her. The gentle rise and fall of her chest. The way her brow curled up as she thought. Before I knew what I was doing, I reached up to touch one of the coils at the nape of her neck. I pulled my hand away quickly when she started talking.

"Him." Jacobs nudged her chin in the direction of a guy sitting at the bar.

I rubbed the back of my neck, trying to take my own advice and not think too much about what I was doing. Why was acting normal around her so difficult tonight?

My eyes found her pick, thankful for the distraction. The guy looked a little older than us. He had locs that stretched down his back and two nose rings.

"Why him?" I asked, curious about her process and type.

"He looks nice." She tilted her head to the side, smiling a little. "Approachable. And I saw him helping a server who spilled some drinks earlier. I'm a sucker for nice."

"Ah, now I see why you gravitated toward me," I teased.

"You're the exception, Morgan," she said in a flat tone.

I laughed. "Alright, practice on me first."

Her voice raised pitch when she asked, "What?"

"What's your opening line?" I moved back to my side of the table. "Pretend I'm him and approach me. Flirt with me."

"Morgan this is a little...embarrassing."

"You're the one who wanted tips, right?"

She sighed. "Right, but..."

"But what? The only way to get better is to practice," I said. "Unless you want to forfeit our bet now and deem me the winner? I'm down."

"No." She straightened her back. "Absolutely not."

I chuckled. "Alright, then. Let's see what you got. Go back a few paces to simulate walking up."

Jacobs gave me a look but followed my instructions. I turned to the window, glancing out to pretend like I didn't know she was on her way over. When I heard Jacobs clear her throat, I didn't turn around. She did it again and I pretended like I was checking a text on my phone.

"Morgan," she hissed.

I started, like her presence came as a surprise. She rolled her eyes at my acting.

"Oh, sorry, I didn't see you there," I said.

She didn't look impressed at my mock surprise, and I smiled wider.

"Stop fucking around." She shoved my shoulder. "I thought you said you were going to help me."

"I am," I promised. "You need to approach me with more confidence."

"I was plenty confident."

"You didn't even sit down. You didn't come into my line of sight. And I could barely hear your throat clearing over tonight's wannabe pop singers."

Jacobs crossed her arms over her chest, but her eyes were soft enough to indicate she was taking in my feedback.

"When you approach someone, you let them know you're there and you're worth it," I explained in a gentle tone. "I've seen you claim your space at the arena. You can do it here, too."

She nodded but didn't look too sure.

"Here." I stood up and grabbed her hand for a second to guide her to my stool. "Relax and I'll demonstrate."

"Okay," she said.

I walked away from our table, ignoring the weird looks we were getting from the people around us. Yes, we were acting strange but the sound of a middle-aged man singing like a dying giraffe felt much more attention-grabbing than my flirting lesson.

When I made my way back to our table, Jacobs had turned to look out the window like I was doing before. I caught her reflection in the mirror and something about her somber expression made my heart tug. Was I being too hard on her? Sometimes I went a little overboard with the teasing. I'd have to be more careful.

"Hi," I said in a voice that carried over the music.

She turned to me. The somber expression was replaced with a fake, confused one. I swallowed a laugh at how cute her eyes were when she was pretending.

I rested my elbow on the table, leaning in close to create some semblance of intimacy. "You're quite distracting. What's your secret?"

"Excuse me?" Jacobs blinked, looking genuinely caught off guard.

"From the moment I walked in here and saw you, I couldn't stop wondering who you were. There's this...fire burning around you."

"Fire?" Jacobs frowned.

"It's a good thing. It makes me want to learn more about you. The curiosity is killing me," I said with striking honesty because it was true.

She laughed. "How flattering."

"I'm serious, I'd like to get to know you, if you're willing. Can I buy you a drink?"

"I don't know—"

"You can tell me to leave at any point," I promised. "Even if it's the second that drink touches your hands. I'll sleep better tonight knowing I could give something to someone like you, beautiful."

She cast her eyes down to where my hand was mere inches from hers. Jacobs wiggled her fingers, and I mirrored her movement. Our hands brushed for a moment. My breathing was unsteady from the slight pressure of her fingers against mine.

"This is the moment that freaks me out," she said, breaking character.

"What?" I took a deep breath, having to push away the building anticipation in my chest.

"The moment where someone could reject me."

"Treat it like the moment you miss a goal. You brush it off because there's no point in worrying about what you can't change. You take note of what you could've done better and then, move on to the next. There's always a next." My chest tightened. I didn't like thinking about what was coming next right now.

"You make it sound so easy."

"With practice, it is. You remember the first time you stood up on skates?"

She smiled, her eyes alight. "Fell right back down on my ass."

I chuckled. "Exactly. And eventually, you learned to stay up, right?"

"That and my ass got harder."

"Even better," I said. "Point is, you keep trying long enough until this feels natural. Like you could do it in your sleep."

Jacobs stared at me with a weird look on her face.

"What?" I asked.

"You give some really solid advice," she said. "Are you sure you want to give me an advantage?"

I scoffed. "Like I said before, execution is a whole other ball game. I have no doubt in my mind I'm still going to beat you, no matter how many lessons I give you because, well, I'm just that good."

She rolled her eyes, but still flashed me a good-natured smile. "Fine. Let's go one more time."

We switched positions. This time, instead of clearing her throat, Jacobs greeted me with a crystal-clear 'hello.' I turned to her and nearly got the wind knocked out of me.

She'd readjusted her dress to reveal more of her cleavage. Her coils were pulled off her shoulders in a high puff, highlighting the curve of her neck. Those small changes seemed to give her the confidence to smile and place a hand on my upper arm.

"Hi, I'm Aderyn," she greeted, leaning into my ear so I could hear her better.

"Aderyn," I repeated with a smile. The feel of her first name on my tongue made my stomach flip. Who knew a name could be erotic? We'd been so formal with one another since the moment we met. Somehow, I felt even closer to her now than I did coming with her in the dorm.

"I'm Sam," I said.

Something in her eyes changed. Did she feel the charge in the air, too? I hoped. Prayed.

"You seem like you're a hockey fan." The teasing glint in her eyes made me want to kiss her.

"Why do you say that?"

She shrugged. "I don't know. I have a sixth sense about these sorts of things. I also sense that you're down for a pool match."

"Oh?"

"We could make a bet."

"You do like your bets." I couldn't resist teasing her. Jacobs stayed on track, though. Determined to get through this practice conversation.

"I'll go easy on you," she promised. Before I could respond she brushed her thumb in small circles around my bicep and added in a whisper, "For the first time, anyway."

Her words went straight to my dick. When I didn't respond, she pulled back and asked in a hurry, "Was that okay? Too cringe with the sultry voice? I need to practice my bedroom voice. My ex always laughed at it."

"N-no." I shook my head. "It was perfect. Very hot."

My cheeks burned from the stammering. I pressed my fingers into a fist, trying to steady myself. Jacobs didn't seem to notice my screw-ups.

"You're not just telling me what I want to hear so I go over there and make a fool of myself, are you?"

"I'm serious, Ader—Jacobs." I cleared my throat. "You were great. You could work on maintaining eye contact the entire time but other than that..."

I'd play pool with you. I'd spend the whole night, morning, and the next day with you.

"It was fine," I said instead, suddenly needing a breath of fresh air. The walls felt like they were closing in.

"Okay, I'll take your word for it." She smiled and shook out her hands. "I think I'm ready. He's still over there."

"You're ready," I agreed even though I wanted to come up with an excuse for her to stick around. Spending the rest of the night with her — even if all we did was shoot the breeze — sounded fun.

"Good luck," I said after swallowing my suggestion to forget the guy and hang out with me.

"I don't need your luck, remember?" She laughed a little, then started for the bar.

I watched, jaw tightening when the guy noticed her, even before she had the chance to say anything. Of course, he'd been paying attention to her. Any guy with half a brain would.

I found myself wishing for something for all the wrong reasons. I didn't want Jacobs to go home with this guy. I didn't want her going home with any guy other than me.

Get it together, I willed myself. This feeling is just because you want to be out there, too. Flirting with whoever, going home with whoever and forgetting them the next day.

No matter how hard I tried to cling to that idea, I couldn't. I didn't want to flirt with anyone. I wanted to flirt with Aderyn.

Chapter Eleven

Aderyn

T he guy at the bar was from Philly. His accent was thick and his humor nonexistent. We weren't clicking on a personal level but physically, it was all there. That's all that should've mattered. Except, when it was time to leave and he offered to take me back to his place, I hesitated.

"Or yours," he offered with a smile that seemed obligatory. Why did that matter? We didn't have to be soulmates to sleep together for one night. Hell, I didn't even have to like him to prove to Morgan that I could be good at this whole sleeping around thing.

"Mine," I agreed with a forced smile.

He grabbed my hand and led me out of the bar. His fingers were dry and cold against mine. His grip was loose enough for me to feel like maybe he was just settling for the night, too. Maybe if I wiggled out of his hand and made up an excuse, we'd both sigh with relief.

I caught a glimpse of Morgan before I walked out. He noticed our entwined fingers and lifted his brow as if to ask if I was okay with what was happening.

I gave him a smile and thumbs up because I couldn't back out. Not on my first go. As soon as I got out of the bar, I winced and groaned under my breath at my fake smile. Did Morgan see through it? God, I hoped not.

"You good?" Philly guy asked. He'd told me his name, but I couldn't hear it over the crowd and I'd been too nervous to ask him to repeat it a fourth time.

"All good." I readjusted my dress, so it covered more of my shoulders. Something about Morgan admiring my body made me excited. When this guy did it, I just wanted to cover up.

"My bike's right over here," he said.

"Your bike?"

"Yeah." He looked amused at my open mouth. "You ever ridden on one?"

The way he phrased that question let me know he was well-versed in using his bike to draw women in.

"Um, no." I brushed back a wayward curl from my face. "Can't say I have."

"I'm a bit of a speed demon," he confessed.

My stomach dropped.

"It's the only way to live if you ask me." He grabbed a helmet from the seat's storage. Instead of offering it to me, he opened the clasp for himself. As far as I could tell, he only had one.

"You sure? Because I heard driving the speed limit is also a very valid alternative," I joked, shooting finger guns because that was the only way I knew how to keep the conversation lighthearted.

He shook his head. "I promise you, it's great. I've only had a few accidents."

Was he fucking with me? "Only a few?"

"Yeah." He waved his hand. "None of them my fault, though. Tons of assholes on the road not looking where they're going. I keep riding because eventually, they'll learn to look out for us."

I shook my head when he pulled on his helmet. "Actually, I just remembered I have a friend that needs me to take them to the dentist."

"Dentist? At midnight?"

"It's early in the morning," I quickly explained. "Bright and early. And I need my sleep because, without it, I get terrible acne breakouts. Just recovered from my last flare-up so...you know."

"Oh, totally," he said in a surprisingly understanding tone. "Scarring's a nightmare. You use masks?"

"Love a good mask."

"Don't," he said, point blank.

"Oh, okay."

"Yeah, they're killers. Minimum face care routines are essential for people like us. Besides, half that shit's got mercury in it anyway."

"You don't say?"

"Yeah, in ten to twenty years, most people who use that shit's going to be in some study about the government purposely poisoning them, getting them hooked on medication. Big pharma for the win."

"That's definitely a theory," I agreed with a smile. His lips didn't move an inch up or down. He was dead serious. "Get yourself plain soap, a lemon, and clam juice."

"Clam juice?" Just the thought of putting that on my skin made me want to gag.

"You'll thank me." He nudged up the kickstand and started his engine before I could say anything else, let alone a 'thank you.' I tried to smile when he gave me a little salute before speeding off into the night.

My chest loosened at the sound of his bike fading in the distance. Sex with him would've probably been fine. Good even because strange guys usually knew how to give good head. But no part of me would've been in it.

This is exactly Morgan's point. You're not a casual hook-up person.

But I could be. I just had to push myself harder than this. And not give up at the first sign of oddness.

"Damn it," I cursed under my breath.

"I take it your night's free?"

I whipped around to find Morgan leaning against the side of the building. He looked incredible in the sweater that clung to his biceps and the pants that hung perfectly on his waist.

"How long were you standing there?" I resisted the urge to wring my hands.

"Just got here a second ago," he promised.

I blew out a breath of relief.

"So? How did it go?" His question made my jaw tighten. I hated when people said I'd fail and I proved them right.

"Fine," I lied. "It was a warm-up, anyway."

"Right, of course." He nodded, pretending to agree. Pretending to care.

"Why are you out here? Trying to resist the urge to take someone home?"

"I don't need to resist." He pushed off the wall, closing the distance between us. "I'm not interested in anyone there."

"You're a good competitor, I'll give you that much."

Morgan's smile widened. "Why thank you."

"Don't get all smug." I shook my head. "I still have time."

"Plenty," he agreed. "But meanwhile, wanna waste some of it together?"

I could feel my heart in my throat. Thank God it was a cloudy night, otherwise, Morgan would see how much I wanted to say yes. I drew my answer out for suspense.

"As long as you promise not drive too far over the speed limit."

"The roads are icy. Who's speeding?"

I felt light with relief. "Lead the way."

We didn't turn on a single light when we got to his room. Our lips were on each other's the second the door closed behind us.

"Where's the bed," I asked between heated kisses. He'd been walking me backward for what felt like ages.

"Trust me?" he asked. I could hear the smile in his voice.

"Kind of," I teased and then, yelped when he lifted me off the ground. My legs encircled his waist, and my hands clutched his shoulders.

"All good?" he asked.

I laughed. "Yeah, surprised is all," I said, breathless.

His chuckle shook his body. I pressed myself harder against him, enjoying the feeling of hard muscle between my legs. Morgan kissed me again, parting my lips so his tongue flicked against mine. I whimpered against his mouth as he teased me with a preview of what his tongue could do. The way his hand rubbed up and down my back felt...romantic. His hands sweetly traced gentle circles against me.

This is foreplay, I reminded myself. *Casual foreplay with a guy you're going to walk away from.*

Morgan lowered me onto the mattress. I relaxed onto the sheets, thinking he'd join me but instead, he moved down my body. His kisses trailed down my neck and to my chest. I arched into him, spreading my legs to accommodate his position in between them.

My dress slipped off my shoulders and down my waist. Morgan tugged down my strapless bra and placed his mouth over one of my nipples. He sucked on the hardened tip, using his teeth to gently tug. My hands held onto the back of his head, holding him steady against my skin.

He moved to my other breast, giving it just as much attention.

"Morgan," I whispered, ignoring how desperate the syllables sounded on my tongue.

He pulled away for a second to say, "Don't call me that while we're this close."

"What?" It was hard to see him in the dark. My eyes took a moment to make out his broad shoulders and thick arms.

"Call me Sam," he insisted.

I swallowed. It made sense. Perfect sense. Yet still, it felt weird because since I'd known him, I hadn't used his first name until we practiced earlier at the bar. Even then, it'd been weird.

"I'm about to eat your pussy, beautiful," he murmured.

My heart stopped. Holy. Shit.

"So, could you please call me Sam while I do it?" he asked. "I need that much. Just for tonight?"

"Okay." I nodded. I could feel his smile against my mouth as he pulled me in for another kiss.

"Ready for me to take these off?" He tugged at the waistband of my underwear. I nodded without hesitation. He slowly glided them off my legs, drawing out the removal. Once they were gone, he placed both hands on my thighs, guiding my knees to my chest.

The cold air on my pussy made my toes curl. I whined when his lips brushed across my thighs.

"You smell like a dream," he said, a hard groan almost masking his words. "I'm so fucking glad you didn't go home with anyone else tonight."

"It was just a practice run," I reminded him.

"Right, right," he murmured between kisses on my thighs.

I frowned because I could hear the doubt in his voice. "It was. I'll be sleeping with plenty of people by the end of this semester."

The noise from his throat sounded disapproving and almost jealous. I laughed at the thought of him being jealous of someone being with me. It was a nice fantasy I could play into tonight. I closed my eyes and pretended to be the one girl Morgan dreamed about.

As soon as his mouth enclosed my pussy, my fantasy was easier to maintain. He licked me carefully at first. Like, I was too delicate to handle his appetite. When I started to squirm and moan, his hands tightened around my thighs so I'd stay still.

I could feel wetness dripping from me. Morgan licked up every drop like he couldn't let it go to waste.

"You weren't this quiet with that vibrator in you," he mused. "If I'm doing something wrong, tell me."

"No, you're perfect…I just don't know if…" I sucked in a breath when he flicked his tongue against the tip of my clit. "…if your roommates are home yet."

"Doesn't make a difference," he insisted. "I want to hear you. I want to see what you react to best. Can you make some noise for me? I need to hear, Aderyn."

"I'll try," I promised through a heavy breath. He resumed his sucking and I pushed away my fear of being overheard. My moans echoed in the quiet space. Morgan responded with moans of his own muffled by my pussy.

"That's it," he encouraged me when my thighs began shaking. "You're so sexy right now. I could spend all night between these thighs. Would you let me? Let me eat you out until the sun comes up?"

"Yes, please," I pleaded. My fingers gripped his sheets. "Please, Sam."

He moaned at the sound of his name, giving me a long lick to reward me. "Say it again? Use my name again."

"Please, Sam. I need you."

"Need me to...?" he prompted and then, flicked his tongue up and down my opening. His hands forced me to widen, stretching me out so everything was available for him to take. My core squeezed, longing for something inside.

"Fuck me, Sam," I whispered, hoarsely. "Please. Fuck me like this."

"Come on my tongue first, and we have a deal."

"Deal." I agreed, tilting my head back to let out another moan as he took my clit between his lips again. His mouth sent my head spinning. I felt tears in the corners of my eyes as the pressure kept building.

"Sam," I said. "Sam, I'm close..."

He moved his hands from my thighs to my waist, tugging my body half off the bed. My ass cheeks rested on his chest and his large hands imprinted on my hard abs. I came as soon as his fingers twisted my nipples. My back arched, forcing more of my body to slide off the bed. Morgan didn't miss a beat, taking on all my weight like it was nothing.

He continued to suck on me until I stopped shaking. When he finally pulled away, he disappeared into the bathroom and returned with a condom. I've never felt anything more satisfying than when he finally slid his dick into me. I arched into him, trying to use his body to stimulate my still sensitive clit.

"That's it," he whispered into my ear. "Hungry for more, beautiful?"

I nodded, heart pounding with excitement at his voice. I've never felt this sexy. Morgan spoke to me like this was more than sex. Like this was an activity where we could ask for whatever we wanted. Sex in the past felt like something I needed only to give not take away from.

"Wanna ride me then?" he asked and didn't have to repeat himself.

We flipped over and I braced my hands on his chest. Morgan's heart was racing. From the small amount of light from the bathroom, I caught the longing in his eyes. His hands cupped my ass, helping me rock my hips back and forth on him.

"God," I gasped when he pressed his hips up to meet my body. The arch allowed for a part of his lower stomach to squeeze against my clit.

"Fuck me like you fucked your toy," he begged. "Grind that little clit on me until you can't take it. I still think about that hot look on your face when you came on my lap. How this hard body melted for me. I want to see it again, beautiful. It's all I've been able to think about."

"Shit, Sam." I leaned in to kiss him, hips still rolling at a steady speed. My pussy clenched around him, and wetness pooled between us as I fell apart. How did I feel numb and yet every nerve in my body was lit up at the same time?

"That's it. Take me. Take every inch you need," Morgan whispered against my lips. He pressed his forehead against mine and I came on him for the second time. With a slight tilt of his pelvis, I rode the next wave. My breath hitched at the feeling of relief and shock of climaxing multiple times. Before tonight, I'd never experienced multiple orgasms before. I didn't know how pent-up I'd been this week.

"More?" he asked, completely willing. "I can give you more, Aderyn."

"No, I need you to finish now. It's your turn." I kissed his neck and ground against his still hard dick. He met every one of my movements, thrusting against me. Eventually, he flipped me over, so I was underneath him. Sam found his preferred rhythm quickly. My stomach fluttered, hearing his hard groan in my ear once he orgasmed. The sound was gruff like he was working his way up a mountain. He buried his face into my neck, whispering something unintelligible against my skin. I could make out the tone though, and it was pleading.

When his orgasm subsided, Sam collapsed beside me. His arms tightened around my waist, pulling me against his chest. We stayed like that for a few minutes. When I finally caught my breath, I was the one to pull away. For a moment, it felt like he wasn't going to loosen his grip. Like he didn't want to let me go. But I must have imagined it because his arms fell as I straightened. He didn't say a thing when I went into the bathroom to clean up.

"I'll see you later for shooting the videos, right?" I asked as soon as I was out of the bathroom, my dress back on. Getting ready to leave wasn't as hard as I thought it'd be.

"Yeah...definitely." He sat up and watched me tug on my shoes. "Hey..."

I paused and glanced at him. "What's up?"

Morgan scratched his cheek and then shook his head. "Nothing. Let me drive you back to your dorm?"

I waved my hand. "I'll order a ride. No point in you having to drive to campus and back this late."

"Take my car if you won't let me drive. I'll pick it up later." He got up, grabbed his keys, and placed them in my hand before I could protest. "It's late, Aderyn. Take it."

"That's quite nice of you. Very boyfriend-level nice," I teased. "Going for bonus points?"

"It's common decency," he argued. "I would prefer driving but you're one stubborn woman who'll probably argue with me until the sun comes up."

I closed my hand around the keys. "You're right. I'm stubborn. But I'll take your car. Thanks."

"Text me when you get back?"

I raised a brow, surprised at his worry. "Wow, you're really dedicated."

"I am. Now, are you going to text me?" he asked with a teasing smile.

"Definitely not," I said.

His smile wavered. "Good for you."

"Great for me." I laughed when he rolled his eyes. "See ya later, Morgan."

"Later...Jacobs."

I'm proud to say, when I walked away, I didn't even feel the need to look back. Didn't even want to spend the night. And on my ride home, I only got a little caught up in his car smelling like him. Only a little. Progress.

I was getting better at this casual thing.

Chapter Twelve

Aderyn

Aderyn: **Which guys are you bringing?**

Morgan and I finally found an opening in our schedules for more than a couple of our teammates to meet up. The plan was to film all our videos in bulk and release them throughout the week to see which ones did best. Since most of my morning was free, I was determined to be productive. I piled my car with extra skates, hockey sticks, and uniform tops. Before coming to the park, I stopped by Dusk + Dawn to buy a dozen Wild Things. My stomach buzzed with excited nerves to get started filming...and because I wanted to see the look on his face when I give him my 'thank-you' present.

Morgan: The ones who are free.

I frowned and glanced up at my tagalongs for the day: a moody Kaya and enthused Mary. We were waiting for the guys at a park off-campus. The lake a few yards away had long since frozen over and provided a near perfect setting for filming—I would've preferred the arena but we couldn't book time last minute.

Aderyn: And who also have active followings, right?

Morgan: You didn't say anything about them having to be active.

Aderyn: That's the whole point of doing this! We're trying to build a crossover audience! Please tell me you're joking.

"Everything alright?" Mary asked, joining me at the trunk of my car. Kaya was close behind her, carrying an overflowing gym bag.

"Did he cancel?" Kaya asked, not even attempting to hide her hope.

"No." I tugged the bag of doughnuts to my chest and locked my phone so Mary's nosy eyes wouldn't catch a glimpse of my panicked responses. "They're on their way and excited to help."

"Perfect! This is going to be so cute," Mary gushed and pulled out her phone to show me the videos she'd sent to our group chat last night. Most of them involve trending sounds and thirst traps.

I snorted at a particularly hot one of a hockey player from Westbrooke University. All he did was eye the camera like it was something he wanted to eat for breakfast. The lick of the lips at the end of the clip was peak comedy in my book.

"God, do you think we can get the guys to do something like that?" I asked, laughing.

Mary shrugged. "Shouldn't be too hard. Some of them already have."

"No shit." My eyes widened and I motioned for her to scroll. "Show me."

Kaya moved closer now, not able to fake disinterest anymore. Mary pulled up the Mendell Hawks men's team page and clicked on one of the top-viewed videos. Lo and behold Lincoln was on the screen and put in even more effort than the guy from Westbrooke. The more Mary scrolled, the better it got.

"Why is this ultimate cringe but also kind of hot?" I muttered when we watched a clip of Jack for the second time. I didn't know much about the guy, but his brown eyes were gorgeous and his devil-may-care attitude was heart-stopping. He didn't like the camera on him, but it liked him. So did the majority of commenters.

Kaya huffed, disbelieving. "Hot?"

"Oh, come on." Mary gave her a look. "I'm one-thousand percent lesbian but still get a little sweaty watching Jack. He's got an undeniable pull."

"Definite pull," I agreed and swiped back to one of his videos. "*Serious* pull."

Kaya's nose wrinkled. "Guess I can't see it anymore 'cause I know the guy."

"Like biblically?" I joked.

"Gross, no," Kaya frowned. "I've known him since middle school."

Mary and I froze and stared at her.

"How did I not know this?" I tried to recall when Kaya and Jack ever interacted. I came up with nothing.

"We were in the same friend group in high school," she explained with a shrug. "That friend group imploded. People took sides and I was naturally on Halle's side."

I nodded, thinking of her cousin, Halle. She was a figure skater at Mendell who'd come to practices sometimes to coach us on the importance of form. The lessons never stuck but we appreciated her efforts.

"So, was he the asshole in your group?" Mary wondered. "He definitely loses all appeal if he was the asshole."

Kaya shook her head. "Jack's cool. I can't share too much because Halle would rather not have her business out there. But, he's fine."

"Well, glad to hear Jack's not an asshole," I said. "Usually the good-looking ones are. It's refreshing the guys on the team don't follow that trend."

"Morning," a voice surprised all of us. We scrambled off the car and Mary shoved her phone in her pocket while the last video played on a loop. The music was muffled but still noticeable.

The smiles on Lincoln, Henrik, Jack, and Morgan's faces let us know they'd heard a bit of our conversation. I elbowed Mary to take care of the still playing video.

"Morning, guys." I smiled a bit too brightly in hopes enthusiasm drowned out our embarrassment.

"This is everyone you could rally?" Morgan crossed his arms over his chest, examining my girls.

"It's early. Most of my team has classes," I explained. "A few others are gonna show up once they get out."

Morgan looked at his watch like he was pressed for time. I raised a brow, thinking about our night together where he promised to dedicate hours to me.

"You in a hurry?" I teased.

He looked back up at me and in a surprisingly hard tone answered, "Well, I don't have all the time in the world."

Damn. Fair but the words still stung considering it was a far cry from the 'call me by my first name' guy the other night.

"No worries. We've cleared the morning for you guys." Lincoln patted his friend's shoulder. His easy smile was almost enough to make up for Morgan's annoyed look.

"We have more than enough time," Henrik agreed and gestured to Mary. "Want to show us what you're planning to start with?"

Mary nodded, excitedly and hurried over to share her phone with the others. Our teammates gathered to share ideas and narrow down filming spots. I joined Morgan's side, hiding the bag of doughnuts behind my back once I was close.

"You're in a mood?" I asked in a whisper.

"No," he said, simply. "Why?"

I shrugged. "I don't know. I just never heard you complain about time. One eighty from the other night."

He scoffed. "Next lesson."

I eyed him, trying to predict where this was going. "Okay."

"Don't think about the past so much. Always press forward in casual relationships. Last night shouldn't exist for you."

My smile vanished and my grip on the doughnut bag tightened. Why the hell did he sound so...cold? "I wasn't bringing it up because I felt something."

"Really?" He didn't sound convinced. Morgan studied me like he could peel back every single one of my layers without much effort. My jaw tightened in annoyance.

"Really," I said, matching his tone. Two could play that game and I could play it better. "I was just making small talk."

"Sounded emotional."

"I think you might be projecting."

He blinked, taken aback for a second before finally shaking his head. "Not a chance."

"Right, because you're the king of keeping emotions out of relationships."

"Exactly," he agreed in a stiff voice.

"Whatever." I looked toward the lake. Suddenly, this morning felt like it couldn't be over sooner. I didn't like cold Morgan. Or being held at arm's length. Somewhere down the line, we'd become friends of sorts. At least, I thought we had, but maybe I was being too hopeful. Maybe this connection between us would only last until the end of our agreement.

Why did I have to go and get these fucking doughnuts?

"How's the search going?" Morgan's question gave me pause. I looked over at him to find his eyes weren't as hard. "What?"

"Your next one-night stand," he reminded me.

"It's going fine," I said, tone clipped. "Why?"

Morgan gave me a one-shoulder shrug. "Just gauging where my competition's at. You seem interested in Jack."

My brow raised. "Do I?"

"From your comments earlier, yeah."

"Comments earlier..." My face warmed. For the first time today, Morgan smiled at me.

"He's a decent guy," Morgan said. "You two would probably get along. For a night or two, at least."

"Are you setting me up?"

"It was only a suggestion." He held up his hands. "I figured our clock's ticking, so it wouldn't hurt giving you some friendly advice."

"I don't need your advice."

"You were singing a different tune the other night," he joked.

"And I'm regretting every moment of it," I snapped back.

Morgan's posture stiffened. "Every moment?"

I took a breath when I saw the worry in his eyes. "No, not every moment. Just the moment where you started to assume I can't make my own decisions."

"Like I said, it was only a suggestion, Aderyn."

My name sounded as soft as the wind after a storm. He said it like he'd spoken it multiple times before. Like he'd been practicing to make sure it sounded perfect. To make sure it sounded like it belonged on his tongue.

"I mean..." Morgan tried to backtrack. He ran his hand across his head, fingers ruining his perfect waves.

"Hey, Captain?" Lincoln called.

"Yeah?" Morgan and I answered in unison. We looked over to everyone else, grateful for the interruption.

Our teammates were staring at us. Some looked confused, others wore knowing smiles. I stepped away from Morgan, just now noticing how close we were standing.

"Uh," Lincoln hesitated, aware he'd interrupted something none of us quite understood. "Are we ready to start?"

"We are," Morgan answered for the both of us.

Before he could move forward, I reached for his shoulder. He frowned at my hand on him.

"Here." I shoved the bag in his direction. I needed to get rid of them and somehow, throwing them away would feel more embarrassing than giving them to him.

Morgan took the bag. "What's this?"

"My thank you. For the car and today," I said quickly."

I walked away before he could respond. Didn't even spare him a glance as I started over to the rest of the group. "Let's get to work."

The guys were always great company on the ice. Now that we'd whittled their group down, we got to know them better. I enjoyed Lincoln the most. He always made sure to keep everyone involved and laughing. And his jokes were never at the expense of someone else—which felt rare for a guy his age.

He and Mary were patient and thorough when teaching us the dos and don'ts of making content. We paired off in small groups to film segments of a current video trend that required split-second transitions and a few dance moves. Jack was my partner and for some reason, we weren't exactly clicking like I thought we would.

Jack wasn't nice but he wasn't necessarily mean either. He existed somewhere outside of those two bubbles, floating in a space I couldn't reach. He'd often voice critiques that came off as harsh. Then, a few minutes later, he'd say he didn't mean any harm and was looking out for you.

"You're swinging very wide," he noted when I tried to mimic the move Mary showed me.

"I thought that was the point," I said with a frown.

"It's going to take up the whole frame. We don't get much real estate with this app."

I sighed and dropped my hands. "This is frustrating."

"The very definition," Jack agreed. "I wonder who thought of doing it. We should probably give them a piece of our minds. Really stick it to them."

I snorted at his sarcastic tone. "Hey, you can leave at any time. You don't have to shake your ass like some prized pig at the fair."

"Don't see why you need to either if you don't want to. Who gives a shit about who shows up to your games or not?"

"The people holding the checkbooks." I stopped trying to do the choreography to look at him. Jack was barely taller than me. He was one of the shorter guys on the team but what he lacked in height he made up for in build. The guy's skin was pale, he kept his brown curls long enough to reach his shoulders, and wore gages in his ears.

"Marketing is a necessary evil," I told him. "You're lucky enough not to have to think too much about it. In five years you'll have some cushy brand deal because you posted a shirtless pic once or twice."

Jack chuckled. "Think so?"

"All your photos give off a vibe of 'I don't care about shit.' And that look on guys never goes out of style."

"All my photos," he repeated, slowly. "Is that an exaggeration or have you been Internet stalking me?"

My cheeks burned because of the knowing smile he gave me. "I've been doing…. research. Like any smart captain would. Can't have just anyone on our page."

"You might be interested to know that I think all your photos give off 'untouchable,'" he offered.

"Is that a compliment or…?"

"Untouchable like you're someone hard to impress. So, I'm glad I've made an impression of some kind. Even if only my shirtless photos are memorable."

I could barely think straight. This was an opening. A chance with a guy who wasn't awkward and a stranger like the Philly guy.

Jack was perfect to add to my currently non-existent list of one-night stands. Charming. Cute. He had a nice amount of attitude to both get on my nerves and challenge me. I should lean into this and yet, my gaze strayed to Morgan. And the part of me—that I so desperately wanted to cut out—felt loyalty to him instead.

I whipped out my phone to block out the feelings about a guy I had no business being loyal to.

"I don't think I have your number yet," I said.

Jack accepted my phone. "Easy fix."

Chapter Thirteen

Sam

J ealousy. It's something I'm very familiar with. Despite how much I've gotten used to casual relationships, my stomach still churned seeing someone else with the person I liked. Up until today, I thought I'd learned to manage the emotion well.

Seeing Aderyn with Jack made paying attention nearly impossible. My stomach didn't just churn, it pinched until that same feeling moved throughout my body.

I'd told her to consider him. Pushed her in his direction. I thought it'd do us both a favor if she finally got with someone other than me. She'd be able to enjoy the dopamine boost from sex, and I'd get a physical reminder that she wasn't mine to keep. She'd never be mine to keep.

My throat tightened whenever Jack invaded her personal bubble. She smiled at him like she smiled at me: open mouth and wrinkles at the corners of her eyes. Apparently, the guy was funny because she couldn't stop laughing. I've never heard Jack tell a joke worthy of a head-thrown-back, hand-on-stomach laugh. But, apparently, he knew some. He even got the hand-on-arm treatment now and then.

I hadn't been lying when I said I thought Jack was a good guy. Sure, he'd made some morally gray decisions. Still, no part of me could, in good conscience, make him seem like anything worse than a misled guy who just wanted to afford college. Anyone who could make her laugh like that deserved a shot. No matter how painful it was to watch unfold.

Aderyn and Jack stayed close to one another throughout the morning. He kept leaning into her to keep their conversations private. She leaned in too, giving him the look I'd taught her.

I wished I'd brought my skates. I needed to move and feel the burn in my lungs and legs. Anything that'd drown out the pain of seeing her with someone else. The pain of pushing her away.

This morning, I woke up with a newfound determination to keep emotion out of my relationship with Aderyn. After sending her away with my car, every part of me itched to text her. The next day, I wanted to invite her to breakfast. Wanted to hear her voice in the gym. Or visit the arena and witness her unstoppable power.

Somehow, her face always popped up when I started to stress. I found myself thinking, at least I'll get to see her later, and it calmed me down.

I wasn't the kind of guy who got calmed down by one person. I've never counted down the moments until I saw someone again. But I was doing that with her.

So, I put on a harder tone when talking to her. Acted more distant...My plan was working until I learned she'd gotten me the doughnuts I loved. Which made me feel even more awful for how I'd spoken to her. Aderyn got up early to wait in some long-ass line to get me something she couldn't even stand the smell of. And here I was, acting a fool and trying to avoid her.

I got fed up at the end of it. We'd filmed a shitload of videos and decided to call it quits when the sun was at its peak in the sky. The girls promised to send over everything after it was edited with tags and handles for us to post. We agreed to stick to their schedule.

As everyone broke off into their own groups to start the rest of their day, I gravitated toward Aderyn instantly. She'd just said 'goodbye' to Jack, and they exchanged lingering smiles. I was going to be sick.

"Took my advice?" I asked, forcing my voice to sound light and worry-free.

She smiled and shrugged. "Maybe. It was a little rocky at first, but you were right about us getting along."

"'Course I was." I forced on a smile, pretending to feel smug when I instead felt like throwing up.

"I see you're in a better mood." She spoke carefully like each word was a step in a minefield.

My shoulders sagged. "Sorry about before. I wasn't feeling like myself."

"You're entitled to wake up on the wrong side of the bed."

"Still. I shouldn't have been short with you. It won't happen again. I promise."

Her eyes widened at my assurance. "Okay...good."

"Thank you," I said in a lower voice like we were sharing a secret. "For the doughnuts."

"Did they help your mood?" Her face brightened a bit a the possibility. There was warm hope in her eyes. I could kiss her.

"They did." Why was my breathing so heavy all of a sudden?

"Perfect," she sang, proud of the outcome.

I cleared my throat, trying to regain control of my body. "So, how did it feel? The flirting?"

"Like I was on the verge of drowning," she said with a laugh. "I had to force myself to ask for his number. It was nerve-wracking."

"Why?"

Aderyn shrugged. "What if he rejected me? That would have been so humiliating."

"You would have been fine," I promised. "Rejection's part of the game. You'll experience it at some point, and once you do, I'll help you through it. I have plenty of experience in that department, trust me."

"Plenty?" Aderyn rolled her eyes.

"I know, it's hard to believe," I teased.

She bumped her shoulder against mine. "In that case, tell me the story now. If you're for real."

"The story? There's more than one."

She placed her hand over her chest in mock horror. "Who dared rejected the one and only Samson Morgan not once but multiple times?"

I chuckled. "Back in high school, I couldn't get a girl to look at me, let alone date me. I was the resident punching bag. The skinny kid with knobby knees and skeleton elbows. Every cliche moment in a high school drama has been acted out on me.

Trapped in lockers, hung by flag poles, and lunch replaced with worms."

Aderyn's teasing smile vanished. "You're serious?"

We were at the parking lot now, passing rows of cars without paying much attention to where we were going. The lot was fuller than it'd been earlier this morning. Family vans filled most of the spaces and the playground was packed with loud kids.

"You seemed like someone who's always been...popular," she said.

"It's been a conscious effort," I promised. "Had an unbelievable transformation senior year. Before then, well, things got bad to the point where I was coming home with bruises every other day."

It was always awkward bringing up my past. I've never done so with the women I've been involved with. Sometimes, I shared my bully stories with guys on the team when they felt like they wouldn't be able to get where they needed to be. I wasn't winning in every aspect of my life. But, I'd come far. And I was proud of the progress I'd made.

Sure, I still stammered over my words when things got overwhelming. Occasionally, I had insecurities about how my arms weren't as toned as they could be or how my body wasn't keeping on weight like I wanted. But, overall, my life was leagues better than a few years ago.

"Constant rejection's been a big part of my life. For a long time, I felt like an outsider. Eventually, I learned how to adapt and become the person I wanted to be," I said. "I don't think I'd be where I am without what happened to me, so for that, I'm grateful."

Aderyn shook her head, a frown on her face. "You'd be here. Without what happened, you would be."

The surety in her voice set my nerves on fire.

"What you went through sounds horrible," Aderyn continued. "I know we live in a world where people say what doesn't kill you makes you stronger. But it shouldn't take all that. You deserved better than that. Sure, maybe it helped you find your strength a little faster, but you would've made it here without the pain. No one deserves that kind of pain."

I smiled, touched by the worry in her eyes. "Honestly, it's fine. It was years ago."

She looked at me and somehow, I knew she could see past my brush-off.

I took a breath, embarrassed and ashamed for bringing it up. She hadn't reacted like I thought she would. Most people preferred leaning into my brush-off. They'd tell me, 'good for you' or 'that's how you deal with it.' My parents encouraged me to move on without addressing it. Sticks and stones. Always look forward, never back.

We'd paused by my car and Aderyn stood close to me. The space between us felt fragile, almost begging us to fill it.

"I'm glad you're here," she said in a low voice. "I'm glad whatever those assholes did to you didn't keep you from being the person you wanted to be."

"Thank you." I could barely feel the words leave my mouth.

"Is that how you got into hockey?" she asked. "To work on bulking up to fight off bullies?"

"Kind of." I nodded and looked down at my feet for a second. How honest did I want to be right now? It didn't take me long to decide—completely.

"I wanted to learn how to be unmovable," I confessed, holding her gaze so she could see my seriousness. "The hockey players I watched growing up were brick walls. They took unbelievable hits and got up without hesitation. It was inspiring. I needed to be like them to survive and eventually, I learned I was good enough to be the best on the team. After that, the respect started rolling in."

She hummed, understanding. "They saw you for more than some guy they could hurt."

"They saw me for a guy they could brag about knowing." I chuckled, shaking my head. "I didn't know what was worse, but I preferred it to getting the shit knocked out of me."

Aderyn sighed. "Hey, if you ever feel like venting about it, I'm always free. I know that was a while ago but stuff like that doesn't go away as quickly as we want it."

"Your experience talking now?"

She nodded. "Kids used to talk crap about my weight all the time in grade school. Told me I should stop working out so I wouldn't be buff— I didn't actually start working out until high school. Buff was a negative thing to them. There was even this rumor that I was this science experiment gone wrong."

She made a face but I could still hear the hurt in her voice. My jaw clenched as I imagined a younger Aderyn just being herself and getting picked on for it. What I'd give to go back in time and be there for her.

"My self-esteem was nonexistent for a long time," she continued. "Thank God I had a mom who taught me how to love the body I'm in. Muscles and all. I embrace presenting a little more traditionally masculine, but still, struggle with bullies' voices in the back of my mind every so often."

I wanted to say something comforting, but from the look on her face, I knew listening would be far more appreciated. Aderyn didn't need sympathies. She needed to be heard, respected, and seen.

"No matter how long ago everything was, those words have enough power to get to me. It probably works the same for you?"

I nodded, heartbeat skipping because someone got it. Like, truly got it. She didn't make one joke about my experience. Didn't make me feel small for a second.

"Sometimes you just need to tell someone who gets it to feel less lonely. I could be your person. I mean, the person you tell the disappointing stuff to."

I nodded, heat coursing through my chest because of how she felt safe enough to share a hidden part of herself. "Same here, Aderyn. Whenever you need it."

She smiled, eyes lighting up.

"Maybe we could—" I stopped short when someone called her name.

Aderyn's expression instantly changed as she looked over my shoulders.

"Shit, it's my mom and sister," she said in a rush. "Don't act weird. And don't mention...us."

"No weirdness. No fuck buddy mentioning," I joked before turning around. "Got it."

She jabbed my side with her elbow at the speed of light and then, greeted her folks with enough energy to power a city. "Hey! I didn't think you guys would get here so quickly. I thought you were still driving."

Aderyn accepted a hug from her mom. The older woman's hair was shaved low on her scalp and completely gray. Her arms were muscular, showing obvious signs of weightlifting. The smile she gave her daughter was wide and didn't falter for a second, even when she glanced in my direction.

"Got out of my doctor's appointment early," her mom explained.

"We dropped you a pin," her sister said, tone indicating an unvoiced, 'duh.' She was shorter than her mom and sister, and like Aderyn, wore her hair in cornrows.

"Oh." Aderyn pulled out her phone to check. "Sorry. I wasn't paying attention."

"Don't worry about it, sweetheart. You were busy," her mom insisted, eyes not leaving me. "You're the captain she's always talking about, right?"

"Mom," the sisters warned in unison.

I chuckled, noting how Aderyn refused to meet my eye. "I suppose so. I'm Samson. Samson Morgan. She's probably told you plenty of terrible things. Promise I'm not half as annoying as she's made me out to be."

"Annoying? Oh, quite the contrary." Her mom laughed and offered her hand for a shake. "Call me Essie. All my kids' partners do."

Aderyn made a noise that sounded like she was choking. "Mom. He's not my partner. We're...just hanging out."

"Hanging out," I agreed with a nod.

Essie tsked, frowning at her daughter. "Just hanging out? With how much you talk about him being the best thing since sliced bread?"

Aderyn tried to brush the comment off with a laugh. "Oh my God, Mom. Stop. Seriously."

"She thinks you're the best hockey player she's laid eyes on," Essie confirmed, ignoring her daughter's glare. "In looks and talent. She knows how to pick out talent—gets that from me. I told her, after a career in hockey, she should take up recruiting."

"Right, okay," Aderyn said. "I'm sure Sam—Morgan's very busy today. And we have a brunch to go to so..."

"You should join us!" Essie suggested.

"It's supposed to be a ladies-only thing," the sister swooped in, trying to help Aderyn's cause.

"We'll make an exception," their mom insisted. "Come on, girls. Don't be rude."

"Is that what we're being?" Aderyn asked, voice low.

I looked at the worry on her brow and said, "It's fine. I appreciate the invite—"

"It'll be my treat, Samson," Essie promised. "I don't get to spoil my kids often. And with you here, it reminds me of my son."

"Terrance wouldn't have been invited either," the sister grumbled. Essie swatted her playfully.

"I..." Again, I looked to Aderyn for a hint at what I should say. I didn't want to intrude on her family time. Meeting the family of a girl I was sleeping with was a huge no-no. Too much risk of attachment.

But a big part of me—a part that clouded my better judgment—wanted to spend more time with her. It didn't matter if we were alone or with others. I didn't want to say goodbye for the day.

When our eyes met, Aderyn didn't look as hesitant as she sounded. Her smile seemed hopeful, and the softness in her eyes told me it was completely my decision.

"Sure, I'll join you guys."

Aderyn's mouth parted wide in surprise. Her sister reached over to tap on her chin so she'd close it. I swallowed a laugh. Though this decision was risky, just seeing that expression made it worth it.

"Perfect." Essie beamed. "We'll start at the thrift shop and make our way to Berry Tea."

My forehead wrinkled. "Thrift shop?"

"It's all part of the experience," she insisted with a casual wave of her hand. "You'll love it."

I looked at Aderyn for an explanation.

"You ready to dive straight into extra?" she teased. "Because that's what you're in for."

"Aderyn, ride with Samson and explain the rules," Essie instructed as she started back toward her car.

"Rules? I thought this was just brunch," I said.

Aderyn snorted. "Nothing is 'just' anything with my family. We strive to take things to unnecessary heights."

Chapter Fourteen

Sam

"Let's go over the brunch rules," Aderyn started as soon as I joined her on the sidewalk. We'd gotten to Tinsel's downtown area ahead of her family since her mom was a slow driver. Her sister, Rae, texted to let us know they were still five minutes out.

"Remind me again why there are rules?" I asked.

"There are always rules." Aderyn removed her jacket as she spoke. I tried not to watch too closely once her arms were bare. She wore a tight-fitted, short-sleeve top that hugged her curves and showed off the faint outline of her nipples. I felt like I should be used to her body by now. Except, I always found something new to admire. Today, it was how she rolled her shoulders back to stretch out. Honestly, there was something alluring about everything she did, from how she lifted weights to when she barked orders to her team and now telling me the ins and outs of how her family did brunch.

"You're already breaking the first rule," she said.

I smiled at the notion. "Am I?"

"You're not family, and you're a guy."

"My bad."

"Apology accepted."

I chuckled, and she continued without falter.

"No talking about what you do for a living or want to do for a living or have plans on doing for a living," she said. "So, in our case, that's hockey."

I frowned. "I'm sorry, what? And why?"

"My mom comes from a family of workaholics. Any time they got together for dinner or whatever, they only talked about their work or productivity," Aderyn explained. "We only talk about our interests outside of work. It's so we can get to know each other and ourselves better outside of what we see as productive.

"Interesting," I murmured.

She nodded in agreement. "My mom's been in therapy for the past decade, so she tries to improve relationships in every way possible. She wants everyone around her to do the same and be themselves."

I considered her explanation for a moment. My family had plenty of rules, but none centered on improving our relationships. We were expected to be respectful and celibate—one of which I've mastered. We were most definitely not encouraged to be ourselves. In any way. My sister was good at breaking that rule. I only felt brave enough to break it when I was away from home.

"No hockey talk," I said. "Got it."

It was going to be a bit of an adjustment not talking about something as big in my life as the sport had become. When I wasn't playing hockey, I was thinking about playing or planning to play. Or—because of the recent issue with Stoll—I wondered how I was going to preserve my right to play in the future.

"Rule number two: accept the outfit your fellow bruncher gives you," Aderyn said. "No ifs, ands, or buts."

"Bruncher?"

"I thought you'd be more interested in the outfit part."

"I'm very interested in both aspects. Everything about yo—this." I cleared my throat, trying to cover up my near slip-up.

Though she'd originally been nervous about her family seeing us together, Aderyn seemed happier around them. There was a noticeable lightness in her voice when she greeted them. And even though Essie had both her daughters cringing, Aderyn did seem to enjoy her presence.

"Before we grab our usual table at the cafe, we go thrifting," she said.

"To what end?"

Aderyn grinned at me. I noticed a small eyelash underneath her eye and, without thinking, reached up to move it away. She stilled under my touch.

"Sorry. I was trying to get this." I showed her my thumb as proof.

She let out a breathy laugh. The expression on her face didn't match the gesture. Instead of looking amused, Aderyn's eyebrows turned downward in confusion.

I pulled my hand back and silently regretted my sudden attention to detail.

Aderyn surprised me by reaching for my hand. Her fingers wrapped around my palm, holding me steady as she blew softly on my thumb. My dick stiffened at the feel of her breath on my skin.

"You're not going to take my wish away from me," she joked. "Are you? Didn't think the guy who wished on baseballs would be the type."

"Wish?" I tried to stand completely still because she was still holding onto me. My breathing slowed as if one deep inhale could scare her away like some stray cat.

But Aderyn didn't scare easily. Especially since this casual touch meant nothing to her. She was playing the game and like always, she played well.

"You never heard of wishing on eyelashes?" she asked.

"Can't say I have."

Aderyn tilted her head to the side. "Serious?"

"Is that something I should know?"

"No, not necessarily. But it's a wildly common thing. Way more common than baseballs, at least." She let go of me then. My heart sank along with my arm. I slipped my hand into my pocket, curling my fingers into a fist. I tried and failed to will away the warmth coursing through my veins.

"Thought you didn't need wishes," I reminded her. "Just hard work."

She sighed and shrugged. "It's been a long morning and now, I have to endure a meal with you and my folks. I need all the help I can get."

We started down the sidewalk. I hadn't been in the downtown area much save for coming to a bar every once and a while after a big game. At night, the streets were packed. But now, only a handful of people were going in and out of stores, most of whom were over the age of fifty. They walked slowly with no need to rush to their next destination.

I've never been a hand-holder. Especially in public where, as adults, it made no sense to hold hands crossing the street. But as we waited for the crosswalk light to change, my fingers itched to grab hers to ensure we'd keep the same pace.

Instead of holding her hand, I moved to her side where most of the traffic waited, in case someone was impatient enough to run the red.

Aderyn gave me a look at my change in position. "What are you doing?"

"Walking. You?"

"You switched sides. Something wrong with this side?"

"I like it better over here, is all."

She didn't look like she believed me for a second but let it go when we saw her mom and sister getting out of their car on the other side of the street.

"Ready for some shopping?" her mom asked as she placed her chunky sunglasses on the top of her head. "Did she explain the rules to you, Sam?"

"For the most part," I said. "Still don't understand the motive."

"We should skip the dressing up this time," Rae said quickly. "It's a bit much...a bit embarrassing."

"I think it's a riot," Essie said and hurried toward the shop. "Besides the theme's pirates, we can't miss pirates. Bonus points for a good story."

"Really, Ryn? You're not going to say anything?" Rae looked at her sister for help.

"Come on, let her have her fun. It's been a long week for her." Aderyn gave her sister a quick side hug.

"We have to suffer for it?" Rae sighed and followed their mother into the store.

"How are we suffering exactly?" I whispered to Aderyn.

"We have to pick out an on-theme outfit to wear at the brunch place," she explained. "It's an upscale restaurant so most folks there are very pinky up. The staff thinks we're hilarious, but the customers hate how we're 'cheapening' the experience. My mom's parents used to get turned away from the restaurant for not being the 'target demo.'"

I frowned. "Sounds racist."

"Oh, it was," Aderyn confirmed. "But with a few decades and some money, Mom's become a regular. And now, she regularly tries to annoy the older customers who still believe we don't belong there."

"She sounds like the ultimate troll. I love it."

"My mom's the biggest troll of them all," she confirmed. "Now, to win, you have to put together a show-stopping costume for one of us."

"Let's do teams today since it's Sam's first go. You two work together," her mom called once we entered the shop behind her. She'd already delved into the racks of used clothes. "And Rae and I will pair up."

"Just my luck," Rae grumbled as she started toward the hat section.

"We only get twenty minutes," Aderyn told me as she hurried to one of the overflowing racks. Her eyes went wide with excitement. "So, don't think too much."

I chuckled, thinking about how this was both the most ridiculous and fun thing I'd done in a long time.

Aderyn was surprised at how willingly I put on the large, pirate hat with lace veil she presented me. Lucky for us, some bachelorette must've dumped her party supplies and Aderyn happened to find the bulk of it before her mom did.

"Why are you pulling that off?" She placed her hands on her hips, studying me as I readjusted the hat in the mirror.

"Because it's not about the item, it's about the attitude," I said as I tilted the brim just so.

Aderyn snorted when I winked at her.

"Come on." I turned to her, accepting the frilly black vest she held out. It was a bit tight around the chest area. "It's okay to admit you're even more attracted to me in this. I've been known to elevate even the ugliest fit."

She rolled her eyes. "You're so full of yourself."

"It's doing something for you," I teased and stepped closer to her. We were in the back of the store, near the changing rooms. Her mom and sister were somewhere behind the curtains, trying on whatever wild pieces of clothing they'd picked out for each other.

"The only thing it's doing is making me wish I picked up the matching lace top." She crossed her arms over her chest and refused to back down—even when I stepped so close her arm pressed against my chest.

"Get it," I dared. "We still have time."

Aderyn laughed. "You really are fearless."

"What's there to be afraid of? I'm only dressed like a pirate's bride." I fluffed out the lace on the vest.

"You make a very memorable bride," she said, still shaking from laughter.

"Why thank you. Now, you ready for your clothes?" I reached behind a mannequin where I hid my selections.

"As I'll ever be." She tried to look behind my back, but I dodged her advances.

"Go in the changing room first. I'll toss them over the top," I instructed. When she flashed me a wary look I added, "I don't want you trying to talk your way out of it."

"Aderyn would never..." Her mother dramatically pushed aside the curtain to reveal her new look. "Break the rules. I raised her better than that."

"Wow." Aderyn whistled. "Rae's outdone herself."

"You look great Mrs... Essie." I smiled, nearly blinded by the amount of white, green, and red sequins on the vest she wore. Rae had paired the atrocious top with neon pink boots and a brown baseball cap that read, "Ahoy."

"It's brilliant," Essie approved as she spun around in the mirror.

"I'm putting my foot down," Rae called from the changing room.

"You can't or we'll automatically lose and have to pay for our entrées. And your bank account was looking a little low the last I checked," their mom called back and received a groan from Rae in return. "Come on, honey. It's not that bad."

"Whoever designed this should be thrown in jail," Rae decided, staying behind the curtain. "And I should be right in the cell beside them for putting this on."

"Hurry and change, Aderyn." Essie nudged her daughter along. "And come out to lead by example. You know your sister will do it if you go first."

"Alright, alright." Aderyn hurried into the changing room. I followed, waiting until she secured the curtain before tossing the clothes over.

"You've got to be shitting me," she said once she saw my selections.

"We're going to look great," I promised. "The story is, I'm the bride and you're the bridesmaid."

Aderyn grumbled something under her breath as she started putting on the clothes. I was about to walk away and give her privacy before she said,

"So, Lincoln invited me to y'all's house on Sunday."

"For the Who Dun It dinner?" I asked, suddenly remembering how he'd been trying to set this thing up for weeks.

"Yeah...is that cool? I don't want to cross any boundaries."

"Of course, it's cool," I insisted. "Why would you hanging out with my friends be a boundary?"

"I don't know. Guys like you are good at compartmentalizing. I didn't want to make that difficult for you to keep doing it."

I smiled, grateful for her thoughtfulness. But, at this point, Aderyn keeping her distance from my friends wasn't the issue. "You should definitely come. It'll be nice having you there."

She sounded relieved as she said, "Great, I'm looking forward to it."

As she continued to get ready, I moved away from the curtain to give her some space. I took the space for myself, too—my head felt light. I was having mixed feelings about spending more non-sexual time with her. She was right that this was usually a no-go for me in my relationships. Yet, I couldn't protest because no part of me had the strength to.

I found myself near her mom again. Essie was still examining her outfit in the mirror.

"You and Aderyn are in the lead," she said to me with a smile.

"She hit the jackpot with the veil," I agreed, brushing the fabric off my face so I could talk without anything between us.

Essie's smile reminded me of Aderyn's. They both tilted their chins slightly up as they did it. "You two make a good team."

"I suppose." I nodded, thinking about how easy it was to spend time with Aderyn. Yes, we argued, but we did so without taking things too far. We anticipated one another, too, like we'd been friends for years and not a few months. She knew when something might be too much for me and vice versa.

"She's very, we'll say, invested in you," Essie said in a lower voice. Her eyes danced with mischief. "I was happy to hear she finally moved on from Erica. Those two were cute as could be but the fights... God, I couldn't stomach them."

"Right." I glanced over at the changing area, willing Aderyn to come out and end this conversation. I was breaching unknown territory. The parent and ex-talk territory—which I clearly had no business being in because I shouldn't have even said yes to this trip.

"She's done nothing but come home and gush." Essie winked at me. "You're a good influence on her. I can tell it's a match."

"I...that's nice to hear." And it honestly was. My stomach flipped at the thought of Aderyn seeming happy enough to talk about me. Of course, a lot of that happiness probably had to do with sex, but I'd take what I could get.

"I have to be a mother bird for a moment, so please, excuse me," Essie said, taking on a more serious tone. "I have to ask. What are your intentions with my daughter? You two are young, I know that. But old enough to make big decisions. I know you're good at what you do. Is professional hockey your goal?"

It suddenly started to feel hot in here. I tugged on my vest a bit. "Uh, I thought we weren't supposed to talk about our careers."

She laughed. "Smart move. And you're right. Breaking my own rule, but I'm a curious, old woman."

"You look more like their sister."

She waved her hand, but I could see the joy in her eyes. "How cliche and kiss ass of you. I love it."

I chuckled. "I was being honest. Lying's something that was disciplined out of me a long time ago."

"That's what I like about you athletes," she decided. "You understand discipline. You know how to commit to something."

My skin warmed because lying was one thing and commitment was a complete other. I still couldn't imagine committing to anyone other than my team.

"My Aderyn is a sweetheart," Essie continued, voice softened with love. "She won't tell you how she really feels at first, but she'll show you. So, you'll have to be patient with her."

"Yeah, I can do that," I said because what else was I supposed to say? Hey, your daughter and I are in a sex bet in which we fuck, and she gets the hell out of dodge as soon as we orgasm?

"She's very headstrong, too," Essie continued. "I'm sure you already know that."

I chuckled, thinking about Aderyn's determination to beat me. "I have an idea."

"I'm glad she found someone like you. From what I've heard, you two are a lot alike. Some say opposites attract, but I've learned that couples who a more similar usually are more empathetic to one another's needs."

I tilted my head to the side, considering. "I never thought about it that way."

Essie smiled. "I think you're a good one, Sam. If you fuck it up, well, she has a lot of people who love her enough to make things right. You get where I'm going with this?"

"Yes, ma'am." I straightened, admittedly a little scared of her tone. "I won't fuck it up."

My shoulders tightened as soon as the words left my mouth. I made a hurried excuse about needing to go to the bathroom. I pulled the hat off my head before escaping into the single stall.

"You should come up with a reason to leave," I told myself as I washed my hands and splashed water over my face. "Something believable and unavoidable."

I wracked my brain, trying to figure a way out of the rest of this brunch. There was no way my conscience could survive the next hour in the company of Aderyn's family. They were so welcoming and kind. Essie looked at me like I was about to get down on one knee. And I kept looking at Aderyn like I'd entertain something after our bet.

That'd been an actual thought I had when we were scouring the racks. I thought they were a fun family, and she was an amazing woman, and I wouldn't mind doing this again sometime.

The Jacobs were so unlike my family. My parents weren't fans of joking or doing weird, random shit. My sister always kept her oddness secret, away from the rest of us.

Do you want to throw out your rules because her family is 'cool' and she's fun? That's ridiculous.

I laughed because yes, it was ridiculous. Everything about this day was ridiculous. And yet, I felt happy.

Before I could come up with a decent excuse to leave, my phone buzzed.

Aderyn: Did you make your great escape?
Sam: I'm still here. Be out in a minute.

Staying would be a mistake but as soon as I went back out and saw Aderyn's smile grow when she saw me, I couldn't leave.

Chapter Fifteen

Aderyn

Morgan was acting strange. First, it was the switching sides while we were walking. I understood sometimes people had a preference for which side of the sidewalk they were on. But his continued switching when we were on the way to the restaurant didn't make sense. If he had a preference, it'd stay consistent, right?

Then came the seating at the restaurant. He pulled out the chair closest to the window. It was the seat with the best light and furthest from the high-traffic walkway.

I nearly moved past it, assuming he—of course—had pulled out his own seat. But he claimed the chair next to it instead. I sat down in the chair he pulled out for me, my brows knitting in confusion.

"You good?" When I leaned in to whisper to him, one of the feathers from his hat tickled my nose. I swiped it away, smiling at how it felt on my skin. My own ludicrous clothing brushed across my body, making me wiggle underneath the fuzzy fabric.

Morgan had given me an oversized sweater with a corset-like detail and a long, brown skirt with a train that kept getting caught under everything.

I kept replaying his reaction to my reveal. Morgan's jaw went tight, and his eyes hunted for a safe place to land. I was downright shocked—and, yes, pleased—by his reaction. The guy acted like he hadn't seen me naked before.

He'd offered to pick me out something else, but I refused to change out of my itchy sweater. Not when it left his mouth agape.

"I'm fine." Morgan didn't meet my gaze but instead scanned the menu with impressive focus.

"Ryn," Rae whispered into my ear before I could press Morgan and potentially torture him with my outfit a bit more.

I leaned toward her with a raised brow. "Yeah?"

She looked at Mom to make sure she was properly distracted with the menu selections, too. "Does something seem off with Mom?"

"No." I frowned and glanced over to find her chatting with Morgan about her favorite selections. She seemed to like him, and that made me proud for some reason.

"Have you talked to Warren, recently? Can you tell something's up with him?"

"I don't talk to him on campus, remember?"

"You know, it hurts his feelings when you avoid him in public," she said.

"Warren has feelings?" I teased, earning an eye roll.

"Come on. No one cares about you and Warren being family," she insisted. "Besides, I don't know how much longer that's going to last."

I frowned. "Excuse me?"

Rae scratched her head. "You heard me. I have a bad feeling. Warren and Mom. They haven't been acting the same lately."

"Couples fight," I reminded her as I glanced at Mom. She was now talking Morgan's ear off about her latest obsession with sci-fi novels. And from what I could catch on Morgan's end, he was a sci-fi fan, too.

"That's just it," Rae said. "They're not fighting. It's all roses and sunshine."

"Why are you complaining then?"

She sighed. "You'd have to see it for yourself. Come home soon and I'll show you what I mean."

"Rae..." I loved spending time with my family. But I also loved the freedom college gave me to do whatever the hell I wanted. My folks were respectful of my age and my choices, yet I couldn't help but feel like a kid when I went back home.

"It'll only be for one night," my sister said. "Suck it up. Because I'm on the verge of freaking out. I don't want to move again. And Warren's like the best thing that's happened to us."

My heart squeezed at the sight of my sister's panic. "I'll come."

"Promise?" Rae offered me two fingers. I linked mine around hers, sealing the deal with our childhood handshake.

"Cross my heart. And it's going to be fine. Whatever's going on."

Rae looked more hopeful once we released hands. Morgan's eyes were on me when I pulled away from my sister. The entertained glint in his eyes made me smile.

"What?" I asked.

"Nothing, it's just..." He cleared his throat. "Nothing."

It took convincing to get Mary and Jas to come with me to the dinner at Morgan's. Sundays were their designated date nights. They usually went full-on old couple and spent the night in with wine and watching old black and white movies.

"You're in your twenties," I reminded them. "We should be out clubbing or at least hanging out with more people our age."

"Since when have we been clubbers?" Jas asked. Their naturally low, husky voice made their protest sound like the beginning of an award-winning audiobook. Like usual, Mary sighed, and her eyes practically went heart-shaped at the sound of her girlfriend's voice. They were cute when I wasn't down about being single. Lately, that feeling had become less frequent.

The friends-with-benefits aspect of this bet was doing wonders for my self-pity. I liked the idea of having someone while also not being afraid they were going to leave me. Morgan was in trouble because I was getting better at our game every day.

"Never," I agreed with Jas. "But we should at least be minglers. Lincoln promised a home-cooked dinner."

Mary's eyes widened. "Dinner? Cooked by who?"

"Henrik."

They perked up then. I laughed at the sound of our stomachs grumbling in unison.

"Get my keys," Mary ordered an already moving Jas. "That man knows how to season. Remember when he brought stuffed pasta shells for us to taste test? I nearly died."

"I've seriously considered paying him to meal prep for me," Jas said. "Obsessed doesn't even begin to describe how I felt when he stocked the bake sale. I still dream about his carrot cake bites."

I laughed at their change of tone. Mary nearly pushed us out the door, citing the importance of being first in line for whatever food was waiting.

The drive to the guys' off-campus rental didn't take long. They invited way more people than I'd thought because by the time we got there only on-street parking was left.

Though the outside of the house could use a little TLC, the inside was warm and smelled like Christmas. Their fireplace had been lit and cider-scented candles were placed around the living room. We shed our coats at the door and accepted the hot mugs of tea offered by their roommate, Naomi.

"I'm glad you guys came. I didn't want to be outnumbered again," she said with a bright smile. I've never seen Naomi without an excited look on her face. She was the kind of girl who could talk to anyone and make them feel like her best friend.

"Of course." Mary waved her hand like she hadn't needed encouragement to come out. "This was too good to pass up."

Mary and Jas were already eying the island over Naomi's shoulder. Dozens of plates and bowls of appetizers filled most of the counter space. The air smelled of warm pastries and buttery rolls. I took a sip of my drink to stop myself from laughing at my friends basically salivating. Our dining hall's food seemed like poorly reheated microwave dinners in comparison.

Quite a few guys from the men's hockey team were here. They were gathered around a coffee table with a deck of cards and bottles of beer. Apparently, the game had already begun so we'd have to wait a few minutes to get filled in on the next round.

My friends were grateful for the extra time and hurried to grab plates. I scanned the room, eyes falling on Jack first. When he smiled in my direction, I gave a small wave. I expected to feel some sort of residual nerves or excitement from our interaction before, but my stomach remained unresponsive. That was a good sign, right? My time watching Morgan act nonchalant was working. I could finally execute an unemotional response.

"Well, look who we have here," someone behind me said.

Speak of the devil. There went my stomach. Flipping like I stood on top of a diving board. Dang it. I'd been so close.

I took a deep breath before turning around to find Morgan leaning against the entryway. He wore a thin T-shirt showing off his arms and dark shorts that fell past his knees. My stomach continued to turn. There was a good chance it was the tea. I wasn't big on sugar and the drink tasted like a Rice Krispie treat on steroids.

"It's late," he noted. "Didn't think you were showing up."

"I wouldn't want to miss out on the potential of stealing yet another one of your favorite spots," I teased.

He raised a brow. "What?"

"There's no doubt in my mind you'll claim the seat cushion I choose to sit on as yours. Or maybe even the tile I'm standing on." I made a show of looking down at the gray and white kitchen tiles. "It's this one, isn't it?"

"The one on your left has a better view actually," he joked, and his eyes danced when I stepped to my left.

"It's a very nice tile," I said. "The light from the window hits it perfectly."

"It's great," he agreed. "Still not my favorite, though."

"That so?"

He nodded and then, crooked his finger, indicating for me to come closer. I swallowed. Before going to him, I glanced over my shoulder at our friends. Most of them were currently shouting 'bloody murder,' while the rest stuffed their faces, feigning horror when they really just wanted their fill of Henrik's famous cheddar cheese puffs.

"Almost," Morgan encouraged when I was a few feet away from him. The entryway was on a small incline, so he towered over me. He didn't tell me to stop until I stood a breath away.

"This one kind of sucks," I said in a whisper, not taking my eyes off his for a second.

He chuckled. "W-why?"

"There's a draft."

Morgan stuffed his hands into his pockets, relaxing his body against the wall. I chewed on my lip when he smiled at me.

This close I could admire the texture of his dark skin and his thick beard. Before we started talking, I thought he was as close to perfect as a human could get. He had the looks, the talent, and the drive. But now, after learning about his past and how he'd used it to become better, I saw the flaws. I saw how his ambition was bred from imperfection. How his leadership skills were shaped by his experience of being excluded as a child. He even stammered when he got overwhelmed and tried to cover it up quickly.

Morgan wasn't who I thought he was. He was better. Braver.

"There's a noticeable draft, sure," he agreed.

"And the lighting is god-awful."

"I prefer eerie," he argued. "Or romantic."

"Those too are definitely synonymous."

"Could be."

When I gave him a look he laughed.

"Fine. You caught me." He sighed, pretending to be disappointed. "You did pick my favorite tile. This was just a ploy to get you closer."

I tilted my head, studying him. "Why?"

"Because I missed you," he said, point blank.

My palms were sweaty. I nearly dropped my mug. "We had brunch earlier."

"And I've been thinking about you ever since."

His words burrowed in my chest and spread through my body like wildfire. I'd been doing so well. I could kick myself right now for wondering if he preferred picnic or beach dates. Personally, I found both to possess equal charm and plenty of excuses to cuddle.

None of that matters, Aderyn! Chill out.

"That's sweet of you to say." I spoke slowly as if not being careful would result in a word vomit request that would be somewhere along the lines of 'we should just make out right now.'

"I can be very sweet," he agreed, voice dangerously low.

My fingernails dug into the mug. "I'm impressed."

"That so? In that case, I have plenty of other ways to impress you if we had some privacy."

My nipples hardened at the look in his eyes.

"Now?" I whispered.

"What can I say? Spending the whole morning and afternoon with you was a turn-on."

I snorted. His acting was getting out of hand. "Very cute."

"I'm serious." He looked over my shoulder toward everyone else. The way he bit his lip as he thought about his next words nearly broke me. "We have plenty of time to sneak away. They're only in the first act of Lincoln's story."

"I wanted to play at least one round," I confessed. "I actually was looking forward to crushing you tonight."

He straightened, excited about my challenge. "You think your detective skills are better than mine, Jacobs?"

"I know they are."

"Alright, then. How about this, I win, and we go upstairs. You win and..."

"We go back to my place," I finished. "It's so much more fun having sex and being able to fall asleep in your own bed right after."

He grinned. "I couldn't agree more."

Chapter Sixteen

Aderyn

We joined the others at the coffee table. A few of the guys switched out, moving to the kitchen so there'd be enough room for new players to have a turn.

"Good luck," Jack said in a low voice as we passed by one another. Our shoulders brushed and I smiled, realizing he'd tried to touch me on purpose. Morgan noticed too. The look on his face wasn't as amused as mine.

"Playing jealous?" I teased under my breath.

Morgan's jaw tightened but he gave me a nod. "I'm a wonderful method actor."

"Don't I know it."

The table was big enough to fit a few plates, a stack of cards, and dice. There were two candles in the middle, casting warm shadows on everyone's faces. The seat cushions on the floor were mismatched with various patterns and color schemes.

"Oh, look, Mom and Dad finally decided to join us," Lincoln teased as Morgan and I sat down.

My cheeks burned at the label, and I scooted a little closer to Mary to put some necessary space in between us. Morgan threw Lincoln a warning look, cementing himself in a 'dad' role.

Lincoln winked at us. "Ready to play?"

"Definitely." I wiggled in my cushion, trying to get comfortable. "How do I win?"

"It's not necessarily about winning," Lincoln said, and he shuffled his deck of cards.

Morgan snorted when my shoulders sagged.

"It's about the journey, not the destination, Ryn," Mary explained to me around a mouthful of pasta. She and Jas were still busy stuffing their faces. Across from us sat Naomi and Finn. She was talking a mile a minute, telling him about something that happened to her earlier. He listened intently as he rubbed her back. Every now and then, he leaned in to kiss her temple. When he did that, her smile got brighter.

"Basically, I give you guys all the clues, and you try to solve the murder," Lincoln explained as he divvied out three cards to each person. "It's best if you work together."

"But we could work alone if we wanted, right?" I picked up my cards, spreading them in and out between my fingers because I didn't know what they were for.

"You know, for a person in a team sport, you really enjoy going solo," Morgan mused under his breath.

I glanced over at him. "I'm a woman of many talents. I shine in any condition. And I like taking opportunities to branch out on my own when able. It's called personal development."

"You do shine," he agreed and studied me with his head tilted to the side. His gaze moved from my face, further down, blatantly checking me out in front of our teammates. I looked away, my heartbeat loud enough to drain out most sound.

"Usually, when we play this game, the guys are on their own," Lincoln said. "But game nights are more fun when the group gets to work together..."

He trailed off, distracted by someone over our shoulders. Everyone with their backs to the door turned. A girl with twists swinging down her back and a face full of makeup stood in the entryway next to Henrik. He'd just let her in and was explaining the food situation. She didn't look familiar to me, but Naomi seemed to know her because she popped up with a squeal.

"Celeste," Naomi greeted.

The girl's eyes were wide. She accepted Naomi's outstretched hand like it was a life raft.

"Is your goalie gonna be okay?" I whispered to Morgan. Lincoln was shuffling the remainder of his cards, absentmindedly. Mary waved her hand back and forth in front of his face. He didn't budge.

Morgan chuckled. "Now, that's a good question."

"Uh. Let's take a break. I think it's a perfect time for a break, don't y'all think?" Lincoln asked, quickly. He stood up and started toward the kitchen where their newest guest was hanging out.

"What? We just started," I called after him. "Wait! I wanted to win."

"Winning tonight is getting seconds." Mary bumped her shoulder against mine. "Trust me."

"You've got to be kidding me." I slouched back and dropped my cards on the table. "What are we supposed to do now?"

Morgan blew out a breath, pretending to think hard. "Arm wrestle?"

I side-eyed him. "You got to be joking."

"Come on, thought you loved doing this. You couldn't stop challenging my guys the last time you were here."

"They were only freshmen," Mary pointed out. When I frowned in her direction, she shrugged and added, "What? They were. Freshmen are notoriously weak opponents."

"I beat Lincoln in one of those matches." I gestured over to our abandoner. "He's not a freshman."

Jas shook their head and in a sweet, calm voice said, "Lincoln got distracted."

"Sounds like him," Mary agreed.

"Oh my God." I sighed. "I can't believe you guys don't think I can hold my own."

"So, prove yourself," Morgan dared. "Go against me."

A low, disapproving noise came from the back of my throat. "It's not the same."

"Lincoln and I bench the same," he promised and moved to the other side of the table. "Finn, you're referee?"

Finn raised a brow, not looking the least bit impressed with our need to compete. But he moved closer to the table anyway. "Sure, I can do that."

Morgan placed his elbow down, opening his hand for me to take. Mary laughed as she unlocked her phone to shoot a video.

"Come on, Ryn. This will be great on our socials." She moved onto Jas's lap to get a higher angle.

"You're not wrong," I grumbled.

"Well then, what are you waiting for?" Morgan's smile was daring but still possessed the right amount of warmness. No matter how much I tried, I couldn't fight off smiling back.

"Fuck it." I sighed and slipped my hand into his. Our fingers wrapped around one another. He applied the tiniest amount of pressure against my palm. Even in a neutral state, Morgan's bicep resembled a rock. I licked my bottom lip, trying to think about holding my own, and not about him holding me the last time I climaxed in his arms.

Finn placed his hand on top of ours. "Ready?"

Morgan and I nodded, not taking our eyes off one another for a second. Something unspoken passed between us. It was an understanding that started in the parking lot this morning and followed us here. We knew each other's strengths and now, weaknesses. Tonight, kind of felt like exploring everything in between.

The second Finn released us from his grip, I braced myself. Mary and Jas were, of course, in my corner. They cheered me on loud enough to capture the attention of everyone in the kitchen. A few people moved over to watch my defeat.

Most people think there's a clear method to winning at arm wrestling. On the surface, it's fairly straightforward. A show of pure strength and might. But, if you've done enough of them, you learn how to hold your own long enough so that the opponent starts to doubt themselves. That was always my go-to: outlasting. Except, Morgan knew how to play mind games with the best of them. And he wouldn't give me an inch—not even for a second to show sympathy. I loved it.

I loved that he wasn't going to roll over and let me win just to make me feel good. That honesty was the marking of a great person. And a good partner. Not that I'm looking for partner material at the moment.

"Shit," I hissed when my arm was halfway down. He'd already won but I didn't let go, determined to see it out. Morgan cocked up a brow, impressed by my attempt, even if I was losing.

"You're stronger than I thought," he complimented once the back of my hand touched the table. Morgan blew out a breath, sounding a bit winded as he laughed. "Had to put my back into that."

"Aw, nice try, Ryn," Mary said. She still held her phone up, recording.

"Impressive," Finn agreed, simply.

"Good game." I offered my hand to Morgan. I was many things, but a sore loser wasn't one of them.

He chuckled and accepted the shake. When our friends were briefly distracted by Henrik announcing dessert was ready, Morgan pulled me closer. I leaned across the table to hear what he had to say.

"I'm ready to put my back into something else," he whispered into my ear. There was nothing but seriousness and longing in his voice. "That was the hottest foreplay I've ever experienced."

My clit swelled at his dark tone. "Really?"

An arm wrestle wasn't your typical pre-sex activity.

"Definitely," he assured and straightened up because a few people came back to the table.

My body ached. I watched him get up, moving to the kitchen to talk to his friends like he wasn't thinking about fucking me.

"You okay?" Mary asked when she settled back beside me. "Losing wasn't that bad, right?"

"No," I agreed and inhaled as I tried to think about how I was going to sneak out of here. I needed him. Now. "It wasn't bad. Not bad at all."

Chapter Seventeen

Sam

The second we got an excuse to slip out of the party, we took it. Aderyn's mouth was on mine as soon as the door closed. Not that I was complaining. She'd never get a protest for me—especially when she took charge like this. She pushed me down on my desk, causing a crash behind us.

I laughed against her lips when a horde of office supplies fell to the floor because of our fumbling. Aderyn pulled back for a second, eyes wide with embarrassment.

"Crap," she whispered, looking at the mess. "I'm so sorry. Did we break anything?"

I shook my head and cupped her face gently, turning her attention back to me. "Doesn't matter."

"But—"

I stopped her with a kiss. She relaxed, forgetting about the mess as soon as my tongue touched hers. I'd been daydreaming about this all night. Her attempt to take me down in the living room had me hard and dying to get her alone. Now that she stood between my legs, everything felt better.

The last time she was here we did this in the dark. I could barely see her. Now, my bedside lamp cast a perfect glow on her dark skin. Every time we took a break to breathe, I opened my eyes to admire her. I wanted to take everything in. Memorize the cupid's bow on her lips and how she tilted her head just right to meet my mouth. She was built solid but felt soft when I held her against my body.

"Why are you doing that?" Aderyn asked.

I frowned. "Doing what?"

"Pulling back so far between kisses. Looking at me. Is there something on my face?"

"No." I shook my head and spoke fast. "You look fine."

"Then what is it?"

I kissed her instead of answering because that felt far less complicated. Aderyn let herself relax against me once more. Her uncertainty disappeared with every swipe of my tongue.

She'd asked a good question. What *was* it? Loneliness, I assumed. Perhaps a bit of misplaced anxiety. Nothing an orgasm or two wouldn't fix.

Aderyn continued to lean into me, forcing me back on the desk. Something else fell. This time it was a textbook and it hit her foot.

She snatched away from me, pulling her leg up in pain. "Damn it."

"Shit, I'm sorry. You okay?" I hurried to pick up the book.

"Don't apologize. It was my fault. I'm fine." Aderyn laughed a little and grabbed the book before I could place it back on the desk. "Wait? You're taking a Theology course?"

"Yeah, why?" I kissed her neck, trying to get us back on track as she studied the book's cover.

"I don't know, I just took you for a math type. Sciences, not liberal arts."

I laughed. "Aderyn, Theology's my major."

Her mouth parted in shock. "No shit."

"Yes," I confirmed and kissed her again. This time moving up to her cheek. "Shit."

"Because your dad and grandpa were preachers." She put two and two together.

"Kind of." My lips were at the apple of her cheek now. I don't know what possessed me to do it. Maybe it was how easily she leaned into me – Aderyn pressed her body against mine like this was her designated spot. Or maybe it was how her free hand absentmindedly massaged the back of my neck? Whatever it was, it led me to playfully bite her cheek. The laugh she let out and her half-hearted attempt to tug away made me smile. I bit her once more before realizing this was new. I didn't tease girls like this.

What in the romantic couple shit was that...and why did I like it?

"Um..." I tried to regain some sense of control but it was all gone. I'd given it up to her and hell, I don't think I cared. I wanted her to have it. "I mainly wanted to study so I could formulate decent arguments during family dinners."

"Oh?" Aderyn looked at me, intrigued and not at all fazed by how I was biting her cheek a second ago.

"My family's super educated," I explained, hoping a sidebar would help me relax a bit. "Sometimes I feel out of the loop in conversations. I figured liberal arts courses could change that. Help me feel more well-rounded. I like being able to keep up with them."

"You want to be more well-rounded? That's really mature of you," she noted.

I chuckled. "Don't sound so surprised."

"I can't help it. Most student athletes I know simply pick the easiest major to get through so they can get the grades to stay on their team—myself included."

"Sports Medicine isn't easy from what I hear."

She shrugged. "Maybe not. But, I'm hanging on by a thread most days. My GPA's just enough to get me by. Meanwhile, you're here actually using school to educate yourself. What a concept! Who would have thought?"

"Not me," I agreed with a smile. "Never would have thought higher education could expand my horizons."

"No one does," she teased and leaned in closer to do some romantic shit of her own. Aderyn brushed her nose against mine. I couldn't take it anymore. I grabbed her chin and held her steady so I could kiss her. She smiled against my mouth.

"Come to the bed with me?" I asked in a hoarse voice once I pulled away. "Please?"

Aderyn smiled and nodded. I didn't waste a second.

We fell into the sheets. My mouth ventured from her lips, neck, belly, and then between her legs. I removed her pants and underwear. She looked beautiful arching herself into the air to meet my tongue. I watched her fingers squeeze my sheets as I tasted her.

"Is that the best you can do?" I murmured against her pussy. "I thought you'd be a little more flexible than that, beautiful."

Aderyn huffed at my teasing. She pulled her legs higher, revealing more of herself. I moaned at the sight of her dripping. This was why I came by just watching her the first time we were together. Aderyn's pussy practically begged to be devoured with how much wetness she produced.

"That's my good girl. I know you're probably upset about your loss but I'll make it up to you." I flicked her clit with the tip of my tongue. "I promise."

"Sam," she begged, fingers gripping the sheet so tight that I heard a knuckle pop.

"Yes?" I asked, innocently. I slipped two fingers inside her. Her walls squeezed around me.

"You look so sexy doing that." Her voice was raspy. And her eyes were half-open as she peered down at me.

I chuckled and made a show of licking her before saying, "And you look hot trying to rub this sweet pussy against me. You in a hurry to come tonight?"

"No, I just can't help it." She laughed a little. "Sorry."

"Sorry?"

"I've been told I laugh too much during sex," she explained. "Which isn't exactly sexy."

I scoffed. "Who the hell doesn't think that's sexy? Especially if *you're* doing it. Laugh until your sides hurt, Aderyn. I'd happily eat you out while you do."

She laughed again. This time, it sounded less guarded.

"When you hang up your player hat for real, it's over. You're gonna be a goddamn keeper one day," she said and urged me up so we could kiss.

"Falling for me?" I half-joked.

"You wish."

I had to check myself when my heart sank.

"You sure I'm a keeper?" I continued, trying to insert as much teasing as I could into my words. It scared me how much I wanted to hear her answer.

"The only thing I'm sure of right now is I want you to fuck me."

Her words sent fire through my body. My questioning was put on the back burner while my dick was so hard it hurt.

"Tell me how you want me to fuck you," I said between feverish kisses. "Tell me how to make you feel good."

Tell me what to do to make you want to keep me.

I moved down to suck on her nipples. Her nails dug into my back when my tongue circled her areola. A deep moan escaped my lips when my fingers dipped back into her pussy. How it was possible that she was even wetter than before, I didn't know. But fuck, I was going to enjoy every drop.

"Fuck me like I'm your girl," she said around a heavy exhale. "Like all I'll ever be is your girl."

Holy fuck.

I kissed her. This time slower, savoring every slight change in pressure and swipe of her tongue. I was in danger. Late night, no phone service, car broke down danger. No one was around to save me from whatever lay ahead. I was usually the one to make sure I got out of things unscathed. This time, I didn't run. Instead, I leaned into her. Aderyn was the night, full of possibilities. I was going to get lost, I realized. There was no map, but wonder outweighed the fear.

I was going to get lost in her—I wanted to get lost in her.

"You are my girl," I promised. "As long as we're doing this, you are mine."

Chapter Eighteen

Aderyn

*F**uck me like I'm your girl?!*

What the hell was wrong with me? Could I sound any more desperate?

I almost pushed Morgan away after those words left my mouth. I wanted to crawl into a hole somewhere, never to be seen again, and forget this. Forget everything. I just asked him to treat me like his girlfriend. Like someone he wanted to be with outside of this bedroom.

Thankfully, Morgan didn't look confused or weirded out. Instead, he kissed me as if I didn't just make this awkward. Then, he promised I was his and I nearly lost it.

"And since you're mine, I want to make you watch," he said in a rough voice. "Make you see how your body gives into mine when I play with your pussy. And how sexy you look when my dick's inside of you."

My heart stopped. "Watch? How?"

Morgan pushed off the bed and started toward the bathroom. Instead of going in, he closed the door. I caught a glimpse of myself in the mirror hanging on the back of the door. My face looked warm, and my lips were swollen from kissing. A large chunk of my hair slipped out of one of my two braids. Despite the wildness of my appearance, I felt sexy—mostly thanks to how Morgan looked at me.

He returned to my side as if to physically co-sign his attraction to me. His hands explored my body, not shying from squeezing the large muscles on my arms or the defined abs on my stomach. I was more hard than soft. My hands were rough and calloused. He moaned at the feel of me. Massaged circles on my hips and left love bites on my shoulder.

"You down for this?" Morgan's gaze met mine in the mirror. He pinched one of my nipples, applying the perfect amount of pressure. There was a knowing smile on his lips when I arched in his direction in need of more.

I could barely speak but managed a hoarse, "Yes."

"Face toward mirror and ass in the air." He moved to grab a condom from his bedside table before claiming the spot behind me.

I clung to the edge of the mattress as I got into position. The sight of Morgan's body lining up behind mine made my stomach flutter in anticipation. I watched as his hands worked up and down my back. He cupped my ass cheeks, squeezing them hard enough to encourage a moan from me. I could feel my pussy dripping, so I pressed myself back into his crotch to get a feel of his dick.

Morgan's low groan sounded tortured. I rocked back again to coax the same dark sound from his throat.

He didn't push himself into me like I thought he would. Not yet anyway. Instead, Morgan tugged me up, so my back was pressed against his stomach and his dick firmly shoved against my ass.

"Look," was his rough order. A captain's order. He kept me close against him, cupping a breast with one hand and massaging my clit with the other. "Look at how fucking beautiful you are."

My eyes didn't know what to focus on, so I scrambled to take everything in. How perfectly our large bodies fit against one another. How pronounced his veins were on his arm. How deeply his fingers sunk into my pussy as he explored beyond my clit. We looked like this was who we were meant to be.

Together.

I pushed away that thought by tugging his hand off my breast. He seemed confused but I quickly assured him everything was fine with a simple, "I need you inside me. Right. Now."

All would be well as long as I didn't have to watch his hands explore my body like I was someone he wanted to keep. Like I was someone he could love.

Morgan followed my lead when I bent over. When he pressed into me, I pushed back, eager to be filled. Our eyes met in the mirror as I took him. We were frozen for a second, hot and dazed at the sight of him completely inside of me.

His fingers imprinted on my waist, holding me still as he whispered, "Damn, I want to be yours."

My pussy involuntarily squeezed around his dick at those words. I parted my lips, letting out a sound that was a mix between moan and gasp. There's no way he just said that. No way he meant it.

"What did you say?" I asked.

"Are you ready to get yours?" His voice was louder and clearer. "Ready to come?"

Had I misheard him the first time? This wasn't exactly the time for second-guessing, so I simply nodded. Morgan's thrusts were slow at first. He moved like he was afraid to hurt me. But with each new stroke, he became more comfortable. Bolder. And by the end of it, he pounded into me so hard I could barely think straight.

I tried to meet each pump with the same amount of strength. I could hold my own in the weight room, so staying steady for Morgan shouldn't have been too difficult. Except, it was.

"You okay?" he asked eyes on me in the mirror. "Too rough?"

"Don't you dare stop," I said between moans. "I can handle it."

He chuckled and resumed his tight grip on my hips. "You might not be able to walk straight when I'm done with you."

"So be it."

There was nothing like seeing myself in ecstasy. I thought I'd be embarrassed at watching him pound into me. It was the opposite. I was mesmerized by the curve of my back and how his fingers traced down my spine like it was some delicate piece of artwork. Seeing the shake of my breasts against the blanket made my nipples tighten even more. But the sight of Morgan's dick entering and exiting me took the cake. He moved in and out of me with confidence and determination. Each stroke felt deeper than the last.

"You're soaking," Morgan groaned. "Going to give me every last drop of cum, Aderyn?"

There he went again with my name. I reached down to rub my clit. My climax started so fast that I almost laughed at how ridiculously easy it'd been to push me over the edge. I whimpered as my core clenched.

"Aderyn." His voice was low and dark. "You're coming, aren't you?"

I nodded and he sped up to help me maintain the high. My wrist hurt from circling and my pussy was already sore from him, but I didn't care.

"You're so goddamn perfect." His eyes met mine in the mirror. "And not just on my dick. Everywhere. All the time."

He leaned down to kiss my back a few times before he started to come, too. I grabbed onto his thigh, needing to touch some part of his body. He convulsed inside of me. His groans had to be loud enough to be heard in the hallway.

"Just a little bit longer," I requested when he was about to pull out after calming down. "It still feels good."

"Fuck, you're right," he said when my pussy squeezed around his now semi-hard cock.

We stayed like that, shuddering in the aftermath for a few more seconds before he finally pulled out. Morgan laid beside me. I buried my face in his blanket since I couldn't bury my face in his chest. We laid in silence for a few minutes before moving to clean up in the bathroom.

I climbed back into his bed with plans to only stay there for a few minutes.

"I just need to catch my breath before heading down," I told him.

The bed dipped underneath Morgan as he joined me. "Same here."

We didn't touch one another. But he was close enough for me to feel his steady breath on my skin. I closed my eyes and enjoyed the warmth and his scent all around me. In a few minutes, I'd get up and pull on my clothes. I'd go back downstairs and hope everyone believed my lie about just talking with Morgan. Then, I'd eat, chat a bit, and go home to my own bed. In a few minutes.

My body began to feel heavy. Something covered my shoulders. A blanket. Morgan's hands tucked the fabric around me. He remained on top of it, but I could still feel his heat. For a second, it felt like he pressed his lips to my shoulder before I drifted asleep. In my exhaustion, I thought I heard him whisper, "I'd give everything to be yours."

Chapter Nineteen

Sam

Somewhere between a thought that should've remained unspoken and a muffled sigh of embarrassment, I fell asleep next to Aderyn.

My bed felt more inviting than ever with her in it. Sometime during that night, we gravitated toward one another. I reached for her waist, and she wrapped her arms around my neck. The new position of her cheek pressed against my chest felt like the most natural thing in the world.

I've always hated cuddling. Refused to do it post-sex. Yet here I was—transfixed and sold.

The sleep was revolutionary. Not only did I make it through the night, I made it through all my dreams. No nightmares. No restless tossing and turning. Just fantasy blended into the reality of Aderyn being by my side.

She was a fucking godsend. I hadn't been able to get a full eight hours of sleep this entire year. My naps never cut it. I'd gotten used to the possibility that small windows of rest would be all I'd ever get.

I'd gone to enough doctors to know it was stress that kept me awake. Learning how to manage it felt impossible. Everything I tried always failed. Now, waking up next to Aderyn felt like a new beginning.

It was the warmth of her body paired with a steady breath and heartbeat. Her scent reminded me of comfort—something I hadn't felt in ages.

I woke up a few minutes before her and was too afraid to move. She murmured in her sleep. None of her sentences made sense but they made me smile. Anytime she readjusted, I froze in fear this spell would be over. My stomach knotted at the thought of letting her go.

I couldn't deny it anymore. I wanted to be with Aderyn. Not just for sex. She'd become the first person I wanted to see in the morning and the last at night. I wanted to get her breakfast and make sure she got home okay. After that, I wanted to text her throughout the day to know what she was thinking. I wanted to bring her dinner after practice and make sure she got enough rest for the next day.

As I thought about our potential, I rubbed my hand up and down her back. I sighed in contentment when she pressed into me more. Her low hum told me I wasn't the only one who felt like they were in the right place.

How am I going to do this?

Did I just tell her I didn't want to finish the bet? That I wanted to take her out on a date instead? Tell her I was the one who fell?

She'd probably laugh at me right before shooting me down. I squeezed my eyes shut at the thought of rejection.

Aderyn was way too good for me. I've never offered anything outside of sex. Never felt like I could. She deserved so much. As soon as this phase of her life was over, she was going to want more. She'd move on to someone who could give her everything.

I should let her.

I flinched at the idea of her with someone else. It felt selfish to tell her I wanted more when I wasn't sure if I could give it. I had no experience being a boyfriend. There felt like so much to learn and not enough time to learn it.

Her eyes started to open while I still argued with myself. She was confused at first but when her brain finally caught up with her body, she shot up.

"Shit," she hissed, touching her hair. The coils were wayward, twisting this way and that.

"You're fine," I said in a low voice, trying to help her calm down. "Everything's fine."

"No, it's not." She scrambled to pull the blanket over her chest. Her hand scrubbed the side of her mouth, trying to rid the dried drool. See, even that was cute. That's how I knew I was a goner.

"I slept over," she whispered in horror.

"It was late." I sat up, too, and pressed a kiss on her shoulder where her muscles strained.

She frowned, pulling away from me. "I was tired and hungover from..."

"My dick," I teased and leaned back on my arms to study her. She took a long look too, eyes traveling down to where my lower body was barely covered by the bed sheet. Aderyn sighed when she realized I was hard.

"Exactly." She scanned the room for her clothing. "This means nothing to me. I feel nothing other than a little regret from not leaving sooner."

My face fell and thank God she had her back turned to me. All my hope that maybe last night helped her come to the realization we were good together was shot.

I watched in silence as she tugged on her clothes. She disappeared into the bathroom, closing the door behind her.

There was still time to ask her. Rejection felt guaranteed, though. And I couldn't stomach it. I literally felt sick with embarrassment over something that hadn't happened. All that talk I'd given her about rejection didn't work on me. I was a hypocrite for not taking this risk.

"Are your roommates early risers?" Aderyn asked as she hurried out of the bathroom. "And do you have any lotion or Vaseline? Preferably both."

"Lincoln and Henrik are but it's easy to slip out of the front door. I'll walk you," I offered as I got out of bed to pull on some pants. "And yeah, in the bathroom's top cabinet."

She nodded her thanks before disappearing behind the door again. Adrenaline coursed through my body as I prepped myself to ask my question. Rejection wasn't going to be like before in middle school. I wasn't some small kid anymore. I was a fucking captain of a division one hockey team. My guys respected me, I was one of the top scorers in the league, and I'd gotten a full ride on my talent alone. I could tell a woman how I felt and handle the rejection afterward.

As soon as Aderyn reappeared, I didn't give either of us a moment to breathe.

"Want to get dinner? My treat? Like a date?" I asked, falling over the words like they were an obstacle course.

She froze and stayed silent for eons. Stars were born and died and born again before she finally said, "You're fucking with me, aren't you?"

I swallowed. "No, why would I be fucking with you?"

"Because you want to win." She laughed like everything made sense now. "That's a good one. Right after we woke up, too. Brilliant."

"I'm...being serious."

"Yeah, right." Aderyn shook her head and rolled her eyes. "No need to play dirty, Morgan. You're killing the game so far."

I don't care about the game, I wanted to insist but her next words made me pause.

"Besides, even if I wanted to, I can't." She shrugged. "I have a thing tonight."

My ears started ringing.

"A t-thing? Like this thing?" I gestured between us.

"Yes, like this thing." She sounded offended at the shock in my tone. "With Jack."

The knife in my heart twisted. "Oh...Okay."

"Playoffs are around the corner and I'm going to meet my quota." She looked pleased with herself. Excited. "You're going down and I'm getting that jersey."

"I'm sure you are," I said, feeling numb all over.

Her face fell. "Didn't think you'd be such a great sport about it. What happened to cocky Morgan?"

"It's a little early for him," I lied with a forced smile.

She didn't look convinced. "Did I say something wrong? I thought jeering was our thing?"

"No, no, you didn't say anything wrong. I'm just not myself until after I've been up for a few hours." I moved to open the door, pausing before I grabbed the handle. My gaze strayed to my desk drawer. I'd gotten something for her. After spending the morning with Aderyn and her family, I walked away not able to stop thinking about her. About making her as excited and comfortable as her family did.

"I want to give you something," I said, moving away from the door and to the desk. There was no point in keeping it now. Even with the rejection, I still wanted her to take the gift.

"What?" She stopped next to me, watching as I opened the drawer.

I grabbed the pair of soft, purple weightlifting gloves. It'd taken me a while to find them. I'd driven to four different sporting goods stores before coming across one that had more color options besides the typical boring black or blue. The stitching was white and there were daisies embroidered on the wrist straps. I didn't know how she'd feel about that part. I didn't know how she'd feel about any of it. But, by the way she let out a heavy breath told me all the feelings were positive. I sighed, relieved I hadn't made a terrible decision.

"I saw your pair in the weight room," I explained. "You could get injured using shitty gloves."

"Morgan, I..." She took the gloves from me and examined them closer. "Thank you. I've been meaning to get new ones for the longest. These are beautiful. I love them."

I took another breath, my chest expanding with pride. "Perfect. I'm glad."

She looked up at me. From the small smile on her lips, she seemed like she wanted to say something more but couldn't. I started feeling awkward at how personal the gift felt.

"I'll walk you out," I offered so we wouldn't stand in silence a moment longer.

"Okay." Aderyn gave me a final look before passing by me. I got her downstairs without bumping into anyone and waited with her on the porch for her rideshare to pull up.

As I closed the front door behind me, I slid down like a dramatic son of a bitch and inwardly cursed myself for doing what I promised myself I would never do—fall for someone so hard, it felt like my body was breaking.

"It's a crush," I said in a monotone voice. "It'll pass."

Lincoln took a breath, trying to come up with something to say. He could tell I was playing this down from the moment this conversation started. But, like the good friend he was, he pretended to play along with my delusion.

"Sure," he agreed as he wiped his towel over his face. I'd been in the gym for about two hours. Got in an hour of cardio before hitting the weights with him. Pushing my body to its limit was the only thing that could distract me from Aderyn right now.

"You get those all the time," Lincoln continued.

I raised my brow, skeptical of what was coming next.

"All the girls you sleep with make you smile when we bring them up in conversation," he continued. "They all make you come to practice extra early on the off chance you'll see them. You stay up late texting all the girls, despite your desperate need for sleep."

My jaw tightened. "We're both night owls."

"Until the other night." Lincoln wiggled his brows. "When you slept like a baby for the first time in forever. Which was after you had very loud—and from your account—mind-blowing, sex."

Scratch that, he wasn't a good friend.

"I told you that in confidence," I complained.

He stretched out his arms, gesturing around to the near-empty weight room. "I'm pretty sure no one here has superhero-level hearing, Sam. Besides...it didn't take superhero-level hearing to know what was going on last night."

I grumbled to myself.

"Look, I get it. You know I get it. What I don't get is how you're stuck pining. I've never seen you this bent out of shape over someone. Why haven't you told her you want something more?"

"I tried."

"Really? Was it in a roundabout way? Because humans are not mind readers."

I groaned when I played back my invite. "Doesn't matter, she turned me down like I knew she would."

"Did she or did you give up?" Lincoln sighed when I didn't answer. "You know, in all the years we've been friends, I've never seen you give up on anything except a relationship longer than a few nights. You worked yourself to the bone in high school for hockey. But when it came to dating you checked out. I always figured it was because you genuinely weren't interested but now this feels like it's about something else."

"I'm not interested," I said, desperate to stick to my guns. Since when did Lincoln get so perceptive? "Aderyn's just good at being perfect. It'd be a struggle to find someone who doesn't fall in love with her."

"So, this is love now?"

My skin burned. "No! Shit. It's not love. Of course, it's not love this soon but...I mean..."

Lincoln smiled. "You mean?"

"You know what I mean," I said through gritted teeth.

It was something that could be more. What I felt for Aderyn was like a new door placed in my path. Whatever was on the other side could change me for worse or better.

"Maybe I do," he agreed with a nod. "You mean you're scared of rejection because no matter how hard you try, you can't guarantee she'll stick around. Hockey's around as long as you want it. People are a different story."

"It's not that deep," I promised, but my voice sounded weak and tired.

"Look, I think a big reason why you don't date is because you don't think you're good enough," Lincoln said. He paused for me to interject but I didn't say a word.

"And a large part of that has to do with what happened to you in middle school. What those bullies did to you fucking sucked, man."

I wiped my hands over my face. "Yeah, it did."

"I wish Henrik and I knew you and Finn back then. Two against the world is hard. Four, though? We would've given them a run for their money."

"We wouldn't have stood a chance," I said, but still smiled at the thought of meeting him before high school. Grade school Lincoln had to undoubtedly be a riot. He'd probably been bouncing off walls back then. Any fight we'd get in, he'd likely lose but be ready to go again the next day.

"You stand a chance now." Lincoln's voice was more serious. "With Aderyn. Don't take yourself out of the running so early on."

I couldn't meet his gaze because I feared he'd see the doubt in my eyes. I thought I'd outrun this raging insecurity the second I became a Mendell Hawk. Imagine my surprise to find that even after I became everything I wanted, there was still this voice in my head saying I wasn't good enough.

"Sam?"

I looked up to find Jack standing behind Lincoln. My jaw tightened remembering that he'd taken Aderyn out a few nights ago. I did my best to push away those feelings. Especially after he said, "Got a minute? Stoll wants to have a quick meeting."

Lincoln's eyes widened. "No shit. This is going down? Tonight?"

"No," Jack's voice was hard and impatient. "It's just a conversation to see if he's in. He wants to see if he can trust you. We got to hurry though because he's on his way out."

"Can I come?" Lincoln asked, quickly. "Two lambs to the slaughter's got to be better than one."

"No," Jack and I said in unison. Lincoln blew out an annoyed sigh.

"I've only talked up Sam," Jack explained. "It'd be suspicious if you tagged along. The point is to get him comfortable with the idea of welcoming someone else into his inner circle. Not to bombard him with two new options."

"I know, I know." Lincoln waved his hand.

Jack looked back at me. "So, are we doing this?"

"No doubt," I said.

Chapter Twenty

Sam

We took the stairs to the third floor of the athletic department building. Stoll's office was at the end of the hall, bigger than his other colleagues.

"Alright." Jack paused before knocking on the door. "Here's the plan. You don't do much talking, okay? Let me lead the conversation and whenever Stoll says something, tell him what you think he wants to hear. You're good at reading people."

I nodded, feeling a slight nervous twist in my stomach. "How many hoops are left after this conversation?

"If you do well, this is the first and only one." Jack straightened his collar like he was anxious to make a good impression. "But you're as good as in with my endorsement."

"He trusts you that much?" I raised a brow. I didn't mean to sound doubtful, but it slipped out. My feelings for Aderyn were definitely jading my opinion of him. I needed to separate the two ASAP.

Jack scowled at my tone. "Yeah, lucky for you, he does."

"Right. Sorry."

"What's wrong with you?"

The color drained from my face. I tried to straighten my shoulders and sound like my usual self. "What do you mean?"

He shrugged. "You're looking at me weird."

"I'm good." I insisted. "Let's just get this over with."

Jack gave me one final glance before deciding to push away his doubt in exchange for the greater good. I did my best to wipe away what Jack had seen on my face. Any thoughts about Aderyn needed to be buried immediately.

"Boys," Stoll's booming voice greeted.

When we stepped into his office, he indicated I shut the door behind us. His space was surprisingly colorful for a man who only wore variations of gray and black.

The couches in his lounge area were bright orange and plush enough for me to sink into when he motioned for us to sit. I felt like I was at my grandmother's house with how the assortment of overstuffed pillows dominated the space. The air smelt of something caramel. My gaze fell on a bowl of hard candies my grandma used to carry around in her purse on Sunday mornings.

"Give me one second and I'll be right with you," Stoll said. He sat behind his desk. The sound of mechanical keys echoed.

Warren Stoll was the youngest athletic director in Mendell's history. He got the role because of his impressive background as a track star who qualified for the Olympics about fifteen years ago. His walls sported awards and medals from his heyday. He didn't place at the Olympics and soon after, tore his ACL which ended his track career early. From the framed diploma on his walls, I could see he held two masters and a shit load of academic awards.

He was the kind of guy I'd aim to be in his post-athletic career. Stoll still got to work in sports, which was a rarity for most athletes. The fact that he was taking advantage of the opportunity made my blood boil.

Stoll got to sit up here and call the shots when he'd already had the chance to make a name for himself. He experienced firsthand the small window college athletes had. Most of us wouldn't make it to any professional league. We got a few years playing the sport we loved. And then, we were left to pick up the pieces.

We would have to figure out who we were when we weren't playing our sport. The majority of us wouldn't know where to start. I sure as hell didn't. Hockey was the only thing I've ever been good at. My body was molded for the sport. Each decision I made from high school until now, I considered how it might affect my ability to be the best on the ice. Now, some asshole with dual degrees came in ready to change things.

If I didn't make it to the NHL because of something I did, if it was my fault it didn't happen, then I would accept it. If I wasn't good enough, I'd accept it. But, if someone else decided to stack the deck, that was another story.

Jack elbowed me as Stoll finished up his typing.

"What?" I hissed under my breath.

"Stop looking so goddamn upset," Jack whispered back with equal bite in his words. "This isn't the time to be an open book."

He was right. I took a deep breath, trying to loosen my jaw. As I stretched my neck, Stoll moved to claim the seat across from us.

"Sorry about that," he said as he got comfortable in his chair. The guy had to be older than forty but didn't look far off from his college years. His black hair was slicked back and there was a tattoo of a dragon on his neck that only revealed itself if he turned his head the right amount.

"There's always something." Stoll crossed his ankle over his leg. "So, what can I do for you boys? I heard this is about the dinner?"

I nearly opened my mouth but remembered Jack's warning about letting him lead. My heart drummed at staying quiet. I didn't like the feeling of putting my trust and my potential future into Whitfield's hands.

"Sam's interested in joining," Jack said, matter-of-fact. "I told him about how great the food is and how the conversation is even better."

Stoll steepled his hands and placed his fingers under his chin. I swallowed a scoff at how trademark villainous that looked. Was I in a Bond movie all of a sudden?

"I think we have a good group for the dinners. Very mixed bunch from various backgrounds," Stoll started, and Jack nodded in agreement. When the two looked at me, I felt the pressure to do the same.

"What do you feel Morgan brings to the table?" Stoll asked.

"He's a great captain," Jack said without hesitation.

Wow, that might have been touching if he wasn't playing his part.

"Sam dedicates himself to the team. He spends extra hours helping those of us falling behind. He even helps us find tutors and suggests going to counseling if we have personal problems." Jack looked at me when he said the last part, "We don't get along but that doesn't matter because he's loyal. As loyal as they come."

He could have left out the not getting along part, but I'd take it. Beggars can't be choosers. And by the look on Stoll's face, it seemed like Jack's words were winning him over. My brow sweat as our AD stayed quiet in thought for a moment.

"I heard my daughter invited you to the cabin this weekend," Stoll surprised us both by saying.

Jack's eyebrows furrowed. "Yeah. She did. It's a getaway trip before playoffs."

I shifted uncomfortably in my seat. I didn't know Stoll had a daughter who was apparently close enough for Jack to vacation with.

"The slopes aren't great this time of year," Stoll warned. "But the views are amazing."

Jack nodded. "So, I've heard."

"How about you, Morgan? Ever been up to the mountains? You into skiing?" Stoll looked at me.

"I've been to the mountains. My folks own a cabin near the lodge. Not that into skiing, though. That's more of my sister's thing."

He nodded his approval. "Very nice. I think I remember meeting your old man. He's a preacher, isn't he?"

"He was," I said. "Now, he advises and works as a dentist."

"I see." Stoll studied me for a moment before getting up and moving toward the door. "Well, boys, I'd love to stick around and chat longer but my wife's expecting me home soon. And you know how traffic gets during this hour."

"Right." Jack popped up and started toward the door Stoll opened.

I frowned, perplexed by what just happened and why my 'in' was giving up so willingly. Jack didn't turn to me when I shot daggers into his back. I know he had to feel the heat of my gaze, but he kept his eyes on the ever-smiling Stoll.

"Looking forward to seeing you two next weekend," Stoll said once we crossed the threshold and stood in the hallway. "Make sure to bring your appetites. Steak's on the menu."

Jack smiled. "Will do, sir. Thank you for your time."

Stoll winked at us. "Of course. Always love getting to know my athletes a little better."

I was still confused as he closed the door. Jack didn't say anything and held up his hand before I could open my mouth. He gestured for me to follow him down the hall and back to the stairwell.

"What the hell?" I asked, my voice echoing off the walls as we hurried down the stairs.

"You did good. You impressed him." Jack looked pleased.

"I barely said two words."

"Exactly. He thinks you're respectable. Especially since you threw that stuff in there about having a cabin."

"It's the truth."

Jack paused. "Your folks really have a cabin? On Burn Mountain?"

"Yes. Black families can buy vacation homes, too," I joked.

Jack's face turned red. "That's not what I meant."

"I'm fucking with you," I assured and patted his shoulder. "Now, what's next?"

"You do what you do in there. Pretend like you're on board one thousand percent. Once we get him talking, he won't stop."

"Hopefully he says something worth recording. Enough to prove our point."

"He will. Get a few beers in that guy and he sings," Jack assured.

Chapter Twenty-One

Aderyn

I swear, every game this season made me feel simultaneously more powerful and more helpless. On the ice, I checked opponents with confidence. When I was on the bench, I looked at the stands with disappointment.

"It's going to take some time," I told Kaya. She was glancing at the stands as often as I was. She wouldn't admit it in a million years but each time her eyes went there, she looked crushed.

"I just don't like wasting our off days," she grumbled and tugged on her helmet so she could shut me out.

Our videos with the guys got triple the views we ever pulled in on our own. Despite the change in audience size, our crowd sizes weren't much different. The stands possessed a few stragglers who watched their phones more than the ice, a couple of girls from the basketball team because they knew our pain and teammates' families. My own family wasn't in the stands, though. Mom worked late and I forbade Warren from coming unless it was an emergency. He was a backseat coach. I loved his energy but didn't need him and Coach Bella getting into a passive-aggressive stare-off. Again.

"Jacobs, Towers." Bella snapped at us. Her face was red with nerves about our close score. "Intermission's over. You ready?"

Kaya and I nodded, joining our team.

"We got this," I promised her with a shoulder bump. "We'll figure the rest out after the game. Don't let it get to you."

"Never do." Kaya bit down on her mouthguard.

I took my own advice, pushing away my worry to focus on what I could do now. Every game requires a little bit of your sanity and your soul. I'd been shoved, pushed, and punched all night. The Southward Tigers won second place at nationals last year. Their whole team came back this year, making them one of the most dangerous set of seniors in the league.

Every team has a unique playing style because of their chemistry and the Tigers played brutally on the edge of the rules. Most of their movements led to body fouls too quick for the referees to catch.

As center forward, I usually called the shots—most of which have failed us tonight. With every move I made, one of the Tigers counteracted it in a heartbeat. I started to wing it more, but my girls weren't great at anticipating my decisions as quickly as I needed. In fact, they were starting to get pissed off.

It was in the third period when I made a mistake that could cost us the game. Instead of trusting my defense to fend off the Tiger's breakout, I went after one of their best defensive players. I clipped her side, forcing her into the boards and she fought back with more bite than I anticipated.

"Watch it, bitch," she said, tone full of venom as she elbowed me in the chest. I shoved her back because if you don't hold your ground, then people suddenly think you like being pushed around.

She took offense to my pushback like I'd spit on her grandmother's grave. The puck didn't matter anymore. She used her stick to shove me to the ice with the kind of determination one should save for a buzzer-beater.

So, she wanted a fight? Lucky for her, I was in the mood to give it to her. Unlucky for me, her teammates were closer than mine.

I lost my helmet early in the scuffle. My head was knocked against the ice with a crack. The sound was nasty enough to scare my opponent, who hurried away from me, surely hoping the distance would help her if I came away from this with a concussion.

Jas and Kaya appeared by my side to help me up and off the ice. Coach Bella took one look at me and told me to get my head checked.

"I just n-need a break," I mumbled with one eye closed. My ears were ringing.

"And you'll get it," Coach Bella promised and nudged her chin in the direction of the tunnel. Jas hurried back onto the ice after Kaya assured them she could take me to the medic on her own.

"Hey, do you have a minute?" a young girl at the end of the stands called out to us. I slowed down at the request—much to Kaya's disapproval.

"We need to get you to medical," she protested.

"Just hold up a second," I insisted when I saw a girl who couldn't be older than twelve leaning over the railing. She wore her hair in micro braids and had a thick pair of glasses that kept sliding down her nose. Her chest was moving fast and her hands on the rail were shaking.

"What's up?" I greeted, trying to smile through the pain.

"You're Aderyn, right?"

Kaya and I exchanged looks. The girl unlocked her phone and showed us the screen. A video of me playing a game was pulled up. It was an old one from my high school's page. I laughed at seeing baby me trying to cling to her hockey stick.

"Yup, that's right," I confirmed. "That's me."

The girl's face lit up with a smile. "I found you online last week and followed all your socials. What you do is amazing. All of you."

Even Kaya was smiling now.

"I convinced my mom to bring me here." The girl gestured over her shoulder to a middle-aged woman who was nose-deep in a thriller novel. "I play softball, but I want to make a switch to hockey. I'm going to make the switch."

"Do you not like softball anymore?" Kaya wondered.

The girl shook her head. "No, I just like hockey better. I've never seen Black girls play, you know? But now, I have, and I don't care what everyone else says. I want to do this and be like you guys."

My head was still spinning so the emotion in my throat didn't make me feel physically better. But I'd struggle through this kind of pain a million times just to see the pure excitement on another young Black girl's face when she realized her world could be bigger than she'd ever imagined.

"What's your name?" I asked.

"Avori," she said. Her hands were no longer shaking. She looked more comfortable and confident the longer we talked.

"Well, Avori, in the next ten years, I expect to see you standing across from me, stick in hand."

She nodded earnestly, bouncing on the balls of her feet. "I'm going to work hard, I promise."

"And have fun," I told her. "Don't do it unless it's fun, okay?"

"Okay," she agreed, still nodding, her face etched with the determination she'd need for the long road ahead.

I smiled. "See you around."

We started toward the tunnel and I began limping again. Trying to feign strength was so much easier with a crowd.

"I'm f-fine." I nudged Kaya away when she reached for me. For a second, she fought against me. Her grip tightened on my waist while I tried to tug out of it.

"Your forehead's bleeding and you're slurring."

"I'm n-not." I pulled out of her grasp, and she finally let me go.

Kaya frowned when I stumbled, reaching for the white, concrete wall to help keep me upright. The tunnel looked longer than usual and the chill in the air bothered me more than it should.

"Whatever," Kaya said but still followed my slow process down the hall. "I'll just watch you struggle to get yourself to medical because you want everything to go your way. Whether you're playing or not."

"Shut up," I said because all sounds made my head hurt.

"I just think one of us should be the realist," she said, voice lower as she considered my pain. "You're working yourself so hard that you tried to take on the Tiger's defense by yourself. Getting injured doesn't prove anything, Ryn."

"I'm not–" I paused for a moment to take a deep breath. "–trying to get hurt. I'm trying to show everyone we have what it takes. And it's working. You heard that girl, right? She's here because of us, Kaya. That means something."

Something more than money and a crowd of people cheering our names.

"Sure, Captain." She didn't sound sold. "Definitely means something. But is that meaning worth getting your lip busted open by one of the best defenders in the league? No."

"What's crawled up your ass, huh?" I stopped walking to press my back against the wall. Up was down and down was up and everything in between made no sense.

"Nothing." She leaned against the opposite wall with her arms crossed over her chest. "I'm tired of looking out for your renegade ass is all."

I tried to laugh but it hurt too much.

"Hey!" someone said at the end of the hall.

We both looked at the entrance of the tunnel. Morgan jogged in our direction—*my* direction. When he stopped right in front of me, I tried to stand up straight and look like I didn't feel like throwing up.

"Why aren't you in medical?" Morgan placed a hand on my shoulder. I leaned into the gesture only because it was helping me stay upright and not because it was comforting.

"She's clawing her way to it," Kaya grumbled, and she gave Morgan a side-eye.

"W-walking," I corrected. "At my own pace, t-thank you very m-much."

"You're slurring." Morgan's forehead wrinkled. He threw a look at Kaya, and it surprisingly made her shoulders sag in guilt. "She's slurring. You need to get someone. *Now*."

Kaya looked at me once more before hurrying ahead of us down the hall.

"Woah, woah." I held up my hand. "I've bashed my head plenty of times. No need to get your horses in a wad. No, panties. Horses in a bunch. No panties. Shit."

"You're thinking about panties at a time like this?" he asked.

"No, you are," I accused with a lopsided smile. "Typical."

Morgan hand hovered near my forehead. His eyebrows knitted at whatever he saw there. "Does this hurt?"

"What?" I reached up before he could stop me. My fingers were painted bright red when I pulled away. "Eh, just a scratch."

"Aderyn," he whispered like he pained him to see me hurt. "That's more than a scratch, beautiful."

My heart fluttered at his soft tone. "I'm fine, I promise."

He held my jaw carefully as he examined the cut for a moment longer. Wheels turned as he tried to decide what to do. I could get used to this. Being taken care of by him.

"Come here." Morgan put my arm over his shoulder. "I saw you go down without your helmet. You girls don't pull punches."

"Why would we?" I tried to tease and let out a groan when I started moving. "I think...I might throw up if I keep walking."

"It's okay." Morgan held all my weight when my knees buckled. Very impressive since I still had most of my gear on. In the blink of an eye, he picked me up and pulled me close to his chest. "I got you. I'll get you there. Throw up on me if it comes to it."

"That's very nice of you to offer."

"Told you I'm generous," he reminded me.

I snorted and pressed my forehead to his chest and closed my eyes, hoping the world would stop spinning. His heartbeat was fast, pounding against his chest like a drummer at a rock concert. I frowned at the sound.

"Your heart's racing more than mine and I just got off the ice," I noted.

"I jogged through the crowd to get here," he said. But even in my state of confusion, I could hear the lie in his voice.

"You skipping cardio days or something? Slacker."

He snorted. "You know I don't skip any days. Can't if I want to keep up with you."

"Right." I'm sure I still sounded unconvinced to his ears because he lifted me higher, readjusting so that my ear pressed against his collarbone.

"You were killing it out there," Morgan said with a smile in his voice.

"Don't lie to me." I closed my eyes again and pressed my head on his chest. He could readjust me all he wanted. I was still going to wonder about his racing heart. "I sucked ass."

"Not from where I was watching."

"And how long was that? I didn't see you out there." If I had I probably would've been hyper-aware, unfortunately.

"The entire time."

I looked up at him to find he was already peering down at me. The honesty in his eyes made my stomach jump.

"Really?" I asked in a low voice, like speaking any louder would change reality.

"I was and I'm not lying," he assured. "You were incredible."

I stuck my bottom lip out, dramatizing how touched I felt. "You do care."

He snorted. "Don't get too excited. There wasn't much else to do tonight. No interesting parties. And crowds at the bar are thin because of the snow."

"You don't lie very well," I whispered.

Morgan's grip stiffened. "Excuse me?"

I poked his chin. "Whenever you lie, you roll your tongue across the inside of your bottom lip."

"You stay taking notes on me, don't you?" he teased, trying to cover up his embarrassment.

"Have to know my competition in and out."

"You do know that sometimes we're on the same team, right? Like now, for instance."

"Sure, but one should never get too comfortable." I avoided meeting his gaze, remembering that this wasn't going to last forever. He wasn't going to keep buying me gloves, or coming to my games and carrying me when I got hurt. Morgan was here because our bet meant he needed to avoid other women. What better way to help keep himself accountable than being near me?

Morgan turned down the hall leading to medical. Kaya and one of the on-call doctors were hurrying in our direction.

Morgan refused to put me down until we got to the beds. I was soaking up every bit of the attention.

"I'm going to stay with her," Morgan told Kaya. "Make sure she's okay."

My stomach fluttered at his insistence. I pretended to be focused on finding a comfortable position on the bed and not on how much I enjoyed Morgan wanting to stick around.

"You sure?" Kaya looked at me for permission. She wasn't going to leave me with him unless I wanted. Kaya's grumpy outer shell was filled with a soft, protective center.

"It's fine." I nodded, wincing a bit at the pain that shot through my neck. "Go ahead. I'll be fine."

"You better be, or you won't hear the end of it," Kaya warned before heading out.

"You have some loyal friends, don't you?" The doctor was a young woman with a honey-blonde afro. She glanced over at Morgan, who'd moved a few feet away to give us space but not far enough so that he didn't know what was going on.

"They just like the adrenaline from my drama," I joked. "We're all addicted, that's why we play."

She laughed and told me to hold still while she shone a light in my eyes. "How does your head feel?"

"Like it's being smashed between boulders."

"Your vision?"

"It was a little blurry at first, but it's better now," I said.

She took my heartbeat and recorded my blood pressure. After another series of questions and tests, she turned to Morgan. "Want to keep your girlfriend company for a bit? Keep her talking for me?"

He didn't say anything about the girlfriend part. Morgan simply nodded and pushed off the wall to join my side.

"I'll be right back with something cold for your head," the doctor said. "Try not to move too much. You don't have a concussion, but you're still pretty banged up. You'll need plenty of rest. No more adrenaline rushes for today, got it?"

"Works for me." I gave her a thumbs up. Normally, I would've tried harder to get back to my team but lying down felt too good to pass up right now.

"Aderyn?" Morgan asked when he sat on the side of the bed.

My heart rate sped up at the sound of my name on his lips. "Yeah?"

"Do you want me to stay?"

"That'd be nice. If you could. If not, I'll survive. My team will come to pester me with updates soon." My stomach twisted because I didn't want to be alone, and it wasn't just anyone's company I wanted. I wanted him and only him. When my team did come to check on me, I'd send them away as soon as I learned how the game panned out. The only person I could stomach being around for longer than a few minutes right now was Morgan.

"Actually, go," I said, quickly.

He blinked, confused. "Why?"

"Because I changed my mind. I don't want you here."

"You'd just said it'd be nice," he countered.

My heart reached my throat, crawling up to reveal itself to him. To offer itself up to him on a silver platter.

"I was lying."

He scoffed. "Yeah, right. You want me here. You need me here."

"You fucking wish." I reached up to remove my shoulder pads. When I moved onto my knee pads, Morgan beat me to the punch. His hands hovered near mine, looking up at me for permission to continue. My throat was too tight for me to speak, so I numbly nodded.

His hands felt like they weren't even there—a far cry from how he'd touched me in the bedroom. Still, my breathing was as uneven as when he undressed me for sex. As soon as the gear was off, Morgan stacked it in a chair for me and came back to sit on the side of the bed.

When settled, he said, "Fine. Then, maybe it's the other way around."

"What?" I frowned at the serious look in his eyes.

He took a moment to respond. His gaze fell to his shoes. "Maybe I need you."

I tried to sit up. He frowned and pushed my shoulders back down.

"What are you doing?" Morgan looked pissed. "You're supposed to be relaxing."

"I'm trying to make sure you're not testing me or something. As you can see, I'm in no shape to deal with a Morgan lesson on fucking around."

His forehead wrinkled. "I wasn't fucking around with you. Why would I do that when you're hurt and exhausted?"

"No clue. Maybe you like the challenge. Little late-night entertainment since you couldn't go pick up someone else tonight?" That sounded ridiculous, even to my own ears. But there had to be a reason why he'd say something like that.

"What part of what I said sounds like a joke?"

"You're a flirt. Sorry if I'm skeptical."

His eyes softened. "I-I know. I see how my words could come off as non-serious."

"Exactly," I agreed.

"So, I promise you with as much seriousness as I can communicate, it wasn't a joke."

"Then, was it something to throw me off?" I raised a brow. "Trick me into thinking I have a shot with you?"

"What? Aderyn, no. I...I didn't realize you thought so little of me."

"I have more respect for you than you do me." I let those words out so fast that I didn't even get to rethink them. My biggest insecurity was laid out right in front of me. I felt like someone had stolen my clothes from gym class. Now, I was fumbling around with everything exposed.

"Are you serious?" He looked pissed and concerned. It was a weird combination that made a vein in his neck twitch.

"Nevermind." I pinched the bridge of my nose. "Forget I said that. I'm tired and a little out of it."

"You don't think I respect you?" he asked slowly, trying understand the meaning of the words. "Seriously?"

"Here you are." The doctor appeared with an ice pack and bottle of water. Morgan pushed off the bed like it'd turned into lava. This would have been the perfect chance for him to leave, but he didn't. He watched as the doctor gave me a pamphlet on caring for head injuries as an athlete. She told me I could stick around until I felt ready to leave. I was supposed to take things easy for the next week. No extensive weightlifting. Easy drills during practice.

The doctor didn't leave when she was done giving me her spiel. But there was enough space between us and her desk where she went back to sit. Morgan re-joined my side. Instead of taking a seat on the bed, he opted on bringing a chair close by instead.

We were quiet for a long while, the weight of our argument before filled the space between us. I kept my eyes closed, hoping he'd think I was too tired and not too embarrassed to talk.

I don't know how the respect thing slipped out. I didn't even realize I felt so deeply about it. Now that it was out in the open it felt more real and raw. I was embarrassed because it sounded like I was desperate for his respect. And I had been at some point. He was someone I looked up to. A hero of sorts. A hero who turned into a guy who fucked me and that was a messy combination.

It was my fault this went so far. I shouldn't have said yes to this silly bet in the first place. The guy barely knew me outside of hockey and I thought him some legend in the making. How in the world did I expect to have a healthy relationship—friendship or otherwise—like that?

"Aderyn," he whispered. "Can you look at me?"

I toyed with the idea of keeping my eyes shut but decided to look at him instead. We'd have to face one another soon enough.

As soon as I met his gaze, my stomach twisted. He looked so... worried. His chin rested in his hand as he leaned back into the seat. He was about a foot away, close enough for me to smell him but far enough for me to not be able to reach out and touch him.

"What is it?" I asked. Why were his eyes so sad? Why were his lips pressed so tightly? Surely, he didn't take that much offense to my words. It wasn't that big of a deal for him. He didn't have to be embarrassed. He didn't have a crush on someone he could never have. He didn't dream about going on real dates and exchanging real kisses. He didn't dream about being in love. About, having someone love him. It was easy for him. He could throw a stone and hit someone who'd fall in love with him in a heartbeat. On the other hand, my track record sucked.

Morgan leaned forward, resting his elbows on his knees so the space between us dissipated. "What did I do to make you think I don't respect you?"

What he did do? My heart squeezed. "Nothing. You did nothing."

"I had to have done or said something," he insisted.

"You didn't. It's just me...And my insecurity talking." I winced. "Can we let it go? For now, at least?"

His jaw tightened but he nodded. "Fine but only because you should be taking it easy right now."

I thought that'd be the end of it. He seemed to as well, so it surprised us both when he added, "Whatever I did, Aderyn, I'm sorry. I'll make it up to you."

"There's nothing to make up." I felt guilty for making him feel bad. "It's more about how I see myself. Not how you see me. It's some inner work shit I'm still working through."

Morgan still didn't look convinced. He didn't push for more though. We sat in silence after that. I dozed while he thought loud enough to nearly muffle out the sounds of my team celebrating in the hall. We won. At least I could feel good about something tonight.

Chapter Twenty-Two

Aderyn

Warren was outside working on Rae's truck when I pulled into the driveway. His face lit up with a smile when I got out of my car.

"What's up?" I grinned back.

His hands were too oily for a hug, so he offered me a fist bump instead. "Your sister needed an oil change. What're you doing here? I thought we were too uncool to visit during the school week."

I rolled my eyes and leaned against the truck. "I'm not a teenager anymore. You guys don't embarrass me—most of the time. I just prefer my space. You know that."

Warren chuckled and nodded. "I do, I do. Still, glad you decided to drop in. Your Mom's going to be happy to see you. It's taco night."

"Tofu taco night?" I winced when he nodded. "If I get back in my car and drive away, would you pretend you never saw me?"

Warren nodded with a conspiratorial glint in his eyes. "Deal. But only for about an hour or so. You know I can't keep a secret to save my life."

My family lucked out when my mom married Warren. He wasn't some guy who longed to be cool for his stepkids. Nor was he someone obsessed with filling in a fatherly role. He fit into a category all his own.

Mom met Warren when I was a freshman in high school. And like most teenagers, I was wary of everyone new. He never tried to win Rae and me over. Whenever he talked to us, he treated us like equals. Like adults who could make their own decisions on who they liked and disliked. From the beginning, he made it clear that he didn't want to replace anyone, and he wasn't in the business of telling us what to do. I warmed to him instantly and now, felt close enough to call him 'dad.'

"How's this season going? Coach Bella says you're killing it." Warren wiped his hands on a stained rag.

I kicked a rock off the driveway and shrugged. "Good so far. I'm the top scorer this year."

"I'm not surprised. Well on your way to that first-place title."

"It's ours this year," I promised.

"So, when you qualify are we allowed to come and cheer you on?" He raised a teasing brow.

I pretended to think about it. "Maybe. If you promise to not yell too much and not get Mom too hyped up. Sometimes she's worse than you and barely remembers the rules, so she just shouts random things."

He laughed. "I promise. Now, want to tell me why you're really here?"

I raised a brow. "What do you mean? I'm here for the tofu tacos, of course."

Warren snorted and lowered the truck's hood. I followed him into the garage where he washed off in the large sink.

"Something happen to you at school?" he asked, talking loudly so I could hear him over the running water.

"No, living on campus is a dream," I assured. "The meal plan sucks, the showers are disgusting, and my roommate calls the room for sex every other night."

"A dream," he agreed with a smile. "You'll look back on these days as good ones."

I claimed an old folding chair we used to bring on beach trips. There was still some sand gathered in the middle of the fabric.

"That's what they keep telling me." I was mostly joking. Living on campus did feel like a dream most days. My parents were never the strict kind, but the freedom that came with staying out all night and falling into bed at two in the morning was unmatched.

"Enjoy it," Warren said. "Before the real adult responsibilities claim you... like, being honest about why you've come home."

"Come on, I told you, I'm here for the food. The awesome company's a close second. Aren't you guys playing charades tonight? Dinner and show for the low, low price of free."

"Did Rae ask you to come?"

I clicked my tongue on the roof of my mouth. "Impressive. How'd you guess?"

Warren crossed his arms over his chest. "She came to me a few days ago, worried."

"Should I be too?"

Mom and Warren fought like a typical couple but things were never serious. From the outside, I learned how quickly Mom lost her temper and how fast Warren walked away from things.

I used to be the peacemaker of the house. It was an easy role to slip into and a skill that helped me become the leader I was today. I won't pretend I was the best at the position—I often brought up things that made them fight more. But I had a knack for seeing both sides of the story and not judging too harshly.

"You girls don't need to worry about us," Warren said. Those words had been repeated so much, I'm sure they could be considered his catchphrase at this point. My stepdad always made sure not to bring us into the drama. Rae and I couldn't ignore it though. Probably the result of seeing our folks argue themselves into a nasty divorce. We wanted to be fixers.

"Oh, come on. I'm old enough to sit at the grown-up table now," I said. "What's going on with you two? What's got Rae concerned?"

Warren's gaze strayed to the garage door that led inside the house. I could hear music playing and Mom singing along in her off-key voice. She sounded in a good mood, so maybe they already made up.

"Your mom and I can handle our differences without you girls getting involved," Warren promised. "I wish you two wouldn't feel like it's your job to help us through fights. That's what we're supposed to be doing."

"Every family is different," I assured. "Sometimes, the kids are more mature."

He shook his head. "I don't like that dynamic. You shouldn't feel the need to come home to referee a fight. You should be somewhere with your friends wasting the night, getting a little too drunk, and cramming for an exam the next morning."

"If Mom heard you say that..." I warned with a laugh.

"She'd disapprove, I know." He smiled and looked at the ground as if he could hear her scolding just as clearly as I could. "But you deserve wasted nights. And you shouldn't be worried about us. We're fine here. I know you miss your dad."

My smile faded. "Warren—"

"No, let me finish." He held up a hand. "I understand that you feel like if you could've done something back then, maybe things would be different."

"I don't want things to be different. Because if they were then we wouldn't have you."

His cheeks reddened. "Thanks, kid. It's nice to hear you say that."

"I mean it," I said, voice soft because it felt weird being so openly mushy. I've been pushing down feelings for months with Morgan. It was therapeutic to finally let something real out.

"I know you do. And I know you want to figure everything out. Be the hero. And that works well in sports. You're an amazing leader. You make your mom and me proud every day."

My heart swelled. I picked at a hangnail just to feel something other than this sheer amount of pride and love. I didn't realize how much I needed to hear I was doing something right.

"It's time to take a back seat and not worry about spearheading family interventions," Warren continued. "Trust me, everything's going to be fine."

He waited until I gave him a convincing nod before moving toward the door. I relaxed my shoulders and got up to follow him inside. Mom let out an annoyingly excited yelp of joy when she saw me come into the kitchen. I accepted her quick hug and then, the stack of plates she deposited into my hands.

"Rae, your sister's home for dinner!" mom yelled, not realizing Rae was slumped on the couch nearby with her earbuds in.

"Yay," Rae said, sarcastically as she pulled an earbud out.

"Nice to see you, too," I teased.

"We literally saw each other last weekend." She turned, resting her chin on the back of the couch so she could more easily watch me set the table. When Warren excused himself to change into a clean shirt, my sister waved me over.

"Did you ask him?" she whispered, keeping a close eye on the kitchen for Mom.

I nodded. "It's fine. Everything's fine."

Rae scowled. "Everything's the opposite of fine."

"I think you're doing that thing where you start catastrophizing." I placed the last plate down and joined her on the couch so she wouldn't have to strain so hard to whisper.

"Easy for you to say, you're not home with them all the time. I could hear the neighbor's bathroom flush from across the street, that's how quiet it's been in here."

I wrinkled my nose. "I think that speaks more to the thinness of the walls."

"What are we whispering about?" Mom joked in her own hushed tone as she carried a salad bowl in one hand and a plate full of hard taco shells in the other.

"Nothing," Rae said at the same time I responded, "You and Warren."

My sister shot me daggers, which I returned with a half-shrug.

"I don't like beating around the bush," I said.

Mom's smile faltered a bit but remained intact for the most part. "There's a bush?"

"Apparently." That word earned me a pinch from Rae. I swatted her fingers as she reached for another once she realized I wasn't done spilling our guts. We were never the kind of family to keep secrets for too long.

Warren entered the room right in time. I pushed away from the couch to stand at the head of the table. "Alright, everyone, sit down. We're going to figure this shit out."

Mom shot me a warning look but was the first to pull up a seat. Rae and Warren claimed spots next to one another.

"Whispers are going down the grapevine," I noted. "Even Terrance texted earlier to ask what was going on and you know how that guy's practically allergic to his phone."

"So annoying," Rae grumbled at the mention of our survivalist, off-the-grid living brother. She wasn't wrong. Getting ahold of him got more difficult each year. He did his best to contact one of us every other week so we knew he was alive, and he still thought we were risking our futures because of our dependence on modern-day tech.

"It's time to squash this so little Miss Sunshine can go back to worrying about high school drama." I gestured my hand to Rae. "And so I can come home to do a load of laundry and steal snacks in peace."

"You actually have a load?" Mom asked. "Because if you do, please just throw in a few of the towels with it. I haven't got around to it in a while."

"Mom, focus," I said. "This is serious. This is about our future."

"Are you joining your brother?" Warren joked. "You sound like you're joining your brother."

"Oh, God, please don't leave here," Rae begged. "I'll give up my phone...on Sunday nights. I can't be left in the silence of these two, it's killing me."

I held back rolling my eyes at Rae's dramatic plea. "See, you two, you're killing her. You don't want to go on trial for murder, now do you?"

"I think I'll manage well on the stand. I've been told I could charm a wall more than once." Mom shrugged as she started shoveling salad onto her plate. She didn't offer the bowl to anyone else before she started digging in. Usually, she was polite, passing everything around until we all got a decent serving.

"Yeah," Warren agreed. He didn't reach for anything but instead watched Mom while she refused to meet his gaze. "We'll get a good lawyer."

"I don't need a good lawyer," Mom said with a little bite in her words. "I am one."

"Of course." Warren shifted in his seat, crossing his arms over his chest like he was protecting his body from her darkening glare.

"Ryn. I. Beg. Of. You." Rae clasped her hands together and pulled them over her heart.

I sighed. "Alright, out with it. What's going on?"

"Aderyn, we talked about this," Warren warned.

Mom frowned and then, looked at me. "Talked about what?"

"That you two are big kids who can work out your problems together," I said in with sarcastic pep in my voice. "And yeah, maybe I shouldn't worry about it. But I know how I get when I dig my heels in. I've learned it from the best. Sometimes, I need a little outside help to push me to say something that has to be said."

Mom's gaze softened and she reached over to pat my hand. "Aderyn, your heart's in the right place. But you don't have to worry about Warren and me. We're fine."

"Hello? Are we just going to pretend you two haven't said one thing to each other since last Friday?" Rae objected.

"It's a personal fight," Warren said, trying to keep control over his growing frown. "Between your mom and me. I know those scare you sometimes, Rae. But fighting's natural. We'll get through it."

When he said the last sentence, Mom caught his eye. Something unspoken was exchanged between them. I couldn't read it but felt less than satisfied with how the air still felt thick with things left unsaid.

"Warren's right," Mom said, pulling her gaze away from him and back to her plate. She stabbed a huge chunk of lettuce and tomatoes. And she kept stabbing, getting more aggressive by the second as she said, "We'll get through it."

Mom's fork was eventually overloaded with salad. And she surprised all of us by taking a huge bite without hesitation. My eyes widened. I looked at Rae and she wore an 'I told you so' frown.

"Now, come on," Mom said as she chewed around her food. "Let's talk about something more interesting. Anything is more interesting than this. What about school, Aderyn? And that boy. Samson."

My stomach dropped and I hurried to take my share of salad in case I needed to stuff my face like she did to avoid conversation.

"Samson?" Warren seemed to perk up. He rested his elbows on the table and watched me reach for a taco shell. "This wouldn't happen to be Samson Morgan, would it?"

"One and the same," I muttered.

"He was such a polite boy," Mom said with a smile. "You have good taste."

My cheeks burned.

Warren cleared his throat. "So, you're seeing this kid?"

"Absolutely not," I said in a voice a little too clipped and too fast. Mom laughed at the denial and Rae shook her head like I was some pre-teen with her first crush.

"The most clueless person in the world could see you two like each other," Rae spoke in a slow, uninterested drawl. She still wanted to squash our parents' beef and hell, I did too. But Mom and Warren were like sharks when it came to their children's relationships. Mom was always a huge advocate that doubled as an annoying cheerleader. Sometimes, I think she liked me being in a relationship more than I did. Warren, on the other hand, liked to play tough guy. Threats and cold stares until he got to know who I was dating one-on-one. It didn't matter what gender they were. Warren was going to be my potential partner's enemy number one until they proved themselves.

"You can like someone and not date them," I told Rae.

"But you do like him?" Warren asked.

I raised a brow. "Sure. Morgan's one of the best players in the league. He's talented, smart, and dedicated. What's not to like?"

"He's also hot." Rae gave me a smug smile. "You forgot to mention that."

I made a face.

"What is it?" Mom's question was directed to Warren. Rae and I stopped trying to look at one another because of the change in vibe.

"Samson's a good kid," Warren said.

"Then why do you look like you disapprove?" Mom asked. "You only joke about disapproving unless something's actually wrong."

"I think the kid's gone through a lot, so I'd suggest Aderyn be careful."

"Aderyn can take care of herself," I assured them. "And I'm always careful though there's no need to be since I'm not seeing the guy."

Not romantically and maybe not even sexually after the way I snapped at him at the arena. I winced at the memory, reaching for my glass of water in hopes drinking would hide my expression.

"We know you can," Warren said. "It was only a suggestion."

"You don't like him?" I asked after studying the lines on his forehead.

"What's wrong with him?" Mom leaned in, putting aside whatever their differences were for some potential gossip. "He seemed like a sweetheart. He's a sweetheart, right? Aderyn?"

I hesitated. "Sweetheart isn't the word I'd use."

Difficult. Competitive. Fucking bullheaded. Seriously charming. Kind. Patient. Considerate. Perfect at getting me to feel like I was heard and seen.

I blinked and realized my folks were staring at me like I'd just belched the ABCs unprompted.

"He's a flirt," I said. "Not in a bad way but in a way that's too noticeable to be called a sweetheart."

Rae snorted. "They're totally doing it."

"Rae," Mom and I snapped.

"What? I thought we were an open-book family," she complained. "But when conversations get hard, that rule goes out the window, I guess. Let's keep this energy up when I start dating, yeah?"

"You know what?" Warren spoke up. "I'm having dinner soon with some of the guys on the team. I believe Samson's going to show up. I'll have a one-on-one with him. Nothing serious, just going to get a better feel for him. I should get to know him better anyway."

All feeling in my body disappeared. "Oh, please, don't. He doesn't even know we're related. And if you have a one-on-one, he'll get nervous and think it's because I like him."

"I thought you did like him," Rae pointed out.

"Not like that, for the love of God." I threw her a pointed look before directing my gaze back to Warren. "Please, don't grill him. Don't scare him."

"I'm just going to talk to him." Warren smiled, seeming amused at my panic.

"Let him look out for you, Aderyn," Mom said. She didn't look as adverse to being on Warren's side anymore. "I think it's a good idea."

I pressed the heel of my hand on my closed eyes. "How did this dinner go from about you guys to about me?"

Warren chuckled. "It's just going to be a conversation. Besides, it would've been happening with or without you getting involved. I've been watching Samson this season and he's got a good head on his shoulders. I want to start introducing him to some NHL recruiters."

I pulled my hands away from my face. "Really?"

"Yeah, he's got what it takes to make a name for himself."

Those words made my stomach jump. That was exciting for Samson. I was excited for him. So much so that I almost texted him.

"He'll do great things," Warren insisted. "I'm going to make sure to get him on the right track."

I smiled at the promise. "I'm sure you will."

Chapter Twenty-Three

Sam

"That's your sixth collar adjustment in five minutes," Henrik teased in a whisper. "A hockey thing or an Aderyn thing? I never know which one's got you anxious these days."

I gave him a look and sounded a bit more pissed than I would've liked when I said, "I'm never anxious about Aderyn."

Henrik chuckled. "Sure, keep telling yourself that."

"Shut up," I sighed, trying to keep the next part in but the words were like an itch begging to be scratched. "Is it always obvious?"

"Only because I know you," Henrik promised.

Henrik, Lincoln, and I stood outside of Andretti's arcade waiting to meet up with a few girls from the hockey team. In our group chat, we agreed we needed a break from campus.

They were running late. And Henrik had convinced us to be devastatingly early. Early enough for me to have time to think about every questionable thing in my life, from the upcoming dinner with Stoll to Aderyn's belief that I didn't respect her.

Aderyn's confession weighed more heavily than whatever information I had to get at Stoll's dinner. She'd become so integrated into my life that I hated the thought of her not feeling as important as she was. She said I hadn't done anything, but I couldn't fully believe that because the look in her eyes told a different story. Somewhere down the line, I misstepped with her. I needed to make things right.

Anxious didn't begin to explain how I felt when I saw Aderyn get out of her car with two of her friends in tow. She didn't greet me at first and instead went in for the hug with Henrik and Lincoln. Andretti's lobby was packed with mostly parents trying to calm their kids long enough to slap on wristbands and decide if they wanted to do laser tag. We stood on the outskirts of everyone, trying to figure out how we wanted to split buying tokens.

"We should get the three-card bundle and split up in groups of two," Mary suggested. "Each person gets five hundred tokens."

Jas nodded in agreement. "We'll get more for our money that way."

"Thanks, moms," Aderyn teased with a shake of her head.

"It is the optimal choice." Henrik had studied the token selection before the girls arrived and came to the same conclusion earlier.

"Works for me," Lincoln bounced on the balls of his feet as he spoke. He'd agree to anything at this point because he was tired of waiting around.

"How about we make this interesting?" Aderyn asked with a teasing glint in her eyes. I wanted to move closer to her, but she stood on the opposite end of our group.

"Whoever wins the most tickets will get their meal for free. Losers pay up," Aderyn finished.

We finally met one another's gazes. There was a competitive spark in both our eyes. I smiled a little, she returned it. Despite the awkwardness that lingered between us, we still had this. Still had a base understanding of each other's motivation.

"I'm in," I said, not taking my eyes off Aderyn. She chewed her lip and looked away like she suddenly couldn't handle eye contact. I imagined taking that lip between my teeth and giving her something else to be nervous about.

"Same," Lincoln said. "You guys don't know what you're getting into. I'm a Skee-Ball champion."

"We're a team." Mary grabbed Jas's hand.

"I call Hen," Lincoln said before I could even open my mouth.

"That's..." Aderyn looked ready to protest but was unable to come up with a decent excuse.

"What's wrong?" Mary studied her friend with a genuine look of concern.

"Nothing. I was just going to say..." Aderyn met my gaze. "That sucks for you guys because I have expensive taste. So, do all your bank transfer stuff before we head to dinner."

"Definitely ordering lobster when we win," Mary said.

Lincoln laughed. "Oh, it's on."

"How do you want to play this?" I whispered into Aderyn's ear once we were in line.

I might have imagined it, but I could've seen her shoulders shiver when I spoke.

"What do you mean?" She didn't move back when I stepped closer to her. I could smell the faint hint of her perfume mixed with the peppermint oil she'd used in her hair. While our friends strategized, Aderyn and I kept looking at and away from one another, both of us unsure of where to rest our gazes.

"Should we split up?" I asked. I didn't want her to be uncomfortable around me.

She gave me a blank look. "Split...?"

"To cover more ground." I frowned, confused as to why she was confused.

"Oh." Aderyn laughed a little. "Right. The games."

A smile crept on my face. "Yeah, the games. What did you think I meant?"

"Nothing." She swallowed, looking a little guilty before she added, "Us. Our thing."

It was my turn to be confused. "Why would I end it now? Here?"

"Because I—" She looked up when our friends got to the counter. Henrik offered to use his card for the purchase. We all pulled out our phones to Venmo him money.

"I know I said some weird stuff to you last time we spoke." Aderyn shrugged like she wanted to not care, though she clearly did.

"It wasn't weird. It was honest," I said, keeping my voice low. "And I've been thinking about it ever since."

Her eyes widened. "Shit, you have? I was hoping it was one of those moments that meant more to the embarrassed person."

"You shouldn't be embarrassed." I stuffed my hand into my pocket to withstand my urge to brush my thumb across her cheek. "I like when you're being honest with me."

There she went again, chewing on her lip. If she kept this up, I'd have to find a dark corner for us to 'make up' in and we'd be buying our friends' dinner.

I closed the remaining distance between us. There was no doubt about it, from the outside we looked like a couple. And thank God we did because, at that moment, we got more company. Jack and a couple of the other guys from the team came through the door. It wasn't lost on me how Aderyn's face brightened at his presence. Nor how he studied our position like he was trying to make sense of why we were standing so close. My jaw tightened when Aderyn stepped away from me to welcome the other guys.

"Didn't realize anyone else was showing up," I said, directing most of the statement to Jack.

"Me neither." Aderyn gave him my favorite smile of hers. I had to look away for a second.

"I thought you said you couldn't make it?" Aderyn gave Jack a quick hug. So they were that close now? Fuck me.

"Other plans fell through." Jack shrugged. He gave me a quick 'what?' look. I returned it with a 'nothing' shake of my head.

"We're all teamed up now," Mary noted. "But, if you guys wanna join in on the bet, we could do some math to factor in a three-person team, right?"

Henrik nodded. "Shouldn't be too hard. We could just add each team's tickets up at the end and divide to figure out an individual average."

"Teams?" Jack asked.

Aderyn filled him in while I exchanged looks with my friends.

"Need a wedge?" Lincoln teased, but the offer was genuine. "You know I'm the king of inserting myself between things."

"No, it's cool," I promised as I watched Jack whispering something into Aderyn's ear. She rolled her eyes but had a good-natured smile on her face. She placed a hand on her cheek, a clear indication that she wanted to laugh but was too nervous to do so. My stomach churned over the fact that I even knew that about her.

Henrik handed me our token card. "Wouldn't have to look like an abandoned puppy if you just told her how you feel."

"I feel like I want to get a free meal tonight," I mumbled. "That's it."

Lincoln blew out a breath. "You sure that's it? Because you're crushing plastic and I'm pretty sure they charge for damaged card replacements."

I instantly loosened my grip on the card. One of the corners was slightly bent thanks to my pressure. My friends tried to hide their smiles.

I was supposed to be the relaxed one. The guy who didn't fall in love. This was supposed to be an easy win.

"Alright, everyone ready?" Henrik asked when the guys got their cards. He raised his brow at me.

"Ready." I nodded and followed the others into the main part of the arcade. The flickering lights, loud music, and the thick crowd weren't as overwhelming as the realization that I was going to tell Aderyn how I felt. Because if I didn't, it'd become bigger than it needed to be. And it already felt like it was crushing me.

Chapter Twenty-Four

Aderyn

"Time to stop conversing with the enemy," Morgan joked. At least, I think it was a joke. The tone and smile were there. But the look he gave Jack didn't feel teasing in the slightest.

"Right..." Jack chuckled. "See you in a bit, Ryn."

"See you." I smiled and waved. Jack and I had been hanging out a little more. Nothing serious. Definitely nothing close to sleeping together. But, it was still nice to make another friend. He was a surprisingly good listener. His snark toned down once I started to get to know him.

I turned to Morgan when Jack was out of earshot and asked, "What's your poison?"

Everyone else had already dispersed with their plans of victory. Mary and Jas were going to kill it in Dance Dance Revolution—like they always did. I think Lincoln and Henrik planned on getting most of their tickets by getting headshots on robots.

"Ryn?" he asked. "He calls you Ryn?"

I shrugged, shocked he pointed it out. "All my friends do."

He hummed, considering. "I see."

"You could, too." I gestured to him, forgetting how close we had to stand in the ever-moving crowd. My fingers brushed against his hard chest. I quickly pulled my hand back. Any physical contact outside of the bedroom felt dangerous.

Morgan shook his head at my offer. "Pass."

I scoffed. "What?"

"I'm not calling you Ryn," he said. "I don't want to be your friend."

My throat tightened but I played it off by snatching our token card out of his hands. "Ditto, Morgan. Now, follow me. I know exactly how we're going to win the boatload of our tickets."

I hurried toward the game I had in mind. With each step I took, I felt a little more grounded and removed from his words. We didn't need to be friends. In fact, it was for the best that he said that. It was a perfect reminder of where we stood.

"Jacobs," Morgan called. He nearly got separated from me when a sea of kids ran in between us. "Slow down."

"Or you could just keep up," I said.

When he finally got through the throng of people, he grabbed my hand. I inhaled sharply at the feel of his palm against mine. He didn't seem the least bit fazed at the contact.

"Well?" The look in his eyes was daring. He wanted me to say something about the handholding.

Our fingers entwined. I couldn't tell if it was him or me who did it.

"You good?" he asked.

I turned away from him before he could coax anything out of me. My fingers tightened around his as I pulled him behind me. It felt so natural to have him following me. His hand in mine was mundane and extraordinary. How did being with Morgan make me feel like I was simultaneously safe and on the edge of a cliff?

"Here." I stopped in front of the basketball goals.

Morgan laughed. "Here?"

"Come on." I gave him a knowing look. "You can't tell me that your family didn't force you to play basketball in hopes you'd give up hockey. It's a rite of passage."

Morgan nodded with an amused glint in his eyes. "My dad's dream was for me to be the first draft pick of the NBA. He still thinks I have time to change my mind. Even told me I'd be a better pick than half the guys on Mendell's team because I'm more 'well-rounded.'"

I covered my mouth to laugh. "Seriously? God, I love a supportive parent but sometimes they really don't understand how things work."

Morgan nodded in agreement. "He tries. Hockey's just not his thing and is probably never going to be."

My smile faded a little. "Does he ever come to your games?"

"No." Morgan didn't look disappointed about it. "The drive's too long and he still doesn't understand the rules enough to be able to enjoy it. But he tapes all my games. He might be one of the last to have a working VHS player and blank tapes. We could own a rental shop and fill all the shelves with my worst moments on the ice."

"I'd definitely be your biggest customer."

He smiled. "I'm sure you would. You are kind of obsessed with me."

I shoved his shoulder playfully. "Obviously, I'd just be in it for the loyalty rewards and the chance to see your mistakes so I can finally have something to hold over your head."

"All I heard was that I'm otherwise perfect."

He moved closer and for a second was only a breath away. I think he was going to kiss me here, in public, with no promise of sex just...a normal kiss.

I whipped the card up, holding it between our faces. The speed of my hand shocked us both.

"I'm going to need your perfection," I said, breathless and my heart racing. "Channel it into the hoops."

"As opposed to...?"

I frowned. "Nothing. Your perfection is needed nowhere else but in these balls."

As soon as those words left my mouth I winced. Morgan laughed, shaking his head.

"You're cute when you're nervous and want to win," he noted.

"Am I?" I swiped our card to release the balls from their gate. They rolled down as the timer went off.

"Very." Morgan winked. Before I could react, he picked up a ball. It went straight through the net, and so did the next one. He wasn't even trying that hard.

I scrambled to catch up. No way was I going to be the dead weight on our team. And no way was I going to let his compliment go to my head.

Morgan and I literally broke a sweat trying to one-up each other in basketball. We'd gone through ten rounds and by my count, I'd won six of them.

"Air hockey," Morgan said, out of breath and slightly frustrated at his defeat.

"Oh, come on. That's a little on the nose," I teased.

"You scared?"

My mouth turned downward. "No. Of course not."

"Come on then." He led the way this time, grabbing onto my hand like it was second nature. I widened my stride to keep up with his quick pace. He walked me to my side of the table before claiming his. I swallowed a laugh at the determined wrinkle on his forehead.

Halfway through our first game, I knew I had him beat.

"Shit." He pulled back when the puck entered his goal for the fifth time. "How are you so good at this?"

I shrugged. "I was born to win."

He chuckled, not looking convinced by the answer so I added,

"It helps to be relaxed when playing. Lately, I've kind of wanted to just have more fun and be chill. Less striving for greatness and approval."

"Is it that easy?"

I smiled. "No, of course not. It's a very conscious effort."

He laughed.

"But I'm trying."

We spent the next hour bouncing from game to game. He got less frustrated and more intrigued with how I managed to keep a level head—even when our scores got close. In the end, I pointed out something about him I noticed a long time ago.

"You kind of retreat into yourself," I said, carefully. "Whenever you think you're going to lose, you go on the defensive and try to maintain a status quo. While you sporadically fight for neutral ground, I figure out a way to get the upper hand."

He blinked, surprised. "Really? I didn't think about it like that. But that's a great note. You're good at that. Catching those small details about people most brush off."

I nodded. I was glad Morgan didn't seem opposed to my feedback. He'd given tips on how to be a better flirt, so it felt right to offer something in return.

"I'm just so used to..." Morgan shook his head, not sure how to word what he felt.

"Fighting so hard to play for today that you're not thinking about next week?" I asked.

"That's one way to put it," he agreed.

"Just remember, survival's great. Necessary. But leveling up is also vital. Like, how my team's trying to be more than only good players. We have to be personalities online, too."

He nodded, understanding washing over his expression. "How's it going by the way? Our comment section's definitely more active than before."

"Great, actually." I smiled and looked over my shoulder to make sure none of my girls were nearby before I shared the next part. I wanted to surprise them with the information later.

"Coach Bella's close with some of the people who work in the tech department on the school's website. A little birdie told her that traffic on the site increased on the women's page by fifty percent. And our upcoming game against the Giants has a slight uptick in ticket sales. Not stadium full level but we can fill more than one section."

"Sounds like a big win."

I nodded. "But wanna hear something even better? I think I helped someone become more comfortable in their own skin. There was this girl at our last hockey game. She couldn't have been older than twelve. She said she wanted to play hockey because she saw us out there. That part feels better than the crowds, the likes, and ticket sales altogether."

My heart warmed thinking about Avori's words at the rink. The determined look on her little face was still clear as day in my mind.

He smiled wide. "That's incredible, Aderyn. You should be proud. We should be celebrating."

I spread my arms out, gesturing around us. "What do you think all this gaming and my winning was?"

Morgan shook his head and laughed. Before he could respond, Lincoln appeared at his elbow.

"We're breaking for pizza and wings because I'm starving and can't wait for a winner to be declared. Wanna join?" His friend nudged his chin toward a booth where everyone else was gathering.

"I could eat," I agreed.

Morgan raised a brow. "Sure you want to disrupt your winning streak?"

"It's not a disruption. I can take all the break I want and still kick your ass in any game here."

He chuckled. "Of course, you could."

Both sides of the booth were almost full. Morgan and I had to squeeze in on opposite ends. Our friends had already ordered for the table but that didn't stop either of us from looking at the menu.

As I half-tuned into Mary and Henrik's musings on capitalism and its effects on the toy-making industry, my foot accidentally grazed Morgan's ankle. I pulled it back instantly and looked his way to indicate it was a mistake. He kept his eyes on the menu, not meeting my gaze. Only a few seconds passed before the side of his foot tapped against mine. He still didn't look at me and decided to join in on the conversation. Underneath the table, his leg stretched, giving me no chance in avoiding another ankle graze.

I tried to keep my smile a normal size. This was by far the silliest game we've taken part in and surprisingly the most fun. There was no prize to win or victory to gloat about. Morgan didn't seem tense when I got the upper hand and placed my foot on top of his.

There was a unique kind of intimacy in our movements. My heart hammered in my chest when Morgan leaned forward in his seat to have an easier time reaching me. I nearly lost all control over my expression when he decided to grab my ankle when I dared to inch it a little higher. The pressure of his fingers on my skin sent sparks up my calves.

He massaged my inner ankle with his thumb. The tight, focused circle made me want to lean back and close my eyes. I didn't, of course. Morgan and I snuck glances at one another. He tugged down my sock to reveal more of my skin. This guy had seen me naked but the feel of him touching my ankle was orgasm worthy. Especially when he started tracing small shapes. Each movement was like an attempt to communicate something. Circles, triangles, squares, and eventually hearts.

I shook my head when he smiled at me. Jesus, he was being cheesy, and I was eating it up.

When the food finally arrived at our table, I expected Morgan to let me go. Instead of releasing me, he rested the heel of my foot on his side of the bench. He ate with one hand while the other gently cupped my ankle. Somehow, this felt better than cuddling. I felt wanted. Needed. Cared for.

I followed his lead, eating while pretending to care about what was going on around us. No one noticed Morgan's possessive grip on me. He didn't even address it afterward.

Such a simple, little thing. Yet, it was all I could think about for the rest of the week.

Chapter Twenty-Five

Sam

I released a heavy breath as I pulled onto Stoll's street. This was it. I was finally getting a shot at forcing this guy out of the program.

Jack was waiting for me at the edge of the driveway. He waved to a few of the guys to go in when he saw me coming up the walk.

"We all set?" He looked over his shoulder like he was afraid of Stoll appearing out of thin air.

"We are." I nodded. "You said the office is upstairs, right?"

Jack nodded and lowered his voice, tone barely audible as he said, "Best time to sneak away is after dinner. He likes to shoot the breeze in their game room. We always play a few rounds of pool. Stoll doesn't pay much attention to who comes in and out. And he drinks...a lot."

"So, you make sure to keep him focused on the game and drinks. I'll slip out and see if I can find something damning," I decided. "Simple."

Jack's face was a little paler than usual. "Simple."

I frowned. "What is it?"

We'd gone over this plan multiple times. He filled me in on the layout of the house, prepped me on some conversation starters in case I ran into Stoll's wife, and even showed me how to pick a desk lock—which was something he refused to elaborate on how he learned.

Jack shifted his weight from one foot to the other. There was already sweat on his brow. I felt a little guilty for dragging him into this and convincing him to be a whistle-blower. Like he said before, the reasons for some of our teammates agreeing to this scam were complicated.

"Look, I know this is hard," I whispered. "Those guys in there trust us. They trust you."

He laughed, humorlessly. "Is this supposed to make me feel any better?"

"You're doing the right thing. The fair thing."

"Fair." Jack shook his head. "Nothing about this is fair."

"It doesn't feel like that now, but one day..." I stopped because that was bullshit. He was right.

"Fair's not in the cards for the majority of people," I tried again. "That's the hardest pill to swallow. But I think this way is better than letting someone on the outside run with the story, you know? If we go to the Dean, we could speak up for the rest of the guys. We'll get them a chance to explain themselves. We'll remind the board that there are gray areas."

"And you're sure you see the gray areas?"

I frowned. "Of course I do."

Jack studied me for a second. He looked like he wanted to believe me but couldn't. "Fred's scholarship nearly got taken away from him when he couldn't make the grades and put in enough time on the ice. He's got no family waiting for him at home. Without hockey, he'll have to drop out. He nearly killed himself when he thought he wasn't going to keep his spot — that's not hyperbole."

My jaw stiffened at the information. Jack continued without falter, "Daniel's mom is in and out of the hospital. He spends most of his nights there. Emerson's folks have been in and out of shelters since he moved on campus. He's been couch surfing since he was in middle school. Those are the gray areas, Sam."

"I... I understand." I hadn't gotten that much out of my guys. They told me things, but I hadn't gotten as deep as I thought. But they'd done so with Jack. Before this semester, I would've felt jealous at this realization. Because first, he'd captured the attention of Aderyn and now, he seemed to be doing a better job at creating a bond with the guys. Instead of jealousy, all I felt was gratefulness for Jack's presence on the team. I couldn't help but wonder if I was in the right position...if I was the right person as the Captain.

"You understand, but I need you to remember," Jack said, earnestly.

"I will," I promised. "Jack, it's not you guys versus the rest of us. It's all of us versus him and whoever else thinks they can take advantage of us. We're on the same team. Always."

S toll's house was an impressive three stories. The outside was designed to look like a Spanish villa. The yard was huge and well-manicured with shrubs shaped like animals.

He opened the door as soon as Jack and I stepped onto the porch. He laughed at my impressed expression when he bragged about his security system.

"Here, I'll show you the whole setup." Stoll grinned ear to ear with excitement. I suppose that's what happened when you become a homeowner. You got a kick out of how decked out you could make your space.

Jack didn't look interested in Stoll's offer and excused himself to join the guys who were already in the living room. "Got a look last time and it's... very impressive."

Stoll pointed at Jack. "Knows what he's talking about. Now, come on, follow me, Sammy."

I winced at the nickname behind his back while following him down the hall. As soon as I entered Stoll's surveillance room, my stomach dropped with disappointment. My mouth went dry as I took in the stack screens.

Why the hell did Jack not tell me about this?

"State-of-the-art technology here," Stoll was saying. "Sensors in the front and back yards. I get a ping whenever something larger than a bug trips it."

I joined him behind a large, mahogany desk. The room looked like it was originally supposed to be a reading nook or sunroom. There was barely enough space for the number of screens and cords running all over the place. My foot almost got tangled in a few as I moved closer to take note of where the cameras were facing.

As I scanned the screens, I saw a camera placed in almost every room on the first floor. The guys were in the living room with drinks in hand and talking in small groups. There was a woman with her back to us in the kitchen, taking something out of the oven.

"Wow." I whistled. I sounded impressed while on the inside, my stomach was churning. There was no way in hell I'd be able to sneak into his office without getting caught. Jack wasn't going to hear the end of this.

"My wife thinks it's a little much but..." Stoll shrugged and placed his hands on his hips. I've never seen this guy smile so easily. It was like obsessive surveillance was a turn-on or something. "When you have a family to protect you go hard."

"Right." I nodded, trying to smile like I could relate. "I get it. My old man's a stickler for rules. He'd be taking notes right now. Maybe I should take some for him."

Stoll laughed. "Once you become a parent, safety's the number one priority. And I have daughters so I'm extra cautious."

Stoll was looking at me strangely now. His smile wasn't as wide, and his gaze was challenging. I continued to smile even though this felt a lot like he was trying to intimidate me. But I don't know why. I didn't know his daughters. I didn't even know he had kids until recently.

"Understandable, sir," I hoped the respectful title would win me some points. From the unchanged look on his face, it was a no-go.

"I'd do anything for them," he said, voice a little lower now as he stared at the screens again.

I didn't know what to say, so I just repeated, "Understandable, sir."

He laughed then and clapped my shoulder. "You seem tense, bud. You alright?"

Well, we took a straight beeline into your fully-equipped security room where you're standing in front of a million screens talking like you're Liam Neeson. Sure, I'm perfect. Never felt more at home.

What I went with instead was: "It's been a long week."

"I'll say. You boys have been really giving it your all this semester. Don't think I haven't noticed all the extra time you've been dedicating to your teammates. You're a huge reason why the team's gotten so far. You're an incredible role model. Honestly, irreplaceable."

"Thanks, I appreciate that." Though I did find it strange that these compliments were coming halfway through the season.

Stoll and I hadn't talked much since the one night when he saved my ass from spending a night at the sheriff's department.

As a freshman, there's nothing quite like that first night away from home when you move to college. Suddenly, the world is bigger than you ever imagined and no one's around to judge you. I got a little drunk and high to celebrate being out from underneath my family's thumb. I was finally able to be myself after years of living in a conservative house.

But that night had consequences.

I called him because I didn't have my phone at the time—but even if I had, I wouldn't have been able to bring myself to ask one of the guys to come get me. And my family was out of the question. I'd always been what Stoll was currently praising me for. A role model. I've always been present, responsible, and respectable. Acting out for a second was fun, but ultimately, one of my most shameful moments. I never had a repeat incident. But anytime I was close to Stoll, I was reminded of it, and that was more than enough to keep my distance.

Stoll kept his distance, too. For other reasons, I was sure. I had a theory—which wasn't much of theory and more of fact now that I'd spoken with Jack—that every guy Stoll's been buddy-buddy with owes him something. And the reason he hasn't come collecting from me is that he can't find a use for me yet.

I didn't need money like the rest of the guys. I wasn't interested in thrill-seeking like I was freshman year. He didn't have a place for me on his chess board yet. I could tell from the look in his eyes that he was anxious to place me, though.

"Come on." He patted my shoulder once more before starting out of the room. "Let's join the rest of the guys. Dinner should be ready soon."

I gave the screens a final look before leaving the room. As soon as we stepped into the living room, Stoll garnered most of the attention—which he relished. And because he was so distracted being the main character of the night, I pulled out my phone to text Jack:

Sam: What the hell? This guy's got a camera around every turn. That might have been something worth MENTIONING.

Jack barely blinked when he saw the text. He even took his precious time responding, finishing his conversation first. I watched him slowly finish his drink and walk to the kitchen to throw away the can. My phone buzzed while he was still outside of the room.

Jack: Relax. There's no camera outside of his office. Second floor's not covered.

Sam: You sure?

Jack: Yeah. His wife didn't want the cameras upstairs so there's only one near the staircase that can easily be avoided. You'll see the blind spot as soon as you clear the stairs.

I breathed a sigh of relief. Well, that was one less thing to worry about.

The night seemed to drag, mostly consisting of Stoll reliving his glory days. We all sat in the living room, listening to stories I'm sure he's told thousands of times. Emerson, one of our defensive players, seemed particularly antsy tonight and decided to bait Stoll into a pre-dinner game of pool. All the other guys looked relieved at this suggestion, hopping out of their seats to ensure this game was happening.

Jack raised his brow at me when the group started migrating toward the family room.

You sure, I mouthed, needing to know I'd be safe.

Jack nodded and nudged his chin toward the stairs.

I cleared my throat and asked Stoll, "Could I use your bathroom?"

"Sure, bud." Stoll pointed down the hall, away from the staircase. "The guest bath is right there."

I tried not to show the disappointment on my face. "Thanks."

"Hey, didn't you mention something about fixing the table tennis net?" Jack asked, talking a bit louder than he usually did but it matched Stoll's energy. He turned his back to me and flicked his fingers quickly, indicating I should hurry.

Jack would have to distract him long enough for me to bypass the downstairs bath, hurry up the stairs to his office and look through as many things as possible. From the confidence in Jack's tone, I had no doubt I'd be covered.

I took the carpeted staircase, skipping two at a time. Jack had been right about the easy-to-see blind spot. As soon as I was at the top of the stairs, I noticed how the lens was facing the hallway. If I slid close to the wall for a few feet, the chances of it catching me were slim to none.

My heart hammered as I kept an ear out for anyone following me up the stairs. I could still hear Stoll and the rest of the guys hamming it up. Once I got to a darker part of the hall, my shoulders finally relaxed. The calm didn't stick around for long because one of the closed doors opened and I slammed right into someone.

She gasped, stepping back with wide eyes. I froze, brows knitted in confusion.

"Aderyn?"

Chapter Twenty-Six

Sam

I grabbed Aderyn's hand before she could say anything and pulled her back into the room she'd exited. Except, it hadn't been a room but a walk-in closet full of linens and cleaning supplies. It was surprisingly spacious, but we still found ourselves standing within a foot as we gawked at one another.

"What the hell?" she asked, eyes widening with confusion when I closed the door behind us.

"Exactly," I agreed. The light above us was dim. I could barely make out her features. She wore a skirt that reached her ankles and a top that fell off her shoulders. It took a lot to not get distracted by how soft her skin looked and the decent amount of cleavage the top allowed.

"What are you doing here?" My voice was hard and admittedly accusatory.

She scoffed at my tone. "I live here. What are *you* doing here?"

"I—wait, you live here?"

She took a step back and crossed her arms over her chest. The pout on her lips shouldn't have made my dick stiffen so easily but it did. "That's what I said."

"With Stoll?" I asked. A thousand possibilities raced through my mind and the main ones made my blood boil.

Aderyn scoffed when she saw my expression harden. "And my mom and sister. Jesus, did you think I was fucking him or something?"

"It crossed my mind," I admitted, relieved I was far off base because damn...I mean, she was supposed to explore her options but the power dynamic in that one would've been concerning, to say the least. Heartbreaking to say at most.

"Gross." Her nose wrinkled. "No, he's my stepdad."

I went tense again. This was a better situation than them sleeping together but still, concerning. "Why don't you sound so sure?"

She frowned. "Because I prefer most people not know."

"You prefer most people to not know?" I laughed humorlessly and pressed a palm to my chest. "I'm most people?"

"Yeah," she said, though that didn't sound so sure either.

"We've been sleeping together for months," I reminded her.

"So I owe you my life story?"

I pinched the bridge of my nose. "Oh, my God."

"What else would you like to know, Morgan? I broke my arm in the second grade because I thought I could fly. Didn't have my first kiss until senior year with a girl from Switzerland. I have a deathly fear of hamsters."

"Hamsters...you're... this is ridiculous." I rubbed my hand over my face. "How long have you been Stoll's daughter?"

"Why does that matter?" She reclaimed the space in between us. The air smelled of her trademark peppermint oil. I had to press my nails into my palm to keep my brain on track. The office. I was here for the office and not to fuck the AD's daughter in a closet.

"I think I should be the one asking the questions since you're sneaking around my house," she countered and gave my shoulder a nice shove. "What are you doing up here?"

"Nothing. The bathroom," I said, quickly.

"Guys use the bathroom downstairs." Aderyn didn't believe me for one second. "Try again."

"I lost my way. I don't take directions very well."

She snorted. "Boy, stop lying. I've seen you in bed. You follow directions like a man on a mission."

"I'm flattered." I smiled.

Aderyn rolled her eyes. "You damn well know your strengths. Now, don't change the subject."

"Of course, I know my strengths, but it's always nice to be appreciated," I murmured and stepped closer to her. Was this the time for flirting? No. But Aderyn was too irresistible for me not to indulge for a minute. I could make time if it meant coaxing a smile out of her.

"Stop that," she said, trying to stay on topic but I could see the twitching of her mouth. "This is serious."

"I'm only saying I appreciate that you appreciate me." As I continued moving closer, she moved back. It didn't take long for her to bump into the wall.

"God, you're ridiculous." She held up a hand to press against my chest. Instead of pushing me away like I thought she would, her grip tightened on my shirt. I bent closer so our noses brushed against one another. Her exhale on my mouth made my dick strain, desperate for release. Only her. She was the only woman who could get me this turned on when I had higher priorities to focus on.

Get it together, man. The office.

"Tell me the truth," she whispered against my mouth. I nearly moaned at the low tone of her voice. She wasn't doing this on purpose before, but she was now. "And maybe I'll give you a reward."

I placed my hands on the wall behind her, hoping that the cool plaster would calm me down. She bit down her bottom lip as she waited for a response. Aderyn was taking a page from my book but hell, I didn't care. She had me hook, line, and sinker. I taught her well.

"You're talking to me like I'm some puppy you've trained," I said, trying to pretend like I was offended. But, honestly, the idea of being on a leash for Aderyn sounded like a good time.

"Not a puppy. Just a typical guy." She shook her head with a small smile that made me want to kiss her until we both forgot why we were butting heads in the first place.

"Tell me, Morgan." She leaned in closer, so her mouth brushed close to my ear. "You don't have long before Warren finds out you're missing."

"I'm..." My smile faded. Her calling our AD by his first name shattered whatever spell I'd slipped under.

Since Stoll was her stepdad then did Aderyn know about the gambling? My back stiffened and I pushed away from the wall to get a better look at her.

"What?" Aderyn noted my change in mood. She cleared her throat like she was embarrassed about her flirting.

"Do you know about these dinners?" I asked.

Her forehead wrinkled. "Dinners? That he has with the guys on the hockey team? Of course. Happens every other week or so."

"It's just dinner to you?"

Aderyn looked at me like I'd grown a second head. "Of course, it's not just dinner. It's networking. Men's team getting a leg up as per usual."

My eyebrows furrowed. "You're upset?"

"Upset's not the right word. I'm more annoyed at the realization that no matter how much I try to help my team, it's the strings behind the scenes that really matter."

"Stoll doesn't have these dinners with the women's teams?" I knew the answer before the words left her lips. Of course not. Why gamble on games for a team who weren't pulling in the crowds? No one was going to bet on a game that only a handful of people watched. Where was the fun in that? I wiped my fingers against my mouth, feeling ashamed even thinking that.

Aderyn sighed. "No, he doesn't. No one in the athletic department does."

I opened my mouth, but she beat me to the punch.

"And no, I don't like asking. It makes me feel weird. But that doesn't mean I have my head so far up my ass that I won't accept his help if he offered it to the team. But he doesn't. So, I'm going to work with or without his help. And we're going to make it. No matter how overlooked we are."

My jaw tightened at the tremble of her tone when she said 'overlooked.' This woman was by far the most capable person I've ever met and the thought of anything that made her feel the opposite angered me. "Fuck, I wish you never felt like that. You never deserve to feel like that. And what you said to me before—in the infirmary—I'm sorry for contributing to that feeling."

"I told you, that was a me thing," she promised. "It's my insecurities creeping in."

"No. I could've done better to support your team in the past. You guys do your best to make our games during the season. You come to every fundraiser and after-party. That energy was never matched on our end. I *will* do better. To support you and your team. I'm sorry for how long it's taken me. I'm sorry for how unfair this is for you."

"Life's not fair," she said, an eerie reminder of my conversation with Jack earlier.

"It's not," I agreed. "But I'm going to do everything I can to make sure that doesn't apply to you. You deserve everything and that's what I'm going to give you. I want to give you everything."

The weight of my words made me feel like we were in quicksand. I didn't flail, though. I refused to backtrack. She needed to know I meant it. I needed her to know I was in this for real.

"What the hell am I supposed to say to that?" Aderyn asked in a near whisper.

"Nothing. Anything." I shrugged.

"You're playing the part of devoted lover a little too seriously. Calm down," she warned.

"I'm not playing. It's not a game to me. Not anymore."

Her jaw tightened. "You're confusing the hell out of me. It feels like you're trying to work me."

I groaned. "I'm not trying to work you."

"Really? Because you still haven't told me why you're up here. If you asked me, I'd say you were looking for something?"

I replaced my hands on the wall behind her. "I told you, the restroom."

She didn't know about the gambling. Aderyn's moral compass wouldn't let her keep it in for this long. I knew that much about her. Her refusal to ask Stoll for help felt like even more evidence of her being in the dark. They never spoke on campus. I've seen them in the same building plenty of times without ever guessing they even knew one another outside of school. Unless she was a master manipulator, Aderyn had no clue her stepdad was running a successful con.

My knowledge of it now posed as a wedge in our relationship. Did I tell her that Stoll wasn't just playing favorites with the men's team but committing fraud? How would that affect her life? Her family? The news would put them under a microscope. Once the inevitable investigation started, would they look at her record, too? Would they wonder if she got onto the team on her skill alone?

"You look like you're about to throw up," Aderyn said with worry and pressed a hand against my chest.

I stared at her for a moment before leaning in to kiss her. She made a noise of surprise but wrapped her arms around my neck in response.

I just needed a moment to think. Time to figure out how I was going to tell her. How I was going to change her life for what might be worse.

Chapter
Twenty-Seven

Aderyn

M organ pinned me against the wall in our linen closet. His grip was firm, one hand on my ass and the other cupped my cheek.

I was going to let him get away with whatever he'd been doing. He won this round because of what he'd said and how he said it.

Everything. He promised me everything with enough surety in his voice to convince me we would last longer than a few months. The look in his eyes told me he meant it. The romantic in me wanted to believe it. And I let myself for a moment. Long enough for him to tug my skirt up and yank down my underwear. I stepped out of them without hesitation. The second he pressed his fingers against my clit, I leaned my head back to focus on keeping my noise down.

My parents were downstairs with a group of hockey players in the living room. This was not the time or place, but I didn't have it in me to stop him.

"I should go back down there," Morgan whispered against me. His teeth lightly raked across my neck. I clawed at his back when two of his fingers sunk into my pussy.

"So go," I told him between moans. The sound of his fingers pumping in and out was far louder and hotter than usual.

He pulled back so I could see the smile on his face. "And leave you this wet?"

I laughed. "I know how to take care of myself. Remember?"

His eyes darkened. The low groan in the back of his throat made my walls clench around his fingers. Morgan thrust deeper. His thumb circled my clit in short, quick motions. I bit down on my bottom lip so hard it hurt.

"I'd like to see that again. You taking care of yourself with that vibrator. That's still the sexiest thing I've ever seen," he said before claiming my mouth. I parted my lips, accepting his tongue.

"Maybe I'll send you something...one day," I teased when he pulled back. "But I'm a very scratch my back, I'll scratch yours kind of girl when it comes to those things."

Morgan laughed. It was deep and dark. If we had the space and the time, I didn't doubt he'd fuck me senseless tonight.

"Deal," he promised. "For now..."

He removed his hand from my face to join the other one on my pussy. One hand went to work solely on my clit, slowly circling. The other slipped inside of me. Two fingers became three once I was wet enough. I tried to keep an ear out for creaking on the staircase or footsteps in the hall, but the sound of my whimpers mixed with his words of encouragement drowned out everything.

"Look at me, Aderyn," he pleaded.

My heart fluttered at his gentle tone. I opened my half-closed eyes.

"I know you can take care of yourself," Morgan said, giving my clit just enough pressure to have me on the edge of climax. "It's one of the sexiest things about you. But I want the chance to do it. Will you let me, beautiful? Let me take care of you?"

I nodded, numbly. At this point, I'd agree to let him have my firstborn child as long as he kept touching me.

"Say it for me." He nuzzled my neck. "Say it."

"Take care of me," I whispered and tightened my arms around his neck. "Please, Sam. I want you to take care of me."

"I'm Sam now? Finally, Sam?" he teased.

"Don't," I warned.

He chuckled but didn't push it. His lips were hot against mine, parting my mouth to remind me that even if he listened to my warning he'd never completely behave. I loved that about him. I loved his determination to go after what he wanted.

I kept my mouth on him as I came because I didn't trust myself to not scream his name. Morgan didn't let up for a second. His fingers still worked me until I could barely stand the pleasure. He took on my weight when my legs gave out. A sudden warm gush of wetness flowed down my thighs in the middle of my climax. I pulled away from his lips in fear I'd somehow peed. Morgan shook his head when he saw the worry in my eyes.

"You're squirting," he said, voice strained from lust. His fingers were still buried deep inside me. "Making a beautiful mess on me. I told you I'd take care of you."

My vision was blurry, and my ears buzzed. Morgan continued to play with my pussy until I caught my breath long enough to tell him I needed him to stop.

"Had enough?" He pulled his fingers out of me, licking each one like I was the best thing he's ever tasted.

I laughed. "I can't feel my legs. So, yes. For now, that's more than enough."

"I can hold you up if you'd like." He smiled to show he was teasing, but the look in his eyes said otherwise.

We both took a moment to catch our breath. Morgan grabbed one of the towels, cleaning me up. I held onto his shoulder once he knelt to wipe my thighs. A shiver ran down my spine when he playfully licked my clit. He chuckled at my post-climax tremors and tugged my panties into place.

"I'm going on a trip this weekend," I blurted when he stood up.

"Okay?" He looked as confused as I felt.

I wanted him to be there. To experience the cabin with me. To experience everything with me. Suddenly, the future felt more exciting with the possibility of him beside me making silly jokes and challenging me to silly competitions. I was going to lose this bet to him. For the first time in forever, I didn't care about a loss.

"Up to the mountains with some girls on the hockey team. And I invited some of your guys, too," I said.

"Oh." Something changed in his eyes "Jack?"

I shrugged. "Yeah, he'll be there."

He looked away for a second. "Aderyn..."

"You should come," I said quickly because it sounded like he was about to reject the invite. "I want you to come."

"You want me?" His eyes search mine, looking for something deeper than a yes.

"Please?" I tried, hoping that'd be enough.

Morgan hesitated for a second longer before saying, "I'll come on one condition."

"What's that?"

"You let me change my prize. I need to change my prize."

My heart sank. He was talking about our bet now? So, all that talk about "everything" was just...talk.

I crossed my arms over my chest, walls slowly going up. "Depends on what it is."

"I want...I-I want to go out with you. For real. On a real date. I want you to give me a real chance," he said.

I went numb, shoulders sagging as his words sunk in. "Are you serious, Morgan?"

"Something real where you always call me by my first name," he continued, sounding more confident with each word. "And we forget about hockey and competition and just be ourselves. Aderyn and Sam. Not captains. Not teammates. Just...ourselves."

"Why?" I didn't believe him. I wanted to but couldn't because the broken part of me thought this was too good to be true.

"It's what I want." He smiled. "I'm going to win...But that doesn't mean you stop trying. I don't want what I feel to get in the way of you experiencing the casual relationships you want this semester. Don't throw this because of me."

My heart squeezed, confused at the encouragement. My mind scrambled to catch up with what this meant.

"Do I look like the type to throw a game?" It was the only sentence I could manage to say. Leaning into cockiness felt safer than telling him I couldn't see anyone else because he took up all the space.

He paused, studying me intently. My eyes widened when he leaned in for a kiss. It was gentle and sweet. He was chock-full of surprises tonight.

"No." He pulled back slightly. "You're as honest as they come. Whoever wins between us will do it fair and square."

Chapter Twenty-Eight

Sam

"**I** should have gone up." Jack pressed his fingers to his temple. "I don't know how long I can take knowing that I'm about to stab those guys in the back. This needs to be finished."

"You're not stabbing them in the back," I assured. It was a feat trying to keep someone else calm when your own mind was frantic.

Henrik shook his head. "He's right, Sam. If you knew something would keep you from handling things, you should have sent him up."

We were in my room, re-grouping and trying to come up with another plan since I fucked us over the first time.

"It's not like I knew she was going to be there," I snapped. "I'm going to handle it."

"Are you?" Jack asked, tone as clipped and vicious as mine. "Because from what I'm gathering, you dropped the ball because you got distracted by the AD's daughter."

"Let's not pretend like you would've done any better."

He raised a brow. "What's that supposed to mean?"

"Don't play clueless. You can't pull it off," I said.

"Alright." Henrik held up his hands. "We can sit here and cry over spilled milk or we can make another plan."

Jack and I stared at one another for a second. I backed off first, walking to the other side of the room. Henrik followed me. He stayed quiet while I pressed my forehead against the cold wall.

"She…" I sighed and lightly pounded my fist against the wall twice.

"What?" Henrik placed his hands on his hips, waiting for my explanation.

"She's…This will change shit for her."

"I would imagine. It's going to change stuff for all of us. But it doesn't matter at this point. It needs to happen because what's the alternative?"

"He gets away with it," I muttered.

"Exactly." Henrik's calm tone was like medicine for my nerves. "If you get a second shot, do you think you can do it?"

"I can." I felt his eyes on me and met his gaze. "I will."

"And you'll factor Aderyn out of the equation?"

My pause spoke volumes.

"Sam, you haven't brought anyone home since you started whatever it is you're doing with her." His voice was too low for the still anxious Jack to hear from across the room. "And you don't seem antsy to move on to the next girl."

"I…"

"You're happy with her."

I sighed but nodded. "So much so that I'm scared of how this could end. I don't want it to end, Hen."

His smile was sympathetic. "I know. But you have to prepare for it regardless. No matter how many times you plan this out in your head, it's still going to change her world. You can't work around it. There's no perfect play for this scenario."

"This might ruin her family," I whispered.

"This is Stoll's doing. Not ours. Not yours," he said.

I nodded, my mind still doing its best to think of anything I could do to soften this blow. There was nothing, though. Hen knew what he was talking about. The only way we got over this was through.

"We'll go to the Dean together. You tell Aderyn you're doing it and you tell her you want to be together. Afterward, we get Stoll fired and deal with the consequences. Together," he said.

"I don't think I can have both"

"Who says you can't?"

"You think she's going to want to be with the guy that ruined her dad's career? Who could possibly ruin hers? They're going to investigate everything Stoll's touched. Her acceptance into the program will be high on their list."

"I don't think you're giving Aderyn enough credit. You're acting like she's not going to understand the nuance. She earned her spot. You know that. I know that."

"But the board doesn't. They could twist it and ruin everything she's worked for."

"Look, you've never been good at handling failure and disappointment."

"Don't. I'm not in the mood for a heart-to-heart."

"I don't care," Henrik continued. "I know your folks put a lot of pressure on you and middle school was hell. But no one around here expects you to be perfect. Let me get the information. I don't need an invite. I still know how to get in and out of places I have no business being."

I shook my head when he raised a knowing brow.

"I'll finish this," he promised.

"No. There is no point in risking you getting into trouble again." I took a deep breath. "I'll do it. I'll start with telling her. It'll be before the next game."

Jack perked up at the declaration.

"Which is after the cabin trip." Henrik sounded disapproving. "I'm assuming you're telling her there?"

"Yes." I looked outside of my window. The drive was covered in snow. This was my favorite time of year and all I felt these days was sick to my stomach.

"In a place dubbed the most beautiful and romantic getaway this side of the country?" Henrik asked.

"I'm doing it," I said, firmly. "Afterward, you guys are coming with me to the Dean, right?"

Henrik and Jack nodded.

"Remember to be ready for our disqualification for the rest of the season," Henrik reminded me. "There's no way the NCAA is going to let us continue while the investigation's going on."

My chest tightened. Jack took a seat in my office chair and muttered an 'oh, shit' into his hands.

"I know. It's a wrap. We'll start over." I directed my next sentence to Jack. "This roadblock isn't an end."

"The way my stomach's turning, it feels more like a ledge," Jack mumbled.

Chapter Twenty-Nine

Aderyn

W e had a party of nine going to Burn Mountain. Mary, Jas, Kaya, and I piled into my car. While Sam, Lincoln, Henrik, Finn, and Jack were split between two rides.

The drive was long. Even with good traffic, we spent most of Friday on the road. Lincoln convinced us to download an app that was like a walkie-talkie, and it was a surprisingly fun way to stay in contact.

"There is such a thing as group calls. We have advanced technology for a reason," Kaya mumbled when Mary yelled into her makeshift walkie. Each channel they tried seemed to have more and more static. Lincoln's voice came through in choppy bits. We made a game of unscrambling his words.

"Where's the fun in that?" I teased just to make sure that the ever-present crease in Kaya's forehead defined itself a bit more. Sometimes, it felt like her goal was to look like a grandma by the age of thirty. "You do know our cabin has a no-technology rule, right?"

Kaya frowned as she tugged at her sweatshirt strings. "Stop playing."

"I'm not. My parents always make us dump our electronics in a basket at the door," I said.

"Well, thank God your parents aren't here."

"I still like to keep to tradition."

Kaya's scowl nearly burned a hole in the side of my face.

"What? I'm nothing if not my mother's daughter." I kept my eyes on the road pretending to be too focused on the snow sticking to the gravel to notice her disapproval.

"That sounds perfect," Mary said. "We already have a bunch of videos scheduled to automatically post."

"How do the numbers look?" I asked, glancing at her through the rearview mirror.

"Good." She beamed. "Always better when it's Sam or Lincoln in the video. Bonus points if they're both there. People even go feral for their off-screen voices."

Kaya snorted. "So much for making people fall in love with *us*."

"It's all part of the process" Mary insisted. "Aderyn and I have already gained over two thousand new followers. Most are far more engaged than any commentors on the guys' pages."

That made Kaya perk up. "No shit?"

I nodded, squirming in my seat from excitement. "I've had multiple comments saying they're happy to see women in the sport. It wasn't just Avori. Quite a few girls said they wanted to start playing because of us."

"That's amazing," Jas said.

"Right? That makes this even more worth it." My smile widened at the thought of some young girl somewhere seeing someone like us on her phone and realizing just how incredible her body could be. "So maybe we don't have the huge, sold-out crowds yet—"

"Or the funding," Kaya reminded me.

"Does that matter? In the end?" I wondered, mostly to myself. We'd made some progress. Broken down some barriers for next year's rookies by reviving our social media pages. It was a slow, uphill battle but we were moving. We were a stepping stone to something bigger."

"Uh, yeah, it matters," Kaya said. "Our whole goal this semester was to make sure Mendell's women's team is on the map."

"Maybe that looks different than what we originally thought," I mused. "Maybe even the smallest amount of progress could make a difference. Like, for the next generation of Mendell players? For women hockey players in general. We've proved we're here. Maybe that's enough?"

"Are you giving up on us?" Kaya looked surprised and a little disappointed.

I raised a brow. "No! Wait, you hate doing this social media stuff. Why do you sound so invested?"

"It was just a question. Not a plea for you to continue," she snapped back.

"Sounded a little like you wanted us to continue," Mary teased. "Come on, it's okay to admit you like spending more time with us."

Kaya scoffed. "Yeah, right."

"You love us," Mary sang.

Kaya slouched in the passenger's seat. "Shut up. I tolerate you guys at best. And I need my phone to do that, by the way. Something, anything to have as an excuse to not have to look at you guys' faces 24/7. Which is why I'm voting no on the tech ban."

"You love our faces," Mary continued and added in a knowing whisper, "Some more than others."

"Mary." Kaya shot her a deathly glare before looking at me. "Do e-readers count as electronics?"

I tilted my head to the side, much more interested in who Mary had been referencing.

"Because if you're going to force me to survive isolation without streaming, I'm going to need some smut to get me through."

"There are four decent-looking hockey players in the car behind us," Jas teased. "You can't get smutty with one of them?"

"Only a knucklehead would get involved with one of them." Kaya studied me for a second. "No offense."

"None taken," I said. "And, hey, it's not like I planned on..."

"On?" Mary scooted up so that her elbows rested on the console. Her strawberry scent made my nose itch. I rolled down the window to sneeze.

"Jeez," Kaya yelped when I swerved a bit during the sneeze. "Are we suddenly in Mario Kart?"

"My bad." I sniffed. "And on...being with Morgan. It just kind of happened."

Warmth crept on my cheeks at the thought of how everything snuck up on me. And how he'd changed his prize. After this bet was over, who knew what the future held for us? I couldn't help but smile when I thought about it.

"Sounds like Sam's taken," Mary decided with a wink in my direction "So, that leaves who for Kaya? Henrik. The know-it-all."

"Ooo, you like intelligence, Kaya," I noted. "You said learning new things was your love language."

"I feel like I'm in a lecture hall with him," Kaya insisted.

"Come on, he's a lot more attractive than any professor we've had," I teased.

"What about Lincoln?" Mary suggested. "He's cute and fun."

"You can't get the guy to shut up," Kaya argued.

"If I fucked guys, I think Lincoln would be the best choice," Mary decided, and Jas nodded in agreement. "He's sweet."

"Very nice," Jas said, simply. "And he quiets down if you talk to him one on one. We've had some awesome conversations."

Kaya's nose wrinkled. "Not gonna happen."

"Since Finn's taken, you just have Jack," Mary said.

Kaya straightened with renewed vigor. "Okay, even if that was possible — remember solidarity with Halle?"

We all nodded.

"The guy's so full of himself he can barely walk straight. I wouldn't be able to deal," Kaya continued. "You know, he tried to teach me how to strap on my gloves properly. Like I haven't been doing this since I was three years old."

I laughed. "You have something bad to say about all of them."

She gave us a one-shoulder shrug. "I have high standards."

"What about Sam?" I baited, giving Kaya a knowing smile. "What's your issue with him?"

"I'm not trash-talking your fuck buddy," Kaya said. "I may not be smart but I'm not that unaware."

"Oh, come on." I flipped on my turning signal a little earlier than necessary, so the guys got a heads-up that we were getting off the main road soon. "I want to know what you think."

"Since when do you care about what I think?" Kaya asked.

"I always care about what you think." I frowned. Kaya felt a bit more snappy than usual. "I care about what all of you think. Y'all are my best friends."

"Aw." Mary squeezed my arm. "You're our best friend, too. And as besties, I must tell you, I think Sam's perfect for you. You guys are like... mountains."

"Mountains?" I considered the comparison. A few years ago, I might have found offense. Now, I kind of like the idea of being compared to something unmovable.

"Solid," she insisted, dramatically—which earned a snort from Kaya. "You two could survive a hurricane."

"That's definitely an opinion," I said with a laugh.

"Compliment," Mary assured. "I wish I was half as strong as you two are."

"You are." Jas grabbed their girlfriend's hand. Mary smiled and slid back to kiss them. They started whispering to one another, easily falling into their intimate world. I stuck out my bottom lip, thinking about how cute it was. Kaya sighed, probably wondering how much longer she had to deal with us.

"But, seriously," I whispered, trying not to interrupt Mary and Jas's moment. "Tell me what you don't like about Morgan."

"Ryn," Kaya warned.

"I want to know because I may and may not be taking things to a new level...soon...ish."

She raised a brow. "You two are going to be together? Like, not just fuck buddies?"

I felt like I was shrinking a little because of her disapproving tone. "Maybe."

Kaya sighed. "Fine. I think he's a collector."

"Collector?"

"Like *Pokémon*. Gotta catch 'em all."

"I still don't know what you're talking about. I don't watch anime, remember?" I turned into the neighborhood, slowing my speed because my folks' cabin was only a half mile ahead.

"You don't have to watch anime to know... never mind. Basically, he wants one of everything. You're someone he's never had."

I readjusted in my seat, causing us to swerve again. Mary and Jas didn't notice since they were now making out. Kaya glared.

"Sorry," I mumbled. "And I see your point but it's not like that."

"Look, I just don't want you to shrink yourself for him. If or when you guys get together, I don't want you to feel like you have to change to fit him. And Sam's the kind of guy who has a certain image. If you shrink yourself, then who will I be big with? Because this shit is hard to do on my own. I like big Aderyn. She's badass. She's my hero."

I heard the strain in her voice. She turned to look outside the window so I couldn't see all the emotion in her eyes.

Throwing all caution to the wind, I let go of the steering wheel for one second to wrap my arms around her neck. She yelped and this time, Mary and Jas joined her.

"The wheel, the wheel, Ryn!" Kaya protested and patted my arm in hopes that returning my quick hug would satisfy me enough to pay attention to the road again.

"We're fine. I got it." I laughed when I heard Lincoln trying to ask us if we were okay through the walkie. "We're on a straightaway. We're fine."

"All good," Mary said while holding her hand on her chest. "Just having a bonding moment. I think."

I smiled at Kaya who snapped her fingers to indicate I needed to pay attention to the road. "I'm not shrinking for him. Ever."

Kaya gave me a disbelieving hum. "That's what they all say."

"How about we make a deal? If you think I'm shrinking in any way, you have full permission to kidnap me and rant. Give me your best Kaya rant."

I felt her gaze on me now. Though I couldn't confirm it, I could hear a little bit of a smile in her voice as she said, "My checking is worse off the ice."

"Sweetheart, I know."

"I will be a bitch but only because I care about you. No matter how gag-inducing this feeling is." She made a face, pretending she couldn't stand herself. "One of us has to be, though. If it was up to the love birds in the back, we'd be picking daisies in a field somewhere."

"That actually sounds fun," Mary spoke up. Jas rubbed her back, nodding in agreement.

"See," Kaya said. "I'm hard so you guys can be soft."

"Thank you for your service," Mary said, sarcastically.

I grinned at them. No words could accurately capture the grateful feeling I got when being reminded my friends had my back. But I tried a simple, "E-readers don't count as electronics. I'm making that rule official."

"Oh, thank God." Kaya let out a dramatic sigh. "I was beginning to worry I'd have to make up the stories myself. Haven't done that since I was in middle school. Fuck that extra work."

We laughed at her relief.

Chapter Thirty

Aderyn

My family's cabin had four rooms, large enough for us to pair off. The guys took the bottom floor. We all agreed on visiting the lodge for dinner. So, as soon as we got our luggage in, we started getting ready.

I was one of the first to get changed. Instead of waiting for my friends to finish, I ventured downstairs in hope of finding some kind of appetizer in the fridge left over from when my aunt and her kids stayed last weekend. Unfortunately, the shelves were mostly cleaned out. I found one water bottle in the pantry.

As I opened my room-temperature drink, Jack came out of one of the rooms. He didn't see me tucked into the corner of the kitchen, so he bypassed it in favor of the living room.

I walked to the doorway, watching him from a safe distance. Morgan's words rang in my ears: doesn't mean you stop trying.

My stomach turned a bit at the thought. No, I wasn't the type to give up when the going got tough. But this wasn't getting tough. This was getting real. It'd feel weird to sleep with someone else and yet, Morgan had encouraged me to do so.

He was right. I did want something different this semester. But did that really matter now?

"Let me guess your genre." My voice made Jack turn around. He'd been standing in front of a small stand of vinyl records.

The smile on his face was undeniably charming. But my stomach didn't do much more than grumble from hunger. Our "thing" a few weeks ago had been a lukewarm study session. Neither of us tried to make a move. I couldn't bring myself to even try and kiss him. I still thought Jack was sweet, though. And his smile made me feel like he was still a good choice.

"Let's hear it," he said, gesturing to the unorganized shelf.

I took a deep breath and joined his side. Outside of his hockey uniform, Jack dressed in all-black. Worn tees, faded jeans, and flannel jackets. He was Hozier on vacation in the mountains. Or a guy who ran a coffee shop that hosted spoken word nights.

"Indie rock." I smiled when his eyebrows furrowed.

"Why do you say that?"

I stepped close enough to feel the warmth of his body. "You seem like the guy who gloats about getting tickets to a band no one's heard of."

He chuckled. "That's code for asshole, isn't it?"

"A little."

"What if I told you I was a top forty guy."

"I'd say you're lying." I studied his eyes and the amusement in them made me rethink. "No way."

"I'm not good at finding alt music," he admitted, a little sheepishly. "Nor do I have the patience. Besides, pop's fun. Could be deep or surface level. I always like a mixture of both."

"You're tearing down my assumptions one by one," I noted.

"You do that a lot, don't you?"

My smile faded. "What?"

"Assume things about me instead of just trying to get to know me."

My cheeks burned and I looked at the record for a second. "Sorry. That's shitty of me."

"No, no," he said, quickly. "I'm not trying to shame you. I'm teasing and trying to see if you want to get to know me for real."

My heart hammered, begging for escape.

"Is that what you want, Aderyn?" Jack asked. When I didn't respond immediately, he added, "Or, is it Sam? Because from the looks of it, you're who he wants. And it seems like the feeling is mutual. I'm not in the business of playing second string."

"Of course not." I stepped away from him, shaking my head. "I'm sorry. This wasn't...I thought I wanted to...You're a sweet guy. And I fully planned on..."

Winning this wild bet. A bet that meant nothing to me anymore. Okay, so I'd fallen for someone again. Someone who understood me more than any of my exes ever did. Who accepted me no matter how obsessed I could get with hockey. Morgan would let me be as big as I wanted. He was insistent on it, in fact.

"Aderyn," Jack said in an even tone. "It's fine. I get it."

"I wasn't trying to string you along," I promised. My pits were sweating now at the realization that I was ready to commit to this decision. Jack's eyes softened because he saw the panic in my expression.

"It's terrifying," he said.

"What is?"

"Falling in love with someone who knows you." He sounded sad and experienced. "And risk getting close enough to lose everything. You're brave for doing it."

"Any tips? You sound like you might have tips." I laughed, my nerves making the noise sound strained.

He shrugged and stuffed his hands into his pockets. "Don't do it. Don't be brave."

"Very reassuring."

Jack chuckled and tried again. "How about this? I know for a fact you're one of the strongest hockey players I've met. Heartbreak on the ice hurts just as much as off. You'll get through it because you've had plenty of practice. Lean into your strength. Trust it."

That was surprisingly deeper than I expected it'd be. "Thank you. I needed that."

"You're welcome."

"I think I need some air. Will you tell the others I'll meet you guys at the lodge? I'll walk."

"Sure thing," he promised.

I didn't go straight to the lodge but opted for walking around the town square. Burn Mountain's resort was inspired by

Santa's Village. During the holidays, all the store owners went all out, pretending they were elves on a mission. The air smelled of cinnamon and peppermint. Most of the people on the sidewalk were tightly bundled up, hands full of shopping bags and steaming mugs decked with marshmallows.

This was my favorite place to be this time of year. I hoped walking through the streets would calm my nerves, but it didn't. One voice did. A worried, deep voice.

"Aderyn?" Morgan asked.

I turned to find him a few feet behind me. I looked over his shoulder to see if our friends were in tow. He was alone.

"What happened?" Morgan's brow worried as he came closer. I waited for his hand to take mine or rest on my shoulder, but he stuffed them in his pockets instead.

"I just needed a walk," I assured.

He frowned. "You sure? Because you bolted from the house. I heard you with Jack. Did he do something?"

"What? No." I shifted my weight. "You heard me?"

"Some of it." He looked away for a second, suddenly enticed by a window display of a small Christmas tree and a toy train circling it. "I was coming out of the bathroom. I wasn't trying to eavesdrop. You two sounded... good."

My heart dropped. "Excuse me?"

"Together." He gestured to nothing in particular. "The flirting. Looks like you're going to prove me wrong after all."

Seeing Morgan admit my success wasn't as satisfying as I thought it'd be. It was downright infuriating.

I scoffed. "You still think I'm going to sleep with him?"

"Of course, why not?" He looked perplexed.

"Because I thought we were going to start something here," I almost yelled. A couple passing by decided to give us a wider breadth. I cleared my throat and Morgan gave them a look that said, 'mind your business, keep walking.'

"We are," he insisted in a lower tone. "But you need a chance to experience something more first. That's what you wanted, right? You wanted me to push you. You knew I'd be able to push."

"I don't want you to push me into another guy's arms. Not anymore." I laughed because we were being ridiculous. "Morgan, fuck the bet."

"Are you sure?" His expression was closed off. I panicked, thinking maybe he'd changed his mind about me. If he did, I would have to deal with the fact that I was ready to give my all to the wrong person again. And for some reason, it hurt more this time.

"Yes. Right now, that's the only thing I'm sure of." I swallowed, waiting for his rejection. Inside, I felt like crumbling but on the outside, I was as solid as ever. Mary was right. We were mountains. I wouldn't give up that classification easily. I'd cry in private and recover that way, too. Whatever was about to happen, I would survive no matter how much I felt like I didn't want to.

"Oh, thank God." Morgan let out a heavy sigh. "Holy shit."

I laughed again. This time it sounded lighter.

"I thought I was going to have to spend this weekend listening to you and Jack go at it and that would have broken me," he confessed.

"Broke you?"

"Everything about you breaks me, Aderyn."

"That sounds bad."

He shook his head, closing the space between us. I moved closer too. The air between us felt light enough to float on. That's exactly what I'm doing. Floating because of how he's looking at me like I'm an answer to an unsolvable question.

"It's the opposite." Morgan cupped my cheeks. When he kissed me, it didn't feel like he was running toward the finish line—sex. Morgan was slow and careful, savoring each second. I wanted it to last, too. My arms wrapped around his waist to keep him as close as possible.

I let him guide me back so I leaned against the brick wall of a toy shop. His hands brushed circles on my cheeks. He kissed me until both of us needed more than small gulps of oxygen.

"You're going to hate me after this," he whispered when we broke apart. His forehead pressed against mine and his eyes remained closed. "Fuck, you're going to hate me."

I smiled, thinking this was some kind of self-deprecating joke. "Come on, I'm sure you won't be that bad of a boyfriend."

He pulled away so I could see his face. The fear in his eyes made my stomach tighten.

"It's not that," he murmured.

"What is it?" I took a breath, fully planning to take whatever he told me in stride.

Morgan kissed me again. This time I wasn't as responsive because anxiety was kicking in. What had him so afraid he couldn't just come out and say it? As soon as Morgan noticed my stiffness, he pulled back.

He let go of my face but remained a breath away. "We can't go forward until I tell you why I was upstairs."

"Upstairs? At dinner?"

He nodded, numbly. I couldn't think of one thing that possibly made someone as solid as Morgan sick to his stomach. Did I really want to know? At this point, there was no turning back. I needed to know so I could help him. I hated seeing the pain in his eyes.

"It's...your dad," he started.

"Warren?" I shook my head in disbelief. At the moment, Warren was the furthest thing from my mind. "What about him?"

"He's not exactly the honest guy you think he is." Morgan let those words hang in the air for a second. My heart sped up as he continued. His words made less and less sense the longer he went on.

"Finn and I started having some suspicions about Stoll," he explained. "We noticed how close he'd gotten to Coach Haynes and how interested he was in our team."

"Yeah..." I blinked, confused. Warren was the AD. Interest was literally a part of the job description.

"Coach Haynes started making weird calls after Stoll started hanging around more often. At big games, the best players were benched for arbitrary reasons," Morgan continued. His fingers were clenching and unclenching into a fist. He tried to maintain eye contact the entire time but I could tell by his rapid blinking it was becoming uncomfortable for him. My own heart squeezed, anxious about where this was going.

"Things didn't add up. So, Finn and I took it upon ourselves to do some snooping," he confessed. "One thing led to another and we found out the Stoll's not only making bets on our games, but he's also running them. Pulling the strings so he and whoever else is in on it can win."

There was air all around me, there had to be. I couldn't get it into my lungs though and my head was swimming because of it.

"From the information I have, he's making a lot of money under the table." Morgan rubbed the back of his neck. "And he's using some of the guys on the team to do it. To ensure they make mistakes on the ice that'll cost us."

I closed my eyes for a second, trying to piece together everything he'd said. "I...This is a misunderstanding. It has to be a misunderstanding."

Warren didn't sound anything like the man Morgan painted him out to be. I've seen him take guys under his wing. Spend his free time talking to new players through the homesickness. Treating Mom to fancy dinners and shows. Whispering 'I love yous' to her when he thought we weren't paying attention. Doing homework with Rae despite being exhausted. He never missed one of her science fairs. Always encouraging us to visit our biological dad. Always trying to build a solid foundation for our family to stand on.

"I wish it was a misunderstanding," Morgan whispered, sounding as conflicted as I felt.

"You...you can't go around accusing people of doing heinous things, Morgan. I've seen how you react to him when he's at the arena. You don't like him and that's fine—"

"Don't like him?" He let out a dry laugh. "This isn't about liking him. I'm not accusing Stoll because I don't like him. I'm accusing him because I have evidence. I'd never dream of telling you this if I didn't think I was right. If I thought for a second, I could be wrong..."

"Show me," I said, sternly.

"Aderyn—"

My voice felt shaky as I said, "I need to see whatever evidence you think you have."

His jaw tightened but he nodded and gave me some space. I wrung my hands as he pulled out his phone.

Gone was our sweet moment and hope of something more. Because as he searched through his phone, I started thinking about how much I'd grown to trust Warren. And that trust didn't come easily, it was built on five years of him proving himself. He was my family.

"Here." Morgan handed me his phone. I swiped through photos of what looked like a ledger. My gut turned over when I recognized his handwriting in the margins.

"This is..." I zoomed in on one photo. The words made no sense, but one jumble of letters looked familiar. It was my initials along with Rae and Terrance's. Mom and Warren often used the combination as banking passwords. I blew out a disbelieving breath.

"The dates correspond with all our hockey games. The losses have larger numbers, which most likely indicate payouts. Aderyn...I'm going to the Dean soon."

I frowned and looked up at him. "With a couple of screenshots and a theory?"

His expression darkened. "I have Jack, too. He's going to confess to working with him. Jack's in his inner circle. He's told me the truth like I'm telling you."

The world was spinning. I tried to take a steadying breath. This couldn't be real. This hurt me but...God, this was going to break my mom's heart.

"What are you thinking?" Morgan sounded hesitant to ask.

"I don't know." I barely met his gaze. "I just...I don't think you understand how nasty this can get. If you're right–"

"I'm right," he promised.

The lump in my throat felt larger. "If you're right..."

He let me have it this time. Morgan sighed, expression softening because he could see the storm in my eyes. The wave of emotions currently drowning me.

"This is going to get nasty," I warned. "You have to be sure if you're going to the Dean. This could ruin everything all of us worked for this semester. Because even if you're wrong, an investigation will happen."

"I can handle it," he promised, voice firm. "I'm right and I will handle this for all of us."

"It's been months and you have nothing more than a couple of photos with numbers and random sentences. If Warren is..." I cleared my throat. It was painful to even entertain this. "...is guilty, he'll have a plan for how to respond. He's a smart guy. You need something more."

Morgan looked annoyed like he'd heard all this before. "What do you think I should do? Playoffs are around the corner, and we need this investigation to start yesterday."

"I'll get you what you need," I decided. My head felt light, and I could hear my heart racing. "If I find it, I'll give you what you need."

Morgan's brows knitted. "What?"

"You're terrible at sneaking around," I noted. "Heavy-footed. The next dinner, you might not be lucky enough to run into me. Best not to risk it. I'll look this time. Besides, I need to see it for myself and make sure."

Morgan nodded, understanding. "Alright. That works. Please, don't confront him, though. It would give him time to destroy everything."

I sucked the back of my teeth. "Of course, I won't. That'd be ridiculous."

"Right, sorry." Morgan looked a little ashamed. "I'm sorry for all of this. Especially for ruining this trip. I didn't want to tell you this early—"

"Doesn't matter," I cut him off and ignored the sad look on his face. I couldn't help but wonder if Morgan started talking to me because of Warren. Did he pick me because I could get him close? He'd used Jack to get inside our house, but I would have given him access if he'd asked.

"This is messy." His words tore me from my internal argument. "But what's happening with Stoll and the league doesn't affect us."

I put my hand up when he tried to move closer. "Let's not, okay?"

Morgan's face fell and my body burned with guilt. I didn't want to hurt him, but I couldn't think straight right now. The least of all make a decision about our relationship.

"Not right now," I said. "I need time. We need to figure this out first. Everything else is going to get in the way of it."

"Okay, yeah, of course." He nodded, sounding relieved since I wasn't closing the door entirely. "We'll wait till after."

I didn't respond because my brain was still trying to catch up. My surety about my future was suddenly in question and the last thing I could do was make him a promise.

There was a change in his eyes when my silence lingered.

"As long as you need. I promise I'll wait," Morgan said, voice firm and sure.

Chapter Thirty-One

Sam

I paced back and forth on the sidewalk outside of our house. Aderyn had texted me a few minutes ago saying she was on her way. Even though her dorm building was a decent ride, I couldn't help but get up instantly to wait for her.

The trip to the mountain had been a bust. Though I'd managed to tell her about Stoll and what she meant to me, nothing turned out how I'd hoped it would.

"How did you think it'd turn out?" Henrik had asked after the trip.

And he was right. What did I think was going to happen? She'd jump for joy at my feelings and then, be on board for ending her dad's career?

It was an impossible situation. After we got back, I kept my distance to give her time. All I told her was that I couldn't wait until the playoffs before going to the Dean. All she said was that she didn't need long. She'd been true to her word. It'd only been a few days since we went to the cabin.

When her car parked alongside our driveway, my heartbeat sped up. I waited at the end of the driveway as she got out of the car. She wore pants that were loose around her thighs and a dark jacket that clung to her muscles.

Even though all this awkwardness hung in between us, I still felt like a weight lifted off my shoulders in her presence.

"Here," Aderyn said. No greeting, just straight to the point. She handed me a large envelope.

I raised a brow and accepted it. "What is it?"

"Everything I could print while Warren was out of the house." She shoved her hands into her pockets. Her eyes were red from crying or sleepless nights or both. I desperately wanted to tell her everything was going to be okay, but I couldn't promise that.

"That." Aderyn nudged her chin to the envelope. "Along with whatever you have should be more than enough to make a good claim. Warren will catch wind of things soon, though. Dean Arnold and him play golf every other Wednesday."

"Right." I nodded, feeling numb and unable to construct a full sentence.

"But the Dean's a good guy," Aderyn said. "He'll listen to you. Don't worry about that."

"Thank you for this. For hearing me out. I know this has to be hard on you."

She shrugged, expression blank. "It's the right thing to do."

"H-how are you?" My throat constricted at the brief flash of sadness in her eyes. She glanced over her shoulder at her car. She wanted to leave. I needed to come up with some excuse to keep her here longer, but my brain wasn't working.

Think of something that'll get her to stay. You need time to tell her...

What? That I couldn't do this without her? That I didn't *want* to do this without her?

"Fine," she said with a sigh. "It's going to get harder, of course, but I'll manage."

"You will," I said.

Her expression changed to something more guarded than before. I didn't even know that was possible.

"Tell me what I can do to help us get back to how it was," I blurted.

Her brows raised. "What?"

"This relationship thing is new to me—"

"Sam, we're not in a relationship."

My skin burned at the sound of my name and the coldness around it. "No, I know. I just...I thought it might be good to talk about what might happen after this."

"What if there's no after this?"

The ground beneath me felt unstable. "I-is that what you've decided?"

"Did you approach me in Harry's because you somehow found out Warren was my stepdad?" she asked instead.

I frowned. "What? No. Absolutely not."

She searched my eyes, looking for a lie. If I didn't know any better, I'd say she was hoping for one. Maybe that would be easier for her? My lying would be the perfect excuse for her to walk away. A perfect reason.

Aderyn crossed her arms over her chest. "I can't tell if you're lying or not. And I can't trust my gut anymore because I never saw this Warren shit coming."

"Aderyn, you know me," I reminded her and did my best not to sound as desperate as I felt. "Better than anyone. You've seen me. More than anyone has ever seen me."

She hesitated before saying, "But it makes sense if you were trying to learn more about Warren, you'd use me to get to him."

I dared to step closer. "I asked Jack for help, remember? He's the one that got me an invite to dinner. I've never once asked you about Stoll or anything to do with the hockey department. Think about it, Aderyn. You know I'm telling the truth."

She stared at me for a moment, still looking for that lie. I wracked my brain, trying to come up with some other proof. As I thought, Aderyn moved close enough for me to touch her. I didn't. I stayed still as she pressed her lips against mine. Moving felt like too much of a risk. I followed her lead, leaning into her hands when she held my face.

We were out of breath when we finally parted.

"Everything that's happened between us has only happened because I'm interested in you. It's you. I want you," I murmured against her lips. "And I swear, you will never go a day without knowing that. I will treat you right, Aderyn. Just please give me a chance to show you."

She closed her eyes. "You make me believe it's possible."

"It is. We are." I touched her then. Wrapped my arms around her waist and pulled her in for another kiss. "You and me, Aderyn. You know we'd be good together. You know I'm not lying. There's nothing wrong with your gut. Look at me."

Aderyn sighed before opening her eyes.

"Look at me." I brushed my nose against hers. "I'm not lying, beautiful."

"I know."

Relief made my chest lighter. Her next words caused that weight to come crashing down all over again.

"But I still need time," she confessed. "My emotions have been all over the place. I can't think straight. I'm scared of everything. What's going to happen to my family? My spot on the team? At Mendell? I don't want my anxiety to push me into a decision I'm not ready to make. You know in my relationships I've always been all-in. Feet first. I put all my trust in one person. Put all my trust in hockey and this program. And I keep hitting walls. I keep getting rejected and overlooked. I can't continue making the same mistakes I always do. I can't keep rushing. Something has to change or I'm always going to walk away from things disappointed."

My chest felt like it was caving in. Heartbreak. Something I haven't mastered. And now, I was paying for it.

"I feel like I need to have control over when and how I decide to get into another relationship. This one thing, I feel like I have to have control over this one thing, and I need to slow down and be sure I make the right decision."

"You do, of course, you do." My grip around her loosened, hands falling away from her. "That makes sense. It's smart. It's what I'd tell you to do if you were asking for advice."

She smiled but it didn't reach her eyes. "I know. I'm practicing my execution like you said."

"I still want to wait," I held onto the little hope I had left.

"You don't have to wait," she whispered, voice shaking a bit. "I wouldn't think any less of you if you moved on."

"I don't want to move on." I winced at the thought. "I want to wait. You're worth it. I need you to see that I'm in this. I know you're done with being all in. You deserve a break from being that person in the relationship. So, let me be the one that's all in. Let me be the one painfully in love."

Her eyes widened at my confession. "Sam..."

"You don't have to say anything." I held up my hand for her to stop because I wasn't ready to hear the rejection. "I just need to get this out so you know."

She nodded, chewing on her lip as she wait for me to continue.

"I respect you, Aderyn. More than just for who you are on the ice. I respect how bold you are every time you walk into the men's weight room. How you will fight to the end of a losing battle. How you will listen to my recommendations but end up choosing your own order...and that respect has turned into something deeper.

I need you to know I love how you smile twice when you're happy. The first time you try to hide your crooked canine. The second time, you catch yourself and it's like you remember how beautiful you are. Then, you smile wider."

That part seemed to hit her. Aderyn blinked, trying to ward off any building emotion.

"I love how you're trying to be better than you were yesterday. You're always trying to be better and that makes me want to do so the same. I love that every time we look at one another after being apart for a while, you give me a nod like we're co-workers. Holding me at arm's length because you can be a bit awkward."

We both laughed. Hers sounded a bit watery. The weight on my chest felt lighter. I should have told her this sooner.

"God, I even love how you hold me at arm's length because it feels better than you..." I pressed my fingers into my palm, willing myself to finish. Every word needed to be said if I was going to feel like I gave this my all. "It feels better than you not reaching for me at all."

I was completely exposed. This woman, whatever she decided, had my heart.

"Sam...I..." she tired.

"I said all that, so you know I'm here for you," I continued, looking down for a second to center myself. "I don't need any promises from you. Now or ever. Don't feel pressured by my waiting. I don't fucking care if this hurts me. The only thing I care about is you knowing that I'm willing to give you my all. I'm going to prove that. I'm here for you."

She nodded, still looking stunned by my words.

"No promises. No pressure," she repeated to be sure.

"Just me. Here for you," I finished.

"How did it go?" Henrik asked when I came back into the living room. I tossed him the envelope and fell onto the couch.

"That good?" he joked and opened the envelope to see what was inside.

Lincoln paused the show he was watching as soon as he sensed the stress in the air. "What happened?"

I shook my head, feeling like I was being held together by safety pins. "Nothing. I just let go of the one person on this planet who understands me in a way I never thought possible. The one person who I understand more than anyone I've ever met. A connection that feels like a once-in-a-lifetime kind of thing."

"Sam," Henrik tried, sobering up.

"No, you don't have to say anything. I know I sound melodramatic as fuck but shit...." I wiped my hand over my face. "This hurts."

Lincoln sighed, sounding empathetic. "I'm sorry. If there's anything we can do—"

I shook my head. "She's better off. This is better."

I repeated the words in my head to try and convince myself.

"This is a bright side, at least." Henrik waved the envelope. "Looks like we've got him."

"Got him?" Finn appeared in the doorway. "Like for real this time?"

Henrik offered him the papers. "He won't be able to bury all this. Check it out. Dates, time, real transactions, and full names."

"This is incredible," Finn said in a low voice as he flipped through the papers. "How did you have time to print this all off?"

"Aderyn," I mumbled.

"When are you going to the Dean?" Henrik asked as he moved back toward the kitchen. There was something in the oven that he pulled out and placed on a cooling rack.

"As soon as Jack's available." I clasped and unclasped my hands. Victory mixed with disappointment was hard to swallow. My mouth felt too dry, and my brain kept replaying my last kiss with Aderyn. I brushed my hand over my mouth.

"Come on." I pushed off the couch, desperately needing to move. If I got into action, I wouldn't have to wallow about something that couldn't be. "I want to head out and pick up Jack now."

"Bet." Lincoln hurried after me. "Let's finally expose this asshole."

Finn nodded, not looking too excited but determined. "Let's do it."

"Give me five minutes," Henrik said, quickly. "I have another pie in the oven, but I still want to come. We're doing this together, remember?"

I smiled a little. Thank God for these guys. Without them I would've cracked a long time ago. At least, I still had them. That thought made me feel a little more sentimental than usual. Aderyn was gone but I wasn't alone. I'd never really been alone.

"What?" Lincoln paused when I froze at the door. "What's wrong with your face?"

I quickly hid my emotions. "Get in the car."

"He looks touched," Finn noted, simply. Recently he seemed more capable of reading expressions. Which was good for him but not for me in this situation.

"Aw." Lincoln smiled and I glared back. "It's been a hard day, hasn't it?"

"Stop," I warned.

"Feel it out, Sammy," Lincoln encouraged. "Do you need a hug?"

"No," I said in a flat voice when he opened his arms.

"It's our generation's job to end toxic masculinity," Lincoln reminded me. "The needle has to start moving somewhere. Might as well start with a hug from me to you."

"He's right, you know," Henrik called from the kitchen. "Take the hug. You need the hug."

"I don't need the hug." I continued to glare at Lincoln. "I'm fine."

"What's going on? Is everything okay?" Naomi asked, standing at the top of the stairs.

"He needs a hug," Lincoln explained. "But is too much of a 'man' to accept one."

"It's been a hard day for him," Finn added.

His girlfriend's expression morphed into one of concern as she came down the stairs. "What happened? And where are you guys going?"

"To ruin the athletic director's life," Lincoln said.

She frowned and looked at Finn. "Excuse me?"

"We're setting wrongs right," I told her.

"It'll be fine," Finn spoke to her in a low voice. He kissed her forehead gently and murmured a few more soothing words to her. Naomi held onto the hem of his shirt as he spoke, pulling him close as if she wanted to protect him from whatever he was leaving her to do. He massaged circles on her arms. Finn's voice was full of so much love it made him give her one of his rare smiles. Those two meant everything to each other. My envy nearly drowned me.

"Come on, guys. We don't have all day," I ordered, stiffly.

Naomi looked concerned and hugged Finn. "Be safe. No fist fighting, right?"

Finn kissed her. "We won't. I promise. And we'll be back soon."

"Don't worry," Henrik appeared in the foyer, exchanging his apron for his coat. "We'll keep an eye on him. Make sure he won't get into any trouble."

Finn rolled his eyes at the teasing and followed Lincoln and Henrik out of the door.

"Sam," Naomi called before I could join them.

"Yeah?" I turned to her.

She opened her arms. "We could...?"

"I..."

"You do look like you need it." She smiled, sounding a bit shy. "But you can say no. That's fine, too."

"It's fine," I permitted. I'm not sure why but something in me cracked. Naomi hugged me. I felt awkward at first and slowly, my hands accepted the embrace. It wasn't as weird as I thought it'd be. Though it wasn't exactly comfortable either.

"Okay?" she asked, pulling away.

"Yeah. That wasn't too bad. I still don't think I'll ever be much of a hugger."

Naomi laughed. "Maybe. But sometimes you need action to know people care about you. Not just words."

"Right." Something clicked then. "You're completely right."

Her smile widened. "See you later."

"Thank you." I squeezed her shoulder before joining the guys.

Chapter Thirty-Two

Aderyn

I went back home after giving Sam what he needed. I wanted to enjoy whatever normalcy my family had before Warren's involvement and leadership in a gambling circle came out.

Only two days passed before my stepdad finally got the warning call. I heard him pick up the call in his office. He'd shut the door and uncharacteristically responded in hushed whispers as whoever was on the other end of the call broke the news.

"What are you doing?" Rae asked when she saw me lingering outside of Warren's office.

I shook my head and placed a finger to my lips.

When she didn't move along, I whispered to her, "I need to talk to him and I'm trying to see if he's done."

My sister's brow wrinkled at the obvious nerves in my tone. "So, knock and ask."

I wiped my sweaty palms on my jeans. "I'm working up to it."

She sighed and pushed past me to knock on the heavy wood door. His response was barely audible, "Come in."

Rae gestured for me to go ahead.

"Thanks," I said, genuinely grateful for her confidence. She gave me a look and muttered, "weirdo" before starting down the stairs.

I took a breath and held it in for a few seconds. Did he know I was the one who gave Morgan those files? Was he going to leave or stick around and face the music? What was he going to tell Mom?

When I stepped into the room, I could feel the heaviness in the air. Warren's knuckles were white as a sheet as he clutched his phone to his mouth. He looked off into the distance, eyes not resting on anything. I always thought he looked so strong and capable in his large, black office chair. Now, with his shoulders sagging and eyes empty, he looked small.

For the past few days, I've felt guilty for talking to him and the rest of my family like I didn't know what was going on. For not preparing them for what lay ahead. But now, seeing Warren look overwhelmed for the first time I realized none of that had been my job. It'd been his job to look out for my family. His job was to look out for his athletes' best interests. He'd have to communicate that failure to everyone he loved. And he'd have to start with me.

"Aderyn." He blinked, coming back to the present. I could tell from how he tried to look calm that he didn't know about my involvement yet. But once our gazes locked and I stared at him for a moment, realization washed over his expression.

"Shit," he hissed under his breath and covered his face with his hands for a second. All pretense washed away.

"Was this the plan from the beginning?" I asked, still lingering at the door. I didn't close it behind me. No closed doors policy was something that both my parents had grained into me. Warren was a hypocrite. So now, I'd hold him accountable for everything. Even something as small as open doors.

"If so, it was ignorant." I sat in the chair on the opposite end of his desk. My confidence was coming back slowly as I started thinking about my dreams of coming to Mendell this year. "And fucking selfish. This was our shot. Not just yours, but our entire family and every athlete at Mendell. You know what it's like to only have four years to prove yourself."

"Aderyn…" he tried but couldn't finish the sentence. Couldn't even look me in the eyes, so I continued.

"You've ruined a whole season for not just the guys but the girls, too. Maybe even all Mendell's sports programs this year. Because who the hell knows how far you took this?"

"It was just hockey," he promised and ran his hand through his hair. "I swear to God I didn't think it'd go this far."

I scoffed. Didn't think it'd go this far? How removed from reality was he? "Do you know how difficult it's been for us this year? How I've been working overtime to make this school care about its women's teams? No one listens to us. Every higher-up is obsessed with making money instead of developing talent. I didn't think you'd be one of them. I thought you'd get around to us eventually. That one day, you wouldn't just say you believed in me, but showed me you did."

"Aderyn, I've always believed in you. What I did isn't any reflection on how much I care about you, your mom, Rae, and Terrance."

"You say that, but I find it hard to believe," I snapped, my voice getting louder with each minute. "Everything I know about you Warren... It all feels like a lie now."

"I got in over my head. Greedy. I wanted it all." He leaned his elbows on the desk. His voice was hard as he willed me to see his side of things. "Not just for me, for your mom. For us. This was my only lie. My attempt at building a better life for us. I wanted you to afford Mendell, I want your sister to go to whatever school she wants, for Terrance to live whatever life he wants, and your mom to retire early—"

I shook my head, interrupting him. "Don't start touting that, 'I did this for us' bullshit. You ruined this. Us. Everything. You forced guys on the team to take part in it. Most of these guys don't have families to look out for them. They feel like they're stabbing each other in the back because standing up to you means getting in the way of someone else's dream. It's so goddamn disappointing, Dad. We trusted you. We all put our trust... I put my trust in you." My eyes stung with tears of anger.

He inhaled deeply and wiped his hand over his mouth. I could see the wheels turning in his head. Warren was thinking of something. A way to get out of this.

"You run and we'll never forgive you," I warned in a hard tone. I couldn't promise forgiveness ever but something in me wanted to dangle that threat and force him to at least consider the people around him.

"I'd never run." He pulled his hand away from his mouth and met my gaze. "Never."

"We'll see about that," I said.

"This won't break us," Warren promised but it sounded more like a wish on his part. "I'll fix it."

"Will you now?" Mom asked. She stood in the doorway with a solemn look on her face.

We both glanced up, surprised and curious as to how long she'd been standing there.

"So, this was what you were hiding?" she said in a calm voice. "I hoped it was something simple like slot machines in Vegas. Should have figured your luck was never that good."

Warren's face was red. "Essie, I—"

"Aderyn, give us the room?" she asked without looking at me.

I nodded and quickly got up to follow her order. As I passed Mom, she reached out to touch my shoulder.

"Did you have something to do with this?" she asked in a low voice. "With people finding out?"

My stomach twisted at the sadness in her eyes. I nodded, numbly. "I gave someone evidence. I couldn't...I couldn't ignore it."

"No, I know," she assured me quickly. "I'm not scolding you. I'm proud of you."

The tightness in my chest faded.

"So proud of you." She kissed my forehead and waited for me to leave before closing the door behind me.

Chapter Thirty-Three

Sam

I went back home after giving Sam what he needed. I wanted to enjoy whatever normalcy my family had before Warren's involvement and leadership in a gambling circle came out.

Only two days passed before my stepdad finally got the warning call. I heard him pick up the call in his office. He'd shut the door and uncharacteristically responded in hushed whispers as whoever was on the other end of the call broke the news.

"What are you doing?" Rae asked when she saw me lingering outside of Warren's office.

I shook my head and placed a finger to my lips.

When she didn't move along, I whispered to her, "I need to talk to him and I'm trying to see if he's done."

My sister's brow wrinkled at the obvious nerves in my tone. "So, knock and ask."

I wiped my sweaty palms on my jeans. "I'm working up to it."

She sighed and pushed past me to knock on the heavy wood door. His response was barely audible, "Come in."

Rae gestured for me to go ahead.

"Thanks," I said, genuinely grateful for her confidence. She gave me a look and muttered, "weirdo" before starting down the stairs.

I took a breath and held it in for a few seconds. Did he know I was the one who gave Morgan those files? Was he going to leave or stick around and face the music? What was he going to tell Mom?

When I stepped into the room, I could feel the heaviness in the air. Warren's knuckles were white as a sheet as he clutched his phone to his mouth. He looked off into the distance, eyes not resting on anything. I always thought he looked so strong and capable in his large, black office chair. Now, with his shoulders sagging and eyes empty, he looked small.

For the past few days, I've felt guilty for talking to him and the rest of my family like I didn't know what was going on. For not preparing them for what lay ahead. But now, seeing Warren look overwhelmed for the first time I realized none of that had been my job. It'd been his job to look out for my family. His job was to look out for his athletes' best interests. He'd have to communicate that failure to everyone he loved. And he'd have to start with me.

"Aderyn." He blinked, coming back to the present. I could tell from how he tried to look calm that he didn't know about my involvement yet. But once our gazes locked and I stared at him for a moment, realization washed over his expression.

"Shit," he hissed under his breath and covered his face with his hands for a second. All pretense washed away.

"Was this the plan from the beginning?" I asked, still lingering at the door. I didn't close it behind me. No closed doors policy was something that both my parents had grained into me. Warren was a hypocrite. So now, I'd hold him accountable for everything. Even something as small as open doors.

"If so, it was ignorant." I sat in the chair on the opposite end of his desk. My confidence was coming back slowly as I started thinking about my dreams of coming to Mendell this year. "And fucking selfish. This was our shot. Not just yours, but our entire family and every athlete at Mendell. You know what it's like to only have four years to prove yourself."

"Aderyn..." he tried but couldn't finish the sentence. Couldn't even look me in the eyes, so I continued.

"You've ruined a whole season for not just the guys but the girls, too. Maybe even all Mendell's sports programs this year. Because who the hell knows how far you took this?"

"It was just hockey," he promised and ran his hand through his hair. "I swear to God I didn't think it'd go this far."

I scoffed. Didn't think it'd go this far? How removed from reality was he? "Do you know how difficult it's been for us this year? How I've been working overtime to make this school care about its women's teams? No one listens to us. Every higher-up is obsessed with making money instead of developing talent. I didn't think you'd be one of them. I thought you'd get around to us eventually. That one day, you wouldn't just say you believed in me, but showed me you did."

"Aderyn, I've always believed in you. What I did isn't any reflection on how much I care about you, your mom, Rae, and Terrance."

"You say that, but I find it hard to believe," I snapped, my voice getting louder with each minute. "Everything I know about you Warren... It all feels like a lie now."

"I got in over my head. Greedy. I wanted it all." He leaned his elbows on the desk. His voice was hard as he willed me to see his side of things. "Not just for me, for your mom. For us. This was my only lie. My attempt at building a better life for us. I wanted you to afford Mendell, I want your sister to go to whatever school she wants, for Terrance to live whatever life he wants, and your mom to retire early—"

I shook my head, interrupting him. "Don't start touting that, 'I did this for us' bullshit. You ruined this. Us. Everything. You forced guys on the team to take part in it. Most of these guys don't have families to look out for them. They feel like they're stabbing each other in the back because standing up to you means getting in the way of someone else's dream. It's so goddamn disappointing, Dad. We trusted you. We all put our trust... I put my trust in you." My eyes stung with tears of anger.

He inhaled deeply and wiped his hand over his mouth. I could see the wheels turning in his head. Warren was thinking of something. A way to get out of this.

"You run and we'll never forgive you," I warned in a hard tone. I couldn't promise forgiveness ever but something in me wanted to dangle that threat and force him to at least consider the people around him.

"I'd never run." He pulled his hand away from his mouth and met my gaze. "Never."

"We'll see about that," I said.

"This won't break us," Warren promised but it sounded more like a wish on his part. "I'll fix it."

"Will you now?" Mom asked. She stood in the doorway with a solemn look on her face.

We both glanced up, surprised and curious as to how long she'd been standing there.

"So, this was what you were hiding?" she said in a calm voice. "I hoped it was something simple like slot machines in Vegas. Should have figured your luck was never that good."

Warren's face was red. "Essie, I—"

"Aderyn, give us the room?" she asked without looking at me.

I nodded and quickly got up to follow her order. As I passed Mom, she reached out to touch my shoulder.

"Did you have something to do with this?" she asked in a low voice. "With people finding out?"

My stomach twisted at the sadness in her eyes. I nodded, numbly. "I gave someone evidence. I couldn't...I couldn't ignore it."

"No, I know," she assured me quickly. "I'm not scolding you. I'm proud of you."

The tightness in my chest faded.

"So proud of you." She kissed my forehead and waited for me to leave before closing the door behind me.

Chapter Thirty-Four

Aderyn

The months following Warren's confession were a shit show that started with a family meeting. It ended with Mom and him on opposite ends of the house. She threatened to kick him out but never actively moved his things. He offered to leave and before he could, Rae begged him to stay. And like usual, none of us could say no to Rae.

On day two of everything going south, Terrance showed up. Which meant this was a whole other level of seriousness. Each day that came held the potential of being the last time we'd all be a family. And despite my disappointment in Warren, I hated that idea.

I loved him. I loved how he made my mom smile after years of tears. I loved how he taught Rae how to ride a bike, swim in the ocean, and drift in Mario Kart. I loved how he supported Terrance even when everyone else in our family gave my brother grief for giving up life in civilization to follow his path. You could still love someone and not condone their actions, right?

Because I wasn't too sure and with each day that went by it felt like I got further and further from the answer.

I wanted an escape. And once the investigation started and word spread about Warren, I decided on one. A fresh start in a new place was what my whole family needed. So, after the investigation and whatever trial followed, we were moving. And I'd transfer.

I'd joined everyone at Zeus as a sort of goodbye party—even though none of my friends knew about my plans yet, And because I needed to see him. I needed to make sure that goodbye was what I wanted.

Then Sam kissed me. He kissed and held onto me like he'd never let go. My surety melted.

In the last couple of months, I cut off all contact with him. I thought quitting him cold turkey would be easier than a slow fade-out. I was wrong.

The first week away from him, I cried myself to sleep. Every tear was for a breakup that happened before an official relationship even began. This was actual heartbreak. When Erica broke up with me last semester, the numbness concerned me. Now, I understood it. I was numb because I didn't feel like that relationship was right. But, Sam and I felt right. Especially after everything he'd said in his driveaway months ago. I knew every word of his confession was true.

I started reconsidering my decision to transfer. Because if I transferred, there was a high chance the distance would kill whatever we had. Thankfully, the drive out to Montville Lake was long enough to help me regain my senses once again. I needed to be close to Mom and Rae. Needed to play at a school not marred by what Warren had done. No matter how much it hurt, those things were my priorities. Hockey was my future. I had to bet on that and not on a maybe with Morgan. Not on a what-if...even though that what-if seemed beautiful.

"All good?" Kaya asked. Out of all my friends, her reaction to Warren was the most surprising. She kept asking if I was okay. And if I needed anything. I didn't get one rant from her about how Mendell was trash for letting a guy like him run things for so long even though that would've been on brand and I would've agreed with every word.

Quite often, Kaya would come to my dorm just to sit in silence and watch whatever shitty movie I wanted. She'd never ask about what my family was doing or about the process of the investigation. After my interview with the review board, she took me out to get greasy fast food and we sat in the middle of an outdoor mall to people watch—one of my favorite things to do after trash days. I appreciated it but a large part of me wished she'd act normal. I needed things to be as normal as possible.

"I'm fine." I opened my trunk and started unloading the extra set of hockey sticks I always kept stored there. "You?"

Montville Lake was in the middle of the largest park in Tinsel. The sidewalks weaving in and out of the park were well-lit with iron lamp posts. There wasn't anyone besides us here because people weren't as silly as we were to be out here on one of the coldest nights of the year.

"Worried that you're going to regret whatever happened between you and Sam," Kaya said.

Her comment made me glance over at Sam. He chatted with his friends while he strapped on elbow pads. I'd only seen glimpses of him since that day I gave him the last bit of information he needed. I avoided most of our usual hangouts. I tried to duck behind something or someone whenever our paths nearly crossed on campus.

"Did he break things off because of Warren?" Kaya asked, speaking so low I could barely hear her.

I frowned. "No. That was me."

She looked surprised. "Oh."

"It's for the best."

"You think so?"

I tugged on my gloves a little rougher than necessary. "You don't like the guy. Shouldn't you be patting me on the back right now?"

"Ryn—"

"Kaya, please. Let's not talk about it. I want to enjoy this night since it's going to be the last…"

She raised a brow. "Last what?"

My jaw clenched. I did a quick sweep of our surroundings. Both teams were heading toward the sidewalk now. Someone brought a portable speaker that blasted music loud enough to drown out conversations.

"Don't tell anyone yet," I whispered. "But I'm not coming back next semester."

The color drained from Kaya's face. "What?"

My chest tightened at how wide her eyes got. "I don't think Mendell's the right place for me anymore."

"Because of Warren," she figured.

"Yeah. And other stuff, too." I shrugged. "My family needs a fresh start. I need a fresh start. And we might as well do it together, you know?"

Kaya shook her head, confusion morphing into anger. "What about the team? Everything we did this semester? You're just going to leave right before we've made any sort of mark? That's bullshit."

I felt my gaze harden at the judgment in her tone. "I can't stay here. My presence will be a constant reminder of what Warren did. People will always wonder if he helped me on the team. If I transfer now, I'll have a chance to have two good seasons somewhere else."

"People in the league already know about Warren," she argued. "Wherever you go, that shit's going to follow you. What's the point of starting over when you've already built a foundation? We need you."

"You guys will be fine," I said. "When I announce to everyone, I'm going to suggest they vote you as captain."

"What? What the hell would make you think that's a good idea?"

Kaya barely liked people and she couldn't stand team politics. Still, she was the most honest and driven person I've ever met. Even though she pretended not to care, she did. Kaya cared so much that it probably hurt. And the girl was talented. Ninety-nine percent of us wouldn't make it to the professional league. I was probably in that percent. But something deep inside of me believed Kaya would rise above us all.

"Just consider it?" I asked.

"I won't," she promised. "Not for a second because being captain is your job."

"Not for long."

Kaya scowled. "I'm vetoing you."

"Excuse me?"

"You heard me. I'm vetoing you. You're not leaving because we need you here. Who's going to talk Mary down from her latest entrepreneurial venture? Or get Jas to open up about what's bothering them? Grace still can't block to save her life and she's only ever shown progress after talking to you. And what about our socials? You spearheaded the whole male team collab and the algorithm eats that shit up. I get thousands of views despite only posting once a week."

"You. The answer is you, Kaya."

"No, it's not. Because...I need you." Her voice cracked a bit. "Just the thought of doing any of this without you...I can't."

My heart squeezed. She balled her hands into fists, trying to calm down. I pulled her in for a hug. I expected her to remain stiff and keep her arms at her sides for most of it. Instead, she immediately wrapped her arms around me.

We stayed like that until someone called for us to join them down the walk. Our group was already halfway to the lake. Mary waved a jacket in the air like a flag to get our attention.

"We should go." Kaya pulled away from me, not meeting my gaze. She quickly wiped her cheeks.

"It's going to be fine," I promised. "Everything's going to work out fine."

Kaya nodded and tried to smile. "Maybe...I just...I'm going to miss you."

I grabbed her hand and squeezed. "I'm going to miss you, too. But I promise. We'll be fine."

"**E**verything okay?" Sam stood across from me on our makeshift center of the ice. Our goalies stood in our DIY goals (stacks of pebbles and pairs of shoes). The sun had long dipped under the horizon so our only source of light was from the park's lamps and the outdoor spotlight my brother gifted me for Christmas—something that I'd never thought would come in handy until tonight.

In any light, Sam looked incredibly handsome. He'd shed his jacket, revealing a long, black sweater. Despite the weather, his lips still looked warm and soft enough to kiss. My cheeks burned, thinking about earlier. My heart ached when I realized this would be the final time I'd get to challenge him on the ice.

"Everything's great," I lied. "You?"

"Can't complain," he murmured. His eyes lingered on mine, and he asked the question again silently. Sam frowned when I shook my head, lying again about being okay.

"What?" I asked when he continued to stare.

"Something's wrong."

"Other than my family being torn apart?" I joked.

Sam's forehead wrinkled. "Aderyn, I'm sorry about—"

"It's not your fault. Don't apologize."

"Still...maybe if I—"

"Ignored your conscience and spent your last few years of college barely getting more than a few minutes playing in a game?" I laughed. "Yeah, no. You did the right thing."

"I know it was right, but it wasn't easy."

"Right things rarely are."

"We were," he said.

My grip tightened on my stick. I couldn't do this. Not now. Not ever. He was making this so fucking hard.

"Stop looking at me like that." I gestured to his face. He caught my hand and held it between us in the air. I swallowed at the feel of his fingers around me.

"I can't," he said in a voice that sounded in pain.

"Try."

"I *have*." Sam kept his hand around mine, lowering them both so that they hung by our side. "And I can't."

"I'm leaving," I confessed and immediately regretted it.

His expression changed. Jaw tight and mouth in a straight line. "What?"

"After the semester's done, I'm transferring. My family's moving and I want to be close to them. It's going to be a tough time for us, and I know we need to stick together. It's the only thing I know for sure."

Sam nodded, looking at me like I was standing on the opposite side of a glass window. "I see."

"I need tonight to be about hockey. About doing what we love. I want this memory, Sam. I want to remember us like this."

"And I want to beg you to stay." He let go of my hand. "But I won't. I'll play. And I'll finally kick your ass in something. Hopefully, that'll be enough for you to remember me."

I smiled through the tight feeling in my chest. "It'll be more than enough."

Chapter Thirty-Five

Sam

She had me.

The moon was high in the sky and the air smelled of pine trees. Everyone was in the best mood they'd been in for weeks. The game we played was a bit lax on the rules but that's what made it fun. And that's how she got me. Aderyn had me.

I let my guard down for a second and she took full advantage. We'd been tied for the last hour. Right when I thought I got the upper hand, bypassing their defense, Aderyn showed up out of nowhere.

She targeted my left side. Aderyn used the knowledge she had on said weakness and forced me to try and block her on my right.

The woman was far faster to pivot than I've ever been. As soon as her stick touched the puck, she speed off toward our goal. I cursed under my breath, hurrying after her. She waited until I was on her tail before passing to Kaya. Together, the two were unstoppable. Kaya avoided any steal attempts. Lincoln readied himself in the goal.

"Ready?" Aderyn called to her.

I frowned because the only thing left for Kaya to do was attempt the shot. Lincoln was her last obstacle.

Kaya pulled her stick back but instead of aiming for the goal, she passed to Aderyn at the last second. Lincoln was too focused on Kaya to react to the change. Aderyn got the puck passed him in the blink of an eye.

I laughed, shocked and impressed. The girls cheered as Kaya and Aderyn grabbed each other's hands, spinning around in celebration.

"Game's not over, ladies," Jack reminded them with an annoyed huff.

"Might as well be," Aderyn shot back but still moved to reset. Her gaze caught and held mine for a second. The painful looks we'd been exchanging were briefly forgotten in place of something warmer.

"That was good," I said.

Her brow raised. "Just good?"

"Great," I remedied. "You're way better than you were at the start of the season. Dare I say, on the road to becoming better than me."

Leagues better, actually. The improvement was massive. This woman was going places.

Aderyn beamed at my compliment. "I know I am. Glad you got to see."

I smiled back. "So am I.

I kept looking at the clock so much that my friends were getting annoyed. Paying attention to game night was far harder when the girl of your dreams was leaving you for good in the next hour. Especially when said girl responded to your, *I'm going to miss you,'* text with a *'Me too. Wish things were different.'*

"Oh my God," Lincoln tossed down his cards. "This is pointless. Do you need me to drive you?"

I blinked. "Excuse me?"

"Drive you to Aderyn's place so you can stop her," Lincoln explained. "You've been re-reading her same text for the past hour."

"No. Absolutely not." I frowned and placed my phone face down on the table. "I can't."

Lincoln groaned. "Why not?"

"That'd be selfish."

"Selfish," Finn repeated the word like it was new to him. "You think telling Aderyn how you feel is selfish? Why?"

"I've already told her how I feel," I said. "Going to her now would be like begging her to stay—which is something I promised I wouldn't do. So, I'm letting her leave in peace."

Finn nodded, looking like he understood a little bit more.

"Does she really want to leave? Or does she think it's her only option?" Lincoln challenged. "Considering the circumstances?"

"Both," I said, stiffly. "Besides, even if she stayed, there's a chance she wouldn't want to be with me."

Finn's forehead wrinkled. "Why?"

I sighed and tossed my cards next to Lincoln's pile. "Because she's always been the girl to be all-in and I'm the guy who sleeps around because he's perpetually afraid of rejection. I scare her. She doesn't trust her judgment right now."

Lincoln raised a brow. "Did you keep sleeping around when you two were together?"

I scowled. "No, of course not. We had a bet of sorts. I didn't break my end of the bargain."

"So, you changed for her, or was it all for the bet?" Finn asked.

"I didn't want anyone when I was with her. She was all I could think of so that made things easy." I ran my hands over my head. "So, yeah, I guess I changed. But, I think I changed for both of us. I stopped running because it wasn't good for me. And I wanted her to be happy. That's why I'm not stopping her. She deserves to do what's best for her and Mendell's not it. I'm not it."

They were both quiet and watching me. I shifted in my seat, uncomfortable at their stares.

"Correct me if I'm wrong," Finn said. "But, from what I understand, she just told you she wished things were different. You're sitting here brooding over the text."

"Hardcore brooding," Lincoln agreed. "You've got Finn beat and that takes some serious effort."

Finn frowned but continued, "My point is, you both are thinking in narrow terms. It's Mendell or nothing in your mind.

All-in right now or nothing. There's got to be more. And if you really want her, you'll do more."

"He has a point," Lincoln agreed.

I opened my mouth to come up with an argument. But Finn's words sparked an idea. Once that idea took root, I couldn't ignore it. I tried not to get too drunk on the new possibility. It could be the worst idea I've ever had but I needed to try. I needed to give us another shot.

"Link," I said. "I'll take that ride."

He smiled. "Let me grab the keys."

She wasn't at the dorm, but Jas was.

"Aderyn's been out for the past hour," they said, voice soft with an unspoken apology.

"Do you have any idea where she went?" I glanced down at my phone to see if she'd responded to my text about talking. She hadn't even read it yet.

"No, sorry." Jas shrugged. "She sometimes disappears for a few hours. To her thinking spot, apparently. Now that I'm saying it, I realize how dangerous it is that none of us know where it is."

My brow wrinkled. "Her thinking spot?"

"A place she found earlier in the semester." They started to look worried. "I'm going to try calling her."

"No, don't," I said, quickly. "I know where she is."

"You sure?"

"Positive." I pushed away from the door and hurried back toward the elevator. It took so long to come that I opted for the stairs, taking two at a time.

Lincoln got me across town to Harry's in record time. He barely pulled up to the sidewalk before I opened the door. Jas had said Aderyn had already been gone for an hour so there was a good chance I already missed her.

Before I even got the front door open, my phone buzzed. Aderyn's name flashed on the screen.

"Hello?" I was out of breath.

"Hey, is this a bad time?" She sounded anxious and unsure.

"Of course not. Is everything okay?"

Silence on her end. I walked inside, weaving through the clothing and camping gear displays. I nearly bumped into one of the employees and quickly apologized. The waterfall on her end started to sound louder as I got closer.

"I wished on your baseball," she finally said.

I stopped walking because I saw her back. Aderyn leaned on the glass fence, staring up at the tree's long branches.

"Really?" I asked. My heart started pounding like it usually did when I was near her.

"Felt as ridiculous as I thought it would."

I kept my distance. Talking on the phone allowed certain freedom. She seemed more willing to be open and I needed that to last as long as possible. "Why did you do it?"

"I..." She cleared her throat. "Had a silly dream."

I smiled and her voice dropped to a whisper. This was a secret that she was only willing to share with me. "What was it about?"

"About something I'll never have if I keep wishing on baseballs."

"I told you. It works. But only if you do it when the sun hits it. Trust the process."

She snorted. "You know, you never explained to me why you think this works."

"I'll tell you if you tell me what you wished for."

"Doesn't that ruin the wish?"

"Only with stars," I promised.

She laughed. "Are you making up these rules as you go along?"

"Naturally."

Aderyn laughed again. This one was a little louder. I inched closer.

"My dream was of us." She spoke slowly, careful with each word that passed her lips.

"Together," I guessed.

"Together."

"We could make that happen. If you really want it."

She sighed, pulling the receiver away from her mouth for a second. "I'm leaving. I need to leave."

"Long distance, then."

"Sam, do you really think long distance is something we'd survive? You'd survive?"

"We could try. I want to try."

"It'd be your first relationship, right?"

When I hummed in confirmation, she let out another sigh.

"That feels destined to fail and ruin what we already have."

"Fine."

Her spine straightened at the possibility of me giving up. "Fine?"

"I'll try something different," I said the next sentence loud enough for her to realize I stood behind her.

Aderyn turned around and let out a disbelieving laugh as she still spoke into the phone. "And what would that be?"

"Follow you." My breath went shallow because I never took this kind of risk when the odds felt stacked against me. I applied to Mendell because I knew without a doubt, they'd accept me. I played hockey because my natural talent was undeniable. I slept with girls who wouldn't need more from me. But now, more than ever, I needed to ignore that small voice in my head that told me to play safe. Ignore that voice in my head that told me I wasn't good enough.

"I'm sorry, what?" She pulled the phone away from her ear, ending the call.

"You're transferring to a school with what I assume will have a great hockey program," I explained.

"Westbrooke," she confirmed.

"This season's not even over. I'd have plenty of time to apply and talk with the recruiters."

Aderyn shook her head. "You love Mendell. Everyone's here. Your friends, your team…"

"It's not a long drive. Couple of hours out. I'll visit on breaks and maybe even play against them." I smiled at the thought of being on a rival team. "It'll be fun to be opposite of them for once. A challenge and adventure."

"You'd move for a girl you haven't even dated? That's so reckless," she said and it sounded like she was trying to convince herself more than me. "We're not reckless. Sam, I can't be the reason you ruin a good thing."

"I wished for my loneliness to go away," I revealed. "That night I tried to get my spot back from you, I wished I wasn't lonely. There was something missing in my life that I couldn't quite figure out until I kept bumping into you. You're the only good thing worth holding onto, Aderyn. I can manage being on another team and starting over at a different campus. What I can't manage is knowing I didn't think of every possible solution for us to be together. You make me want to be brave. Ever since we started this thing, I've wanted to be brave enough to finally go after what I want. I am now."

She took a deep breath. "Are you sure?"

I grabbed her hand, lacing our fingers together. "More than anything. I swear, more than anything."

"You'll probably get sick of me after a few weeks."

"Or fall in love with you," I countered.

She laughed. "God, does this mean you win? I didn't even kiss another guy and here you are, transferring schools for me. You were right, you can pull an Aderyn better than I could pull a Sam."

I smiled and pressed my forehead against hers. "Gonna be a sore loser about it?"

"I just really wanted that jersey," she teased as she stared at my lips.

"We can always make a new bet," I offered. "But you have to pay up on the original one first."

"Right." Aderyn laughed, eyes twinkling. "What was your prize again?"

"You and me on a date. Giving us a chance."

"Fair's fair," she agreed.

I kissed her. Her arms wrapped around my neck, immediately pulling me close. I backed her up, so she was pressed against the glass. The warmth of the sunset from the windows overhead felt like a blessing for what lay ahead.

"Maybe you are onto something with that baseball," she whispered against my lips.

I brushed my thumb across her cheek. "I told you so."

Aderyn laughed a little. "How long have you been waiting to say that to me?"

"Not as long as I've been waiting for you to look at me like that." I moved my head back a little to study her better. Her smile was shier than usual.

"Like what?" she asked.

"Like I'm someone you can see yourself with for longer than a fling."

Her grip around me tightened. "Much longer. I hope that doesn't scare you."

"It doesn't scare me." I shook my head. "It's everything I never knew I wanted."

"Just like me?" she teased.

"Exactly like you," I confirmed.

THE END

Epilogue

Aderyn

Sam pressed kisses against my cheek until I started to smile. We were standing in front of his old rental house, waiting for his sister to show up.

"You're not getting away with this that easily," I mumbled even though my wall had fallen as soon as he'd wrapped his arms around my waist.

"We were running out of time," he reminded me in a low voice that was supposed to soothe me.

"There was plenty of time to drop me off at Kaya's place for a shower..." The knowing look he wore made me trail off.

"You take forever and a day to get ready."

"Fine, you could have just dropped me off if you didn't want to wait," I countered. "Helped Eden move in and came back to get me."

His deep frown made my chest heavy with guilt. "You've been avoiding meeting my sister for a while now. Any of my family for that matter. What gives?"

I shrugged, not able to come up with an answer that didn't sound as wimpy as my genuine emotion: I was scared out of my mind.

"It's a big step."

"Bigger than the brunch step?" he asked. "She's not going to dress you up as a pirate."

"That's not the same and you know it. You weren't even my boyfriend then."

"And your mom still instantly loved me." He nodded, smugness practically drowning his next words. "Yeah, you're right. My ability to charm surpasses yours."

I snorted and swatted his chest. "Don't get all cocky on me right now."

"I'm only teasing." He laughed. "From the moment I met you, I was charmed."

"Stop lying."

"Okay, fine. Moderately intrigued."

"You play too much." I pulled away from his next kiss with a smile. "I'm nervous, Sam. Nothing you do is going to distract me."

"It's going to be fine," he promised, cupping my face gently. "What's the worst that could happen?"

"She meets me, hates me, and convinces you to break up with me."

"I have a mind of my own, thank you very much." He rubbed circles on my cheeks with his thumb. "And I've decided I'm in love with you. I will be by your side as long as you'll have me."

"How sweet," I said in a teasing voice because joking felt better than giving into the knot currently lodged in my throat.

Sam had kept his promise and never let a day go by without showing me how much I meant to him. I thought he'd tire of the reminders but each day, he found a different way to express how much he cared. His openness helped me feel comfortable doing the same.

We'd been adjusting well to life at Westbrooke. It was early in the school year, but we were already finding our footing and rhythm. Sam lived in a dorm with some of his new teammates. They'd already started pre-season training which—from Sam's observations—indicated an amazing team chemistry. Of course, he still missed his friends but spreading his wings seemed to make him even more confident than before.

I opted for living at home with Mom and Rae—for this first semester, at least.

Things at home were slowly feeling normal but there was still some way to go. Mom and Warren were separated. Their issues before the investigation were magnified. Apparently, Mom felt like he'd been putting distance between the two of them. After everything came out, she finally understood why.

Warren still wanted to be in our lives. Rae and I didn't have the heart to cut him out completely. Our group chat felt awkward at times. But it was nice to have a part of him in my life. The part I grew to love and consider as family.

"Get through this meeting and maybe you'll get a reward?" Sam bargained.

I laughed. "It's not like I can't convince you to do anything I want."

"You can't..." He cleared his throat when my hands trailed dangerously close to his belt.

"Sure about that?" I asked.

Sam sighed. "Not entirely."

"Thought so."

"But what I'm talking about isn't a sex reward."

I perked up. "A trip to Italy?"

"No, not that. Not yet." He chuckled. "Let me graduate and pull in some NHL money first."

"New car?"

"Again, I need time for that stuff." His eyes danced, amused. "You're going to be really spoiled in a few years, you know that?"

"I'm counting on it."

"Your wish is my command." He kissed my cheek. "But, for now, let's keep our guesses realistic. And to ourselves, because here comes Eden."

I would have stayed frozen if Sam hadn't turned me around. A tall woman with freeform locks and black lipstick climbed out of a black Chevy Impala. Tumbled out might be a better description. She laughed at her clumsiness and the few boxes that fell onto the ground behind her.

"You okay?" I asked and quickly hurried over to help her gather her things.

"Oh, I'm fine." She waved her hand at me. "This happens all the time."

"She happens to be a bit...chaotic," Sam said under his breath as he helped his sister to her feet. "And tends to go overboard with her belongings."

She frowned at his statement. "I'm a maximalist. Sue me."

Eden wore a black T-shirt with a cutout heart safety pinned to the front. Her plaid maxi skirt grazed her ankles, nearly hiding her white socks and chunky platforms. She gave off the vibe of a cool teaching assistant who might give you an extension on a paper if you didn't tell the other TAs. My shoulders relaxed as soon as she met my gaze. There'd been absolutely nothing to worry about.

"Aderyn, right?" she greeted with a wide smile. I noticed piercings on her cheeks. They accentuated her dimples. "It's so great to finally meet you. I've been begging Sam to bring you over."

"It's great to meet you, too," I said, feeling silly about dragging this out for so long.

"I don't have any sisters," Eden confessed. "And always wanted a little one, so you might get an overwhelming amount of invites to hang out. Feel free to say no at any time."

"Lots of babying, too. You'll get lots of babying during those hangouts," Sam spoke up. "Just saying."

Eden rolled her eyes. "I can be a bit bossy."

"A bit?" Sam's voice raised as he teased her. She swatted his shoulder.

"It comes from a place of love," Eden insisted as she shot a playful glare at her brother.

"Well, we're both in luck because I've always wanted a big sister," I said. "Don't get me wrong, love bossing around my baby sis, but sometimes you just need someone to go to for solid advice."

Eden clapped her hands. "I'm your girl. My first bit of advice is, don't let this guy push you around. He thinks he's the best at everything."

"I wouldn't dream of it," I promised.

"Have you finally picked someone who can keep up with you?" Eden threw a surprised look at her brother.

"I told you." He shrugged, not taking his eyes off me. "She's perfect for me."

My cheeks burned and Eden stuck out her bottom lip in awe.

"Oh, my God, this is the perfect way to start my semester," she mused. "Mendell really worked its magic on you. Finally, you're in a mature relationship."

"Maybe it'll do the same for you?" Sam asked in a teasing tone.

She shook her head. "Let's hope not. Let's not even think about it so it's not put into the universe."

Sam and I laughed at the disgusted face she pulled.

"Did you bring what I asked?" Sam looked hopeful at his sister.

"Yeah, and never ask me to cart around an item this big again," she said and started back to her car. "It was a fucking nightmare getting it to fit into my trunk. Plus, every turn I made I thought the glass might break."

"Come on," Sam instructed me as he followed Eden to her car. "Claim your reward."

"What are you talking about?" I fell into step behind him. It took both of them to get the frame out of the car. I offered to help but Sam waved me off, indicating I should stand back a few feet. Once he set it on the ground, my eyes went wide.

"Is that…" I gawked. "O'Ree's jersey?"

"Check the signature." He nodded, face bright with a wide grin.

I stepped closer to see that in addition to Sam's name, O'Ree had signed mine with a short note,

Sorry about the bet. Win some, lose some. Always get back up, though.

"How the hell…?" I pressed my hands to my cheek, laughing with blurry vision.

"I have my connections." He shrugged, looking extremely pleased with himself—as he should be.

"I have no idea what this means," Eden said as she read the note. "But it seems like a special moment. I'll give you two some space. But only for a few minutes because I have a ton of stuff to unload before tomorrow. I need to make a good impression and get to my first class early."

"We got you," Sam promised. "The guys should be home any second and they'll help us, too."

"By the way, your room better be as good as you said it was," Eden warned teasingly. "Or it's you and me in these streets."

As soon as she left to start unloading, I practically jumped into Sam's arms in excitement.

"Even when I lose, I win," I joked. "I like this."

Sam laughed. "You deserve this. You worked hard."

"We worked hard," I corrected. "First at Mendell. Next, Westbrooke. And then, the NHL and PHF. We're going to make it to the top, Sam. I just know it. You and me."

He kissed me until I was breathless. "You and me, Aderyn."

Bonus Epilogue

Sam

Ruby stumbled over her feet as she hurried to me. She clenched two small, blow-up dumbbells in her tiny fists.

"Let's go," she declared. "I ready to own."

I laughed and scooped her into my arms. "I think you mean you're ready to tone?"

Our daughter nodded with a grin.

"*Own*," she repeated and put on her "mean" face as she tried to flex like her mom.

It was my day to watch her, and we'd done everything from eating dinosaur nuggets for breakfast to playing dress-up for lunch—had to prep her for brunch days with her grandma—and watching her favorite Disney movie three times in a row.

I looked at my watch, trying to gauge where Aderyn would be in her workout by now.

"Momma's probably about done," I said and started down the hallway toward our at-home gym. "So, we can go say hi."

Ruby bounced up and down, excited at the prospect of being allowed to go to the gym. Because she was so young and small, most of the places in our house were off-limits to her. Aderyn and I bought our two-story villa in the early years of our marriage without much thought to practicality—babyproofing had been a huge feat.

Our home had gorgeous wall-to-ceiling windows in most hallways, letting in enough light to make us feel like we were outside. We had an interior courtyard complete with a small pond and trees that reminded us of the landscaping at Harry's. And tons of decor that centered our journey as professional hockey players.

"Ben," Ruby said, pointing at one of the many photos on the wall.

"Your Uncle Finn, yeah." I corrected, stopping for a moment to look at the photo. It'd been taken five years ago when Finn and I won our first Stanley cup with our team, the Evansville Eagles. Since then, we'd won two more times.

"And here's your mom." I pointed to another photo. "Killing it, as per usual."

Aderyn's team photographer sent us a candid shot of her with her teammate, Kaya, on the ice. They were in mid-celly and a large crowd cheered them on in the background. Nowadays, most of Aderyn's games were packed and the noise was near deafening.

"Look, I know she has more championship wins than me," I said to my daughter who looked up at me like she knew exactly what I was talking about. "But, this year, I think we're finally going to catch up to her. Our rookies are top tier. And my knee's on the mend."

Ruby smiled and knocked her dumbbell on my nose.

I chuckled. "You don't believe me, do you?"

She bopped me again.

"Definitely your mother's daughter," I confirmed and continued down the hall.

Aderyn had the stereo playing but quickly turned the music down when she saw us at the door. A smile lit up her face as we walked it. I grinned back. It never ceased to amaze me how excited I got at seeing my wife. It didn't matter how long we'd been apart, my heart tugged in her direction as soon as I laid eyes on her.

"How are my favorite people?" she asked, popping up from the weight-lifting bench. With both of our incomes, we could afford some of the best equipment around. In fact, buying Aderyn the newest and latest equipment had been my highest priority when we got our house. We had a fully decked-out gym before we had a mattress.

The look on her face when I surprised her with the workout room was priceless. I'd taken the surprise even further, donating money specifically to Mendell's women's teams so they had the equipment and support they needed. I got most of my old teammates who were now pros to do the same. The next generation of women hockey players finally had the right kind of people looking out for them.

"Is it okay if we interrupt?" I asked. "She was excited to get a set or two in."

Aderyn laughed and reached for Ruby. "Of course. I missed you two anyway and was about to call it quits early. How is you guys' day going?"

"Did her favorites," I said. "And she humbled me about my career. All in all, I'd say it's been a great day."

"Speaking about humbling," Aderyn started with a grin.

"Uh oh," I teased.

"You remember that face-off we won?" Aderyn asked as she moved Ruby from one hip to the other. "Back at Montville Lake during our last year at Mendell?"

I scoffed. "You guys won?"

"Yes, of course, we won." She feigned offense that I'd even question it.

"Momma won!" Ruby cheered.

"Exactly." Aderyn kissed her cheeks. "You remember, don't you, Ruby-girl? I knew you'd back me up."

"She wasn't there," I protested with a chuckle.

"She was there in spirit," Aderyn argued.

"Beautiful, I love you. I would go to hell and back for you. Die for you," I swore. "But you didn't win that night. Not when Kaya fouled against Finn during the final goal. We all agreed."

Aderyn laughed. "Oh, my God, we did not agree. Since when?"

"When!" Ruby cheered .

I cupped my wife's cheeks and leaned in to kiss her forehead gently.

"Since it was the truth," I teased and kissed her lips this time.

"Your truth." She tried to look pissed, but I could see the softness in her eyes.

"Why are we arguing about this?"

"Because Lincoln called." She smiled down at a squirming Ruby. Our daughter loved all her uncles, but Lincoln was by far her favorite. As soon as she heard his name, she wanted to hurry out of the room to look out for him at the front door.

"He's not coming today, baby," Aderyn tried to calm her.

"What did he want?" I reached over to brush Ruby's wayward coils. She had her mom's tight texture. I'd gotten tons of lessons from Aderyn, Rae, their mom, and even my own sister on how to braid hair. But I still had a way to go. Everyone could tell when I did Ruby's hair because it'd never last through the day. In my defense, we were raising a very active daughter. She barely napped and wanted to run everywhere. Don't even get me started on her obsession with rolling around on the carpet.

"He wants a re-match," Aderyn said. "His words, not mine. Which, leads me to believe, he knows my team won."

I scoffed and shook my head. "I'll talk to him. Jog his memory."

Aderyn gave me a look. "Come on, Sam. It's okay to admit defeat. You're at the top of your game now. Who cares about a little loss so many years ago? No one but us remembers anyway. No one but us knows who had the better team. I'll keep our secret."

"No, no." I laughed and pointed at her. "I see what you're doing and I'm not falling for it."

She stuck out her bottom lip. "I have no idea what you're talking about."

"You're trying to bait me into another game."

"What? No. What for? My team can already say they beat a Stanley cup winner. They don't need to prove themselves another time."

"You're unbelievable..." I chewed on my lip, trying to tame my smile.

She shrugged. "So, I guess I'm telling Lincoln no?"

I stared at her for a minute, trying to conjure up enough maturity to resist. No matter how old we got, Aderyn and I always found ways to challenge each other. We still wanted to be the best and urged each other in that direction. Her determination and love made my world so much happier and more beautiful. Not a day went by when I didn't feel grateful for following her. Next to marrying her, it'd been my best decision.

"When?" I exaggerated a sigh.

Her eyes grew big with excitement. "When?"

"Yeah, when did Lincoln say when he wanted a re-match?"

Aderyn squealed and started dancing. Ruby bumped up and down on her hip, giggling and waving around her dumbbells.

"He said as soon as the lake's frozen over."

"Alright then." I nodded and pulled out my phone. "Looks like we're going to have a lot of calls to make."

"My girls are already in," she said without hesitation.

I raised a brow, shocked. "Really?"

"I sent out a bat signal," Aderyn explained with a shrug like getting together her crew from college was no biggie. "Some girls from Mendell and some from Westbrooke. They're ready to kick some A-S-S. Ruby can join in too, won't you, baby? Come help Mom beat your Dad again?"

Ruby giggled and tried to mimic Aderyn's scrunched nose.

"Such a bad influence," I joked, tugging on one of Aderyn's braids.

"I'm raising a champion." She waved me away and turned toward the weights to show Ruby how to properly set things up. I smacked her ass before she could get too far away.

"I'll show you an A-S-S kicking," I said in a lower voice.

She rolled her eyes but by the way she licked her lips, I knew we'd probably be calling one of our folks to babysit tonight.

As Aderyn used words that most definitely went completely over our daughter's head, I made my first call. The voice on the other end sounded tired.

"Were you asleep? Isn't it eight in the morning where you guys are?" I asked. "I thought you two were early birds through and through?"

Henrik chuckled. I heard sheets rustling and a familiar voice mumble something to him. He said something that sounded like a sweet nothing before addressing me again.

"I had a long night," he said.

I snorted. "Ah, the honeymoon phase."

"This important or can I call you back when I have pants on?"

Definitely didn't need that visual. Henrik had become less suit and tie and more relaxed over the years. Which meant, he overshared sometimes.

"I'll make it quick," I promised. "You down to get the gang back together?"

"What for?" He sounded a bit more awake.

"Rematch against Aderyn's team. This time, we're not leaving until we have an indisputable victory."

He laughed. "Count me in."

"Exactly what I wanted to hear. Spread the word?"

"Will do," he agreed before saying goodbye.

After we hung up, I called a few other guys. All were down. Those who didn't live in the state promised to fly in. I felt nostalgic talking to them. And it was exciting thinking about all of us in one place again.

Right before my last call, I looked over at Aderyn and Ruby. They were staring out the window. The sun shone on them as Aderyn explained something to Ruby in a low voice. I paused, taking a moment to soak in the image. My family. My everything. Something bigger than hockey. Something better. Something that had my whole heart and then some.

Aderyn sensed my eyes on them and turned to me.

"Everything okay?" she asked, looking a little worried.

"Everything's fine," I assured with a nod. "You're going to lose again, but everything's fine."

Her smile was effortless, lighting up her beautiful face. "I've spent years learning from one of the best players. I know all your weaknesses. My advantage is undeniable."

Aderyn joined my side again and handed Ruby over. She gave me a kiss that made my body warm.

"Promise you won't hold back, though," she whispered against my lips. "Fight till the end."

I nodded. "Fighting till the end is my specialty, particularly when it comes to you."

"You've always known exactly what to say," she murmured.

I kissed her. "And you've always loved it."

"Now that, we can both agree on."

Also By Deanna Grey

Mendell Hawks

Sunny Disposition

Westbrooke Angels

Just Please Me

Just Fall For Me

Printed in Great Britain
by Amazon

18830375R00212